THE NIGHT MAN

ROBERT CHAZZ CHUTE

EX PARTE PRESS

The Night Man
The Nightscape Series

ISBN (paperback) 978-1-927607-54-1
ISBN (Ebook) 978-1-927607-55-8

Cover design by Rocking Book Covers

✼ Created with Vellum

WHAT READERS SAY ABOUT ROBERT'S THRILLERS

5.0 out of 5 stars Do Not Miss This Book!

Chazz is the master. Every story he writes immerses you so deeply in its world, you can barely crawl out when the pages are closed. "Brooklyn in the Mean Time" might just be his best yet. I don't know which parts of the story are reality and which are fiction. Chazz presents a version of himself where it might just be autobiographical. Then again, he may be messing with we readers to up the ante in our suspension of disbelief. Either way, it's an amazing book. I loved every syllable. Chazz ranks among the top tier of our generation's storytellers. Do Not Miss This Book!

~ Amazon review by Alex Kimmell, author of *The Key to Everything*

Move over Elmore

Love the dialogue and the character studies ... definitely a blend of Mickey Spillane and Elmore Leonard

~ Amazon reviewer Alex Adamson

A unique and engaging novel with a compelling plot and well-drawn, idiosyncratic characters.

~ David Pandolfe, Amazon reviewer

Robert Chazz Chute is a versatile author, with books ranging from zombies, vampires, hit men, the end of the world, robots, dreams and time travel. Each book and series is well written, smart and leaves the reader wanting more.

~ Cavewoman reviews

Another good story from a master storyteller

Once again I got completely sucked in by Robert Chazz Chute. I could not put this book down once I started it. My only regret is that I got this book in November and waited until now to read it. The story is imaginative, engaging, and really not like anything else I've ever read.

~ Amazon reviewer Deborah630

DIG CHAZZ CHUTE

His writing style makes you part of his thoughts & conversations: you are part of his dimension Dear Reader and will "SWING" his every day. Only in Brooklyn can the 90's thrive and remain true. You can never truly return home after you ran from its hurts and pains, when naturally embedded during formative years are often hard to run from. Yet, the raw perspectives of your past with eyes wide open; does allow you truth and thus clarity. From there, knowing the negatives and going ballz to the walls with a cuppla hail Mary's; Chazz rocked it and lives the life he was meant to live and believed in. HIGHLY RECOMMEND!

~ Amazon reviewer MIKALA RATED

Bigger than Jesus **Captured My Imagination and Ran!**

I have always liked the detective style books of the films from the 30-50's. This book captures all those best features. While reading the book I felt I was transported into a world that was inhabited by all the people and characters that made up the Humphrey Bogart movies, the Mike Hammer books, and the other gritty pulp fiction that I have always liked but somehow could not fully embrace. What helped me do that was the witty style that Robert Chazz Chute writes. It is funny, humorous, often serious and he speaks in a way that mixes the old style and current cultural references that make every one reading it feel included in the story.

~ Tidal Ashburn, Amazon reviewer

The writing is just superb.... From beginning to end, this is one top notch crime novel. It is a smooth, easy read.

~ David Wilde, Amazon reviewer

Robert Chazz Chute proves that genre fiction can be inventive and unconventional in its use of language while delivering a suspenseful story.

~ Dream Beast, Amazon reviewer

An Excellent Read

I loved this book. It is well written, fast paced and unusual for a gangster book.

~ M Slott, Amazon reviewer

Bigger Indeed!

Oh wow. What can I say? Mr. Chute pulled me in with his POV and kept the twists coming through the whole book. I found the ending to be delightful and perfect. With comedy throughout and a wonderful cast of characters.

~ Jo Michaels, Amazon reviewer and author of *The Fury*

Excellent, fast paced romp

This book plays out like a Guy Ritchie film. The pacing is frenzied, the plot convoluted yet easy to parse, and the characters larger than life. Half the fun is trying to who's trying to betray who. I would wholeheartedly recommend this novel to action fans and can't wait to grab the author's next work in this series.

~Amazon reviewer Rev357

What a fun ride of a crime thriller!

In a short span of a couple of short stories collections and a few novelettes, Robert Chazz Chute has seriously become one of my favourite authors! You can count on him for well-written stories that pack punch, plot twists, clever dialogue and even some hidden wisdom in their pages.

~ Amazon reviewer johligo

Five Stars

Great treat, fun, unpredictable and gritty.

~ Kindle customer, Amazon reviewer

Love

Suspense, humor, love!

~ Shirleyjack, Amazon reviewer

Genuine characters, full of ups and downs. Intricate plot.

~ Julio Wickham, Amazon reviewer

Good Thriller

Kept my attention. Real page turner could not stop reading till I finished the entire book. Read it in one day.

~ Amazon reviewer A. Alpuch

ACKNOWLEDGMENTS

I'm a lucky person. I have J, C and C.
You help me live my life on my terms.
You are the why.

Special thanks to Gari Strawn of garistrawnediting.com
for her prowess and conscientiousness.
Also many thanks to Russ whose beta reading skills are always
helpful.

To my lifelong bestie Peter Hawkins. We're so close to twin speak,
it's always funny.

"...he subjected his heroes to the gruesome rewards of their passions..."

~ Michael Chabon
Wonder Boys

～

When the good man loses his patience, the devil shivers.

~ Unknown

1

I told my prisoner to stop struggling. "Those zip ties will chafe your wrists raw."

When I graduated from high school in Lake Orion, Becky Clee-shaw gave the valedictory address to our class. Becky was my girl-friend at the time. She loaded us down with the usual conventional wisdom. Her words were meant to be motivational but came off as an impossible dare. She kicked us in the ass on the way out the door with, "Ask yourself, what special thing do you have to offer? What can you do to change the world? Go do that."

Pretty high and mighty for a bunch of kids from next-to-nowhere Michigan. We'd slung hay on farms. The lucky few got shifts at Dunkin' Donuts. Nobody I knew thought they'd cure cancer, get rich rapping or move to San Francisco to develop killer apps for a tech giant. For most of us, the choices were unemployment, chronic underemployment or joining the military. Of all America is, my hometown might be the American-est.

We all had the bug to get out and make our mark, though. We wanted something more, to pursue careers our parents wouldn't even understand. To our surprise, the class valedictorian hardly left town. The girl who swore she'd get out of Lake Orion and never look back.

However, five years later she was back after attending school in Connecticut and a brief foray in Los Angeles.

She'd found a husband at Wesleyan — somebody's older brother. Rud Bench was a lawyer from Chicago looking to be a big fish in Lake Orion's tiny pond. Becky Cleeshaw became Becky Bench full-time and a real estate agent part-time.

The story would end there if Becky was the type to be satisfied. She wasn't.

I'll tell you a little about me you might not know. I went away for seven years after graduation. Maybe ran away is more accurate. I thought the military was my way out. Lake Orion was too small for me. I figured three hots and a cot and close order drill might make for some great stories someday. The trouble was, I didn't get any great stories in the Army. All I saw was sad stories nobody wants to hear unless we're both drunk. I don't want to get into the gory details of my injury but, suffice to say, I got out of the Army and kicked around for a while. I always felt like a round peg in a world of square holes.

Just like Becky, I returned to Lake Orion, too. Stories are constructed of lies, mistakes and conflict. If it's done right, the truth leaks out between the lines. I'm going to confess some ugly things but I will also say this: Through Becky, I found my calling. If it weren't for her, I would never have figured out what I could give, the talent I had to change the world.

"Keep walking, relax and listen," I told the prisoner. "I'll tell you everything, exactly as it happened. When we're done, I'll decide what to do with you."

2

It's a curious thing to return home after a long absence. There was that weird moment of debate. I'd been away too long to act too familiar. Do I ring the doorbell? Should I knock and poke my head in and announce, "Hey, Dad! It's me!"

The late summer sun was still bright, burning into the back of my head. I adjusted my sunglasses, cursing the orange light. I'm not a vampire, but I live like one. If there were support groups for the blood-sucking undead, I'd be stuck in the sharing circle commiserating with them.

My father, Ernest Jack, ambled around the corner of the house. He stopped by the azaleas and stared at me as if the gears in his head needed to take a moment to get back up to speed. I was in shock, too. I'd been away almost seven years. He'd aged twenty. His shaggy hair, once salt and pepper, was now all silver.

"Junior?"

Who else? I thought. *And he knows I hate being called Junior.*

"The dogs started barking," he said. "I wondered who was here. No car in the driveway — "

"No car," I replied. "Walked from town."

"Quite the walk, wasn't it?"

"Yeah."

"Feet sore? How's the leg?"

"Not bad and stiff, in that order."

"My feet are sore," he said. "Been up since five." Dad always wanted to establish he'd won some competition between us, some race I was usually unaware I was participating in until he informed me that I'd lost. Getting up early had always been a point of pride for my father. Being up before everyone else and clean-shaven meant he could hold it over me for the rest of the day. I think he kept score, building up points in his head. He was also insufferable at cribbage, grubbing up points other players missed. If you didn't do the math in your head fast enough, he'd take those points, too. He'd always had a head for numbers.

"What are you doing here?" he asked. "Did someone call you?"

"Um, first, things first. Hi, Dad."

"Hi."

"And no, no one called me. Who would call me? Should they? I thought I'd come home for a bit. That okay by you?"

"No job to rush back to, huh?"

"Nothing special."

"What's happening with the Army?"

"Oh, they're out there doing their thing somewhere, I'm sure."

He made a sour face. "You know what I mean, smartass. Did you get a medal for the secret stuff? Above and beyond and all that?"

"Told you, I'm out of all that, dumbass."

He gave me a grudging grin. "I see. Poverty recruited you and now you're back, still poor as us church mice, huh?"

"I did what good soldiers do, Dad."

"Follow orders, you mean?"

I shrugged. "Sacrifice is what I mean. There's some mumbo jumbo about doing the hard thing for the greater good. It was in the recruitment pamphlet."

He gave a slow approving nod. I didn't see that sort of thing from him often so I made a point of remembering it. "You surely did sacrifice. I didn't know quitting was a sure thing. Thought you might stick it out considering you don't have anything special lined up for whatever comes next. I never quit one job before I had another one."

"Those were different times. There's no new vine to swing to at the moment. Besides, the leg's a problem. I could make it through the obstacle course but I'd be in pain for a couple of days. They don't approve of that so much. The Army wants guys who can haul packs and haul ass."

"They can't fix that?"

I took a long breath and said nothing. I didn't want to get into that with him.

"How're the nerves?" he asked.

I held out my hands to show I had no tremor. "I could wait tables and serve tea. The cup wouldn't chatter on the plate if that's what you mean."

"But?"

"I stay away from fireworks and air shows. The sound of a jet overhead makes me antsy."

"Antsy?"

"Like ants are crawling all over me. Dogs and fireworks, me and fireworks. Same same."

He gestured toward my face. "And then there's the eye thing — "

I rushed in, eager to change the subject. "I've got you to visit, don't I? That's special, right?"

"Yeah, come in and take a load off. It'll be dark soon."

I didn't know how to take that. Was he saying that he would have turned me away if I'd arrived earlier in the day? Was that an invitation to dinner? To come in so I wouldn't be eaten by wolves? What it didn't sound like was a warm invitation to stay indefinitely.

He approached me warily and for a terrible moment, I wondered if he was building up to giving me a hug. Instead, he gave me his standard handshake: firm grasp, two pumps, staring me in the eyes. To a casual observer, it would probably look like he was setting me up for a sucker punch.

The house was smaller than I remembered. Everyone says that and it's always true. I wasn't quite done growing when I achieved escape velocity from Lake Orion. I was 5'11" when I graduated and when I joined up the Army doctor told me I was six feet even. Still, the house looked much smaller than the difference one inch of height would make.

"I got hodgepodge on the stove," Dad said. "You wanna Speedway?"

I accepted the offer of the black beer but turned down the hodge-podge. A few drinks might make a bowl of vegetables and warm milk go down easier. I looked in the steaming pot. The carrots were the small misshapen stubs Dad had always grown in his garden. I sat on the one kitchen chair and the wood gave a familiar creak. My mother told him to fix this chair or throw it out years ago. Sophie Jack had been dead almost a decade. Same chair, same old Dad.

Dad and I hadn't always gotten along well, especially after my mother's death. Depression sometimes brought out his nastier instincts. Mom wasn't around to tug his leash when he spoke out of turn so the friction increased over time. I wondered if we were working on inertia, only playing at being the loving father and dutiful son because that was what we were supposed to do. Maybe we only tolerated each other now because of the people we were when my mother was alive. Family ties: Unbreakable bond or knotted tangle?

Recent history pressed and compressed me. Age and gravity had begun to make him shorter. We were getting smaller again. We weren't the people we set out to be. We weren't even the people we used to be.

I didn't see the dangerous turn ahead. I didn't know we would become dangerous again.

3

"How's the trucking business?" I asked him.

Dad stared at me for a beat, maybe deciding how much to give away. "Same same."

That wasn't good. Throughout my father's business endeavors, the profits never seemed to amount to much. It was often difficult to figure which business was his prime game and which was the side hustle. Through it all Dad had one sentimental note: Not only did he call every dog Sophie, but he'd also named his old Kenworth semi after his dead wife, as well.

"The rig still running okay?"

"*Pfft.* That old eighteen-wheeler's got too many miles on her. Should put her out to pasture. Between gas prices and upkeep, it's hard to stay ahead. You know how it is."

"How do you manage with the dogs when you go off on a long haul?"

"Kerry from down the road. You remember him? Kerry Robar?"

"I do not, not really."

"Oh, c'mon. He went to your school."

"A lot of people did, over time."

Dad chewed on this, looking annoyed. "I suppose Kerry woulda been a few years younger than you. He doesn't know dogs like us but he can feed and exercise them fine when I'm away. He makes a good rabbit." My father's gaze strayed to my left leg. "Kerry's a good runner."

I'd been the rabbit many times but I guessed I wouldn't present enough of a training challenge anymore. Not that speed was really a factor. In takedown training, nobody outruns a German shepherd. They always catch up and take you down. I didn't miss it, either. Bite suits are hard to run in and bite sleeves get hot pretty quick.

"What's your action word for this litter?" I asked.

"Sweetie pie."

"Good one." Dad came up with a unique order to attack for each training group. In the past, we'd used a lot of random go words: mantra, oobie, crush, Kissinger, Cheney, hipster and honey bunch.

"I used to have a different go word for each dog, you know," he said. "One order is easier, especially now."

"Oh?"

"I'm tired all the time, Junior. I need Kerry to come over more often to get the dogs proper exercise. Just letting 'em loose on the property isn't enough. Everything's slowing down. I haven't been driving the truck much lately. Haven't felt up to it. Too many miles in that seat gets hard on my back and my ass. I get Rollie to drive more now."

"You got a subcontractor?"

"Yeah, have for a long while now. You forget Rollie, too?"

I shrugged.

"Sure you remember," Dad insisted. "You haven't been away that long. Rollie? Rollie Gallagher?"

"Uh … "

"The kids called him Sleepy Rollie."

"You hired a guy to drive Sophie and his nickname is Sleepy?"

Dad ignored my jab. "I guess he would be a few years older than you, prolly still is."

"The time-space continuum is pretty consistent in that way, yeah."

Dad gave me a tight smile that meant: Shut up, smartass. "Rollie lives over toward Ecorse now."

"He's got Sophie at the moment?"

"He took a shipment of air conditioners to Colorado. When the Kenworth gives up the ghost, I'm out of the trucking business altogether. Overstayed my welcome anyway. The work is drying up and petering out. It's getting to be unreasonable. To make any money, you have to be hauling constantly, puttin' on the miles and growing hemorrhoids. I got the piles, hangin' like grapes."

"Jesus, Dad!"

I chuckled but Dad looked away. He wasn't embarrassed to have hemorrhoids. His face was red because his cash had so little flow. When he shrugged, his shoulders looked more sloped than I remembered. He looked thin and pale.

"The wolf's always at the door," I said, hoping to soothe him.

He brightened a little. "Sure, things are tough all over. I was crossing back into the US from Canada not long ago. There's a rusty old factory on the road down to Dearborn, abandoned. Made me think of a useless old ship run aground. Every pane of glass was knocked the fuck out. It looked like it had been bombed. You traveled the globe to see the Third World. We got a bunch of the Third World just down the road."

"I didn't join up to see anything, Dad."

"Just to get away, then?"

"It's more complicated than that."

"Uh-huh, and how'd that turn out?"

"I'm back." I didn't have to guess why he would cross the border. He'd long dabbled in bringing guns to gunless Canucks and bringing back prescriptions to drugless Americans. He'd resold the cheaper drugs with very little markup to old folks in retirement homes in Auburn Hills and Sylvan Lake for years. Training dogs didn't pay the bills and apparently, long-haul trucking wasn't the profitable enterprise it had once been. To make money, he had to be a little more entrepreneurial and lots more illegal.

"Over in Detroit?" Dad continued. "Still so messed up! Big wildcats sun themselves on roofs all day and yowl all night in the Badlands. The plants are taking back civilization, boy. Vines creeping in the windows, claiming hulks of rotting houses. Ivy's making planters out of what was once somebody's home, some carpenter's pride."

"I've heard it's still bad."

"After the crash, a bunch of Detroit just picked up and disappeared one day, left the keys and the dreams to the bank. Some even left mid-meal. They called 'em walk-away mortgages but they were runaways. Nobody knows where all them upside down mortgage people went. Could be aliens or government camps or their Auntie Sadie's house, who knows? Meanwhile, there are people out in the 'burbs still out on Saturday nights playin' in their pickleball leagues, tellin' each other everything's a-okay. It ain't."

"People still want dogs, don't they? I would think, the way things are, people would want more guard dogs."

"Can't afford 'em and if they can, they want cute little puppies, not guard dogs so much," he complained. "Once or twice a month, somebody will pull a minivan into the yard. People with little kids will ask if I've got labradors or spaniels. I tell 'em what I tell everybody — "

"The sign says Sophie's Choice Alsatians, Licensed Breeders and Trainers," I finished for him.

Mom wept long and hard when she saw the movie *Sophie's Choice*. She came up with the name as a dig against bad guys everywhere. She preferred the term Alsatian, too. She wouldn't call any dog a German shepherd (emphasis on the *German*) unless the animal behaved very badly. Her great-uncles had fought and died in World War II and Mom knew how to carry a grudge. An immense capacity to hold a grudge was something I inherited from her.

"You ever think of raising any other kind of dog?" I asked Dad.

"A black lab is a handsome and docile canine but he can't cute you to death," he replied. "My father raised guard dogs so I raise guard dogs."

"And me," I added. "You raised me."

"You're more your mother than you are me. I couldn't tame her or you. If I had managed to keep you home, what happened to you wouldn't have happened."

"Stuff didn't just happen to me, Dad. I made choices."

"We should have made sure you had more choices. Still and all, like your mother, you got a bit of the wolf in ya. You never could abide gettin' fenced in. Can't stand a collar, won't take to the leash."

"You, either, Dad."

"Not a wonder we're both here, is it?" he asked.

It was the sort of question that is uncomfortable to answer.

4

It took Becky a week to figure out I was back in Lake Orion. She found me in the pens shoveling dog shit. The dogs, five in all, barked at her approach. They must have caught her scent before I did. She sprayed her sweet perfume on so thick it was hardly sweet anymore. Many women who smoke do that. I'm not sure if they're trying to mask the cigarette smoke or maybe they don't stop pumping the mist until they can smell it on themselves.

"I heard you were back in town," she said. "I had to come out and see for myself."

I straightened and turned. I wished she hadn't caught me shoveling shit. I dropped the shovel and came to the edge of the enclosure. A wall of chain link separated us. That was good. I wasn't sure if this was a hug or a handshake situation.

"You look good, Easy," she said. "Those big sunglasses make you look like a bug but you still do look good."

She wore her raven black hair shorter now. The pixie cut made her look more sophisticated somehow. Her large blue eyes studied my face. Her smile told me that I was okay. The jean jacket reminded me of the Becky I'd known. Her tight jeans were still ripped but she'd no doubt got them from the store shelf that way.

She didn't look like a real estate agent to me. She dressed like Teenage Becky.

"Good to see you," I said. "I heard you moved back."

"Who did you hear that from?"

"Donny."

"Down-to-the-Store Donny? Yeah, he wears the crown as King of Town Gossip but every small town is full of pretenders to that throne."

"Wasn't gossip so much as making conversation. I think he gets bored behind that counter. We hardly spoke in high school but he's a chatterbox now. I just went in to pick up a toothbrush and he bent my ear for twenty minutes."

"He's always extra friendly to me, too."

I imagined a lot of men went out of their way to be extra friendly to Becky. She'd moved back to town but she still didn't look like she belonged in Lake Orion. I pictured her walking the Miracle Mile in Chicago carrying a bunch of shopping bags from expensive stores. Despite how she dressed down, she had an air of confidence I admired. I imagined her at the head of a conference table saying things like "Alert the shareholders" and "Offer them twenty percent less and we'll buy the whole supply chain."

"Dude?"

"Huh?"

"I asked you a question."

"What was it?"

She laughed. "Still daydreaming?"

"Was that the question?"

"No, it was, how's your dad?"

"Out somewhere. The dog breeding and training biz are a bit slow. Long-haul trucking isn't much better these days but he always finds a way."

"Your dad's still hustling. He always was a hustler."

The dogs started barking and I turned back to tell them to be quiet. For a pack to listen, you have to be the alpha. When I put bass in my voice, they settled down quickly.

Becky looked me up and down, taking her time. "You still got it, I see."

"Er...thanks."

The moment passed and I wondered what to say. She had a fat diamond ring on her finger but she looked at me like she was hungry. "What's going on with you?" I asked finally.

She ignored the question and stared at the dogs. "Does Ernest still call the dogs by your mother's name?"

"Yep, they're all still Sophie, male or female."

"Still? That's kind of sweet, I guess."

"You'd guess wrong. It's not entirely."

"But he must miss your mom terribly."

"Yeah, but I'm not sure that's why every new litter is an abundance of Sophies. Could be spite, too. She left and he's resentful."

"She didn't leave. She died."

"Same thing in my dad's book. He says she quit as soon as she heard the diagnosis."

"I get that. Every time I even hear the word cancer I knock on wood. You taught me that."

"And what if there's no wood around?"

"I remember," she said. "Then I bite the tip of my tongue. Do you still do that?"

"Ever since Mom, yeah."

"You still think that'll keep the cancer away?"

"So far it has, yeah."

She smiled. "Same old Easy. I'm glad you haven't changed. Not much. The short hair looks good on you. You always looked like you belonged in a band in high school."

"Before I signed up, seems like every damn day Dad was telling me to get a haircut."

"Where's your dad today?"

He'd left early that morning. Rollie was back from Colorado so he took off, leaving me in charge of the dogs. "Off to Missouri. Some tables and chairs need to get somewhere and he's still got his license so — "

"Is he still selling guns on the side?"

"He gets around to the gun shows from time to time, yeah."

"Good thing, given all he's got to deal with, given his health and all."

I took a beat to digest that. Then, "What about it?"

"Y'know," she said. "Bills. Insurance companies are such crooks. They're your friend as long as you're sending in the premiums on time but try to make a claim and suddenly they don't know you."

"Um, yeah." I didn't like that Becky seemed to know more about my father than I did. I played along, pretending all this was old news. The way she looked in my eyes, I suspected she knew that I didn't know. I hated that. When people know too much about you, they hold the power. It had been years since we'd spoken but that didn't lessen the power she had over me. If anything, absence and being unattainable increased her edge over me.

"What have you been doing since...you know?"

Our messy breakup? I didn't give voice to the unbidden thought. "Traveling, mostly."

"Where to?"

"Miami, New York, L.A., Seattle. I could only visit. I don't know how anybody can afford to live there. I did a bit of roofing and house painting, odd jobs — "

"I don't know whether I should say that's cool or ask if you're a drifter."

"I dunno either."

"How did you choose those places?"

"Just curious. I checked out the graves of a bunch of dead celebrities."

"If they're in graves, I sure hope they were all dead."

"I didn't hear anybody pounding on the inside cover of their casket."

"Who'd you visit?"

"A bunch. Bruce Lee is buried in Seattle. People are still leaving flowers."

She smiled. "How many times did we watch *Enter the Dragon*?"

"Yeah. There aren't that many good martial arts movies anymore. Now we've got MMA every Saturday night."

"Is that how you're spending your Saturday nights? Really?"

I shrugged. "Still figuring out what to do with my life, I guess. Our high school guidance counselor ... what was his name?"

"Ike Trimby?"

"Yeah, he didn't know what to do with me, either. As I recall, he had big plans for you, Becky."

"And yet, here we are, both back in Lake Orion. Oh, well, Trimby spent his life as a high school guidance counselor. What does he know?"

"He still alive?"

She nodded. "I've seen him around town. Retired now but still around. Most of the people we went to school with moved away. No jobs. You had a kickass job, though, right?"

"Turns out I'm not really cut out for a career in the military."

"Why's that?"

"The getting up early and running thing isn't me. I also can't seem to say the word 'sir' unless I mean it ironically. My superiors caught my vibe."

"I like your vibe." She looked me up and down again. I felt the weight of her stare. We'd seen each other naked and I was pretty sure that could happen again. I didn't want to want her. I didn't want to be the ex-boyfriend who came back sniffing for more. I didn't want to be the guy on the side, still shoveling dog shit in his dad's backyard.

"Donny told me you married a lawyer. Rudy Bench?"

"Not Rudy. Rud, short for Rudyard."

"Rudyard?"

"He's American but his family's British."

"Cool."

"Not really." Her phone buzzed and she pulled it out to check the screen. "Speak of the devil. Gotta go but it was good to see you. I was just in the neighborhood and thought I'd say hello. So...hello."

She waved goodbye and I watched her go, checking out her ass in those tight blue jeans. She still had the wiggle. I could pick that ass out of a police lineup.

There was no way she was "just in the neighborhood." We were on a dirt road far from town. The nearby farms were mostly abandoned and the nearest living neighbor was more than a mile away.

The seeds were planted. I'd see her again. If I was a touch smarter, I would have caught the next bus out of town, bound for anywhere. I've come around to thinking that no one really chooses their fate. Opportunities wax and wane. Obligations pile up. For the most part, we fall into the future. That's what happened to me.

My father raised guard dogs. I was destined to become a guard dog, too.

5

There was still beer in Dad's fridge but I needed to get out of the house. I didn't want to hear him complain about me cleaning him out, so I walked into town. It's a long walk and I limp. I wanted Pabst, though.

The frogs were loud and the road was dark. I would have brought along a dog or two for the exercise but I didn't think the Sophies would be welcome in Paddling's Bar. We didn't want the dogs to take to strangers easily, either. It had taken a week of feeding and training them for the pack to get used to me.

Lake Orion hadn't changed much in the time I was away. There were fewer stores that sold things people actually needed. The township used to have three hardware stores. Now it was down to one. The building that used to house Stanneman's Hardware was empty. The one that had housed Mill's Hardware Needs was now a candle store. How many candles does anyone need? I assumed the new owners made the rent by selling diffusers, bongs and weed out the back of the place.

The township had replaced some sections of sidewalk. In an act of puppy love, Becky and I had written our names in cement with a stick once upon a time. We'd defaced the freshly poured cement sidewalk by the bank. When she drew a lopsided heart around our names, I assumed our vandalism, like our romance, would last forever. After a thorough search, I decided the town had erased us. In little towns everywhere, lots of people feel erased, I guess. Everything exciting and important seems to be happening somewhere else.

Paddling's was the local bar we wished we could get into when we were in high school. The name always sounded to me like a preschool that practiced corporal punishment. There was no way to bull your way in with attitude and a fake ID, though. Too many people knew each other in Lake Orion. My father was a regular. To get my underage drinking done, I had to go to Flint or arrange for someone older than me to buy a six-pack. Then we'd go drink in the woods and talk about how great it would be to live somewhere else, in places where things happened. After my experience in the Army, I can say those dreams of far-off exotic places are overrated.

Even if Dad didn't spot me at Paddling's, there was a good chance the guy behind the bar would know who I was. Mike Paddling was a fixture behind the bar, barely moving. Somehow he seemed to know everyone. It was Mike who spilled the beans that the local Anglican minister was messing around with the industrial arts teacher's wife. That revelation ended with two divorces. The Anglican minister left town to become a shoe salesman in Saginaw.

I'd seen the inside of the bar a couple of times when I was seventeen, but only to pick up Dad. He'd taken my mother's death hard and became a sloppy drunk. After a couple of falls on his face on too many drunken nights, Mike banned him from the bar.

"Tell Ernie he's welcome to come back after he finishes grieving," Mike told me. "And tell him if he wants coffee and a chat with me, that's always free."

A decent offer. However, my father never returned to Paddling's after that. I don't think it was out of embarrassment. Dad carried his grudges in a bucket, always fresh, always handy.

Walking into the bar on a Saturday night, the place seemed smaller and sadder, just like home. I ordered a Pabst.

"You wanna start a tab?"

"Nah, I'll pay as I go." Too much alcohol didn't agree with my medication so I had to keep the liquid refreshment under control.

"Good man," Mike told me. "Nobody runs out of dough that way."

I shrugged and took my drink to a small table at the back. The place was not bright, busy or loud and I liked that about it. When I was in high school, I thought any place I wasn't allowed to go had to be exotic. This bar seemed to cater to an older crowd. The music wasn't to my taste but at least it played low in the background. I'd been in a lot of bars since. Most of them were too loud to have a real conversation and I wasn't much into dancing anymore. My left leg ached from the walk so I washed a couple of Advil down with my second beer.

A couple of pool tables stood nearby. The felts had seen better days and no one was bothering to play. I took a look at the cues on the wall rack. I couldn't find one that wasn't warped but chalked one and racked some balls, anyway. I used to be pretty good at nine-ball, but playing pool is a skill. Skills require practice to keep them sharp. Though it was true that the pockets were a bit tight for recreational play, I was out of practice. I'd lost my touch.

Just as I was telling myself how glad I was that no one was watching, a guy in a windbreaker walked up. He was almost as tall as me but thicker through the neck and chest, like all he did in the gym was the bench press and shoulder shrugs followed by a heavy investment in cheeseburgers. The guy didn't ask for a game. He just stood nearby and watched me knock and flail.

"Hey," I said. "You want this table? You can have it, man. I'm just killing time."

"Nah, go ahead. Looks like you need a lighter touch, dude."

"Uh-huh."

He didn't budge so I decided I hated him. I was far too incompetent to have a spectator. I never wanted to do anything unless I could excel at it. As a result, I hadn't done much besides train dogs and shoot guns.

"I notice you got a bit of limp there."

"Must have a rock in my shoe."

"Must be quite a rock."

"Maybe I twisted my ankle playing racquetball."

"Did you?"

"No." Ready to leave, I left the balls in their triangle on the table and replaced the cue in the rack.

"You sore?" he asked.

"No."

"I'd hate to think I chased you away." His smile told me he'd love that.

"I'm good."

"You look familiar. You got a name?"

"I do." I started to walk away.

He called after me, "I know where I know you from."

I looked back and studied his smug face. I couldn't figure his angle but I was sure he wanted something from me I didn't want to give. "Don't know you, man. We've never met."

"You know my wife. Becky."

"I know a Becky."

"You do. I've seen pictures of you two together in her yearbook."

"That so? I never got my high school yearbook. Didn't know we had pictures in there. You're Rudyard, right? Tell Becky I said hello."

"Not super necessary, is it?" he asked. "You just saw her as soon as you got home."

It was at that moment I wondered if I should have held on to that pool cue. My dad had already been banned from this bar. I wouldn't love it if "like father, like son," got around town. "She came by for a visit, is all."

"That's what she said but I don't know whether to believe her. She's acting different since you came back to town."

"Different how?"

"I don't know. Happier, I guess."

"Sounds like you've got something to work out with your wife," I said.

"Does it? Maybe I should work it out with you."

"Pleased to meet you, Rudyard." I didn't offer my hand. I just nodded and kept my distance. "It was nice to catch up a little with Becky."

"You're a lousy pool player." His fists were balled and his legs were braced. For a second, I thought he might take a swing at me. I was sure he wanted to. Then it occurred to me he was trying to get me to throw the first punch.

"Out of practice." I smiled. "I guess I don't have a light touch, not with a pool cue, anyway. Good luck making Becky happy, Rud bud." I nodded to Mike behind the bar as I limped out. Rudyard Bench did not follow me into the street but I knew that wasn't the end of it. He'd go out of his way to run into me again.

In a city, you can go for years and easily avoid an enemy. A small town has too few places in which to lose yourself. Worse, the rumor mill is always spinning, churning up old blood feuds. People have good memories and like holding on to old news. The only history anyone remembers is the bad stuff and I already had a bad history in Lake Orion. Even if you make one enemy accidentally, trouble is always waiting around the next corner. One enemy easily becomes many.

6

The next night Becky was at my door. Her right eye was black and she wore a small bandage on her left hand. I spotted a bruise and some swelling along her jaw, too. As soon as I saw her on my doorstep, I knew her husband was left-handed.

"I have to talk to you," she said.

"Dad's place is a mess and smells weird, but come on in."

She gave a little laugh. "Then nothing's changed."

I'd changed plenty. I thought about the pain in my leg but decided not to be argumentative.

Becky hurried in. She took a deep breath and looked around the living room. The crummy couch had sagged in the middle. Dad's ugly plaid chair still pointed at the television. I imagined the only spots of carpet that were relatively clean were probably under the furniture.

Becky gave a bright smile as if she'd been allowed behind the velvet rope at a museum and was allowed to touch the exhibits. "I've driven past this house quite a few times in the past year. It feels weird not to be allowed to where you were once welcome. I used to come here all the time."

I wondered if she'd intended the double entendre. She certainly had come here a lot. She'd come on that couch and in that chair.

As if she read my mind, Becky asked, "Remember all our movie nights? You still love old movies?"

"Better dialogue in the old ones," I said. "The new ones depend on special effects too much."

"Same old Easy."

We had watched a lot of movies in this room. Then, after my father went to bed, we fooled around. There was something extra sweet about our teenage sexual adventures. Eventually, our love-making became more athletic and urgent but when we were virgins together, we took our time. We had slowly escalated to the mutual deflowering so it was a special event. We'd built up to intercourse so long, it felt like there should be a plaque commemorating the event over that couch.

"It's a bit strange coming back, isn't it?" I asked. "Had a similar feeling going into Paddling's place. We wanted to hang out in there when we were in high school. Not being allowed in was the real draw. I went in last night to check it out. It wasn't so great. One of the customers was kind of rude."

If she knew the rude stranger was her husband, she gave nothing away. I wondered if she was going to make me ask about her injuries.

I invited her to sit down and offered her a drink. She didn't do either of those things. Instead, she stood a foot away from me and, slowly and painfully, pulled the bandage away from her face. Her chin was raw and red. The contusion along her jawline was fresh, turning blue. Her ice blue eyes watched my face, gauging my reaction.

"How'd you get that burn on your chin?"

"Rud dragged me backward by my feet. It's rug burn."

"I see."

"Not the kind of rug burn I want."

I ignored her obvious flirtation and focused on her problem marriage. "What did the cops have to say about you charging him with domestic violence?" I asked.

"I didn't talk to the cops," Becky said.

"Why not?"

"I'm talking to you."

"A guy who hits a woman is a piece of shit. Can't take that back. You should talk to the cops."

"What are they going to do?"

"Depends on you, I guess. Are you up for kicking him out and getting a restraining order and — "

"Restraining orders are just pieces of paper. It'll never get to a divorce. Rud is gonna kill me one day. Paper won't stop him. He's a lawyer and he's shifty. He'll find a way to get away with it, too."

"Have you thought about leaving?"

"What? Just hitting the road? Sounds like something that would be easy for you. I need money and to get that I have to have a plan."

"Divorce him. Then, when you come back for a visit and you look at me like that, we could do something about it."

"You still want me, don't you? Even like this?" It was more a statement than a question.

"Oh, no. You're hideous."

She laughed and hit me in the center of my chest. "Ass!"

"Hey, you go fishing for compliments, sometimes you don't get a rainbow trout. Sometimes you get an ugly old eel."

She took another step closer and kissed me hard on the lips. While she was doing that, the heel of her hand found my crotch and she rubbed me up and down for what seemed like a long time. But not long enough.

Becky pulled back to look me in the eyes. "I want the old eel."

We laughed together and that was nice, too.

"You've got bruises on top of your bruises," I said. "I can't imagine you're up to it."

Becky pulled her shirt over her head. She wasn't wearing a bra. "If you're up for it, I am."

I was up for it. We weren't laughing anymore. I'd never made love to a woman with a black eye. Turns out, I didn't mind. It was my first time with a woman in a long while and Becky had been my first. Nostalgia is powerful, difficult to resist. I have a hard time letting go of grudges but old loves don't fade easily, either. With grudges, every insult feels as fresh as the moment it was inflicted. Nostalgia is the longing for something good from the past, something to last. I didn't have enough good memories and Becky was a memory to treasure. I wanted to feel like a teenager again, as if my whole life was still in front of me instead of half of it burned away already.

Becky was in a hurry and I tried to slow her down. I missed the shyness of our first explorations, the timidity and the fumbling. Still, it was good and hot and sweet.

We didn't turn back time but for a few moments it almost felt like we were teenagers again. At least, that's how it was for me. Every shitty thing that had happened to me since I left Lake Orion was erased.

Her phone rang as we were finishing. We ignored it and kept going until we were both done. I felt good for a few minutes afterward. Then Becky spoiled it by giving me a smile instead of a kiss. She pulled away and giggled. "Thank you for your service!"

I don't think she noticed as I looked away to make my face do something other than scowl.

Becky's phone let out the long drawn out sound of a mournful foghorn. Her cheeks were still flushed but she didn't take time to enjoy the afterglow. She checked her texts.

I asked if the message was important.

"No and yes," she replied. "It's Rud. He's on his way here."

7

B ecky finished pulling on her clothes and rushed to leave. "It'd be best if I'm not here when he shows up."

"You aren't going back home, are you? Not after he hit you."

She paused. "Thanks for the hospitality. You never disappoint. You were always easy."

"No pun intended?"

"Rud's not easy. He's complicated."

I couldn't afford to offer her money for a motel. A gentleman would do that. I offered to let her stay with me instead.

"Thanks, but that would make things even more complicated."

"If he breaks a cheekbone it'll hurt when I kiss you."

"You don't have to kiss me," she said. "We can still have fun."

"Is that all we were doing?'

"You didn't have fun?"

"I did," I admitted. I thought about saying something more but kept my mouth closed. If I'd spoken, I would have said something sappy. I wasn't sure what Becky was doing but I knew I was the only nostalgic person in the room. At first, I thought her coming over was about receiving comfort. She could have had that with a hug. When she switched positions from missionary to doggy style, it occurred to me the sex might be about getting revenge. I understood the inclination toward vengeance.

"How's your husband know you're here?"

"I don't know. Maybe he followed me or had someone else do it. Doesn't matter. I'll stay at a girlfriend's tonight."

"Then keep one eye on your rearview mirror when you go."

She didn't so much kiss me as brush her lips across mine. She had large pouty lips, warm and soft. Nostalgia packed a powerful punch, but this feeling wasn't just that. It felt good in the present, too. I hadn't felt good in quite a while.

"Becky?"

"Yeah?"

"I want you to be safe."

"Too late for that. I was born. Once that happens, all bets are off."

"Call me." I remembered my father's code to dodge bill collectors. "When you do, let it ring once, hang up and call again."

"Thanks, Easy."

"If he shows up here, can I tell him you went away and you're not coming back? Or do you plan to let him hit you again?"

"I don't plan on either of those things. Let me handle it."

"And what if he doesn't like what I might have to say about it?"

"Try to stay out of it. If he comes at you, do whatever you think is best."

She squeezed me tight and left in her car, a sky blue Audi.

Watching her go, I felt a twist in my gut. I wasn't sure how much I could do for her. She needed a divorce lawyer, not me. Becky was always a little out of my league and that new Audi she drove down the dusty driveway told me I'd always be too poor to support her luxurious tastes. The sex had been great but with me, she'd always be slumming.

Rud must have texted from his car because he pulled into the driveway within a few minutes of Becky leaving. I sat out on the porch and waited in my father's rocker.

Rud Bench pulled halfway up the driveway and left the engine running as he got out. He drove an Audi as well, but this one was black. He left the door open so the annoying bell recording chimed. *Ding! Ding! Ding!*

The alarm continued as he ambled toward me slowly. He staggered a bit, taking his time. I don't know if he was trying to intimidate me or if he was building up his courage for a confrontation. I understand dogs but I have a hard time reading people's intentions.

"Hello, Rud bud," I said. "You been drinking?"

"No."

"Shouldn't drive if you've been drinking."

"I haven't," he said.

"That's just a little disappointing."

"Oh? Why's that?"

"If you'd been drinking, that might give you a little leeway with some people for bad behavior."

"But not you, I take it?"

"A guy who loses control and hits a woman shouldn't drink in the first place, so no, no excuses with me."

"She here?"

"Do you see her car?"

"Where is she?"

"Not here."

"What's going on with you two?"

"I'm not here to play twenty questions with you, Rud. I'm just out here listening to the frogs."

"Stay away from my wife!"

"I don't tell other people what to do. If someone wants to take the trip out of town to see me, I won't tell them to stay away unless they're rude."

He didn't come for a conversation. He came to sock me in the jaw and yell at me. When he got to the bottom step, one of the Sophies let out a low growl. That gave him pause. Then the other Sophies joined in and he took a step back.

"How many dogs you got?"

"Usually half a dozen or so, depending."

"Depending on what?"

"Depending on how many guard dogs we sell."

"That legal? To have so many dogs?"

"We're outside of town, so yeah, it's legal."

He tested the dogs then, jumping up to the second step. The dogs rose from the shadows around me and barked a serious warning.

Rud almost fell backward as he retreated to the bottom of the stairs. The dogs were not satisfied and jockeyed for position at the top of the stairs. The lead dog, the biggest male, bared his teeth.

"See how his ears are flat against his head, Mr. Bench? That Sophie doesn't like you."

"Sophie?"

"They're all named Sophie. Dogs are sensitive, much more sensitive than humans. They pick up on their master's moods. I don't like you so they don't like you."

He retreated a few more steps. He was almost to his Audi before he started cursing me out. "I'll be back!'

"I wouldn't recommend it."

"It would be a shame if something happened to your dogs!"

"It surely would," I said. "You ever see *John Wick*?"

"Wh-who?"

"Not who. What. *John Wick*, the Keanu Reeves movie. Somebody kills his puppy and he murders the entire Russian mob for it."

"That sounds stupid."

"Maybe so," I said, "but as a dog person, I have to say I understand the impulse. I also like Becky. You might say I'm also a Becky person. Do you hear what I'm sayin', Mr. Bench?"

He stared at me bleary-eyed for what seemed like a long time. The dogs' growls and barks and the annoying sound of the door alarm seemed to fill the space between us. *Ding! Ding! Ding!*

Even the frogs stopped to listen. Frogs are good listeners, better than people. Animals of all sorts stop to listen when there's tension in the air. A jungle, for instance, can be a surprisingly loud place. The bark and rattle of a single AK can make all the animals go silent as they listen for danger. Even the insects seem to go still.

Rud Bench wasn't as smart as he thought he was. He wasn't even as smart as the insects in the jungle. As he climbed back into his car, I was sure he had not received the signal I sent.

I would see Becky again. Rud would be back, too. I have a hard time reading people but of that much I was sure.

8

The next morning sunlight dazzled me as I entered the living room. I closed the blinds tight and switched on Dad's television. After adjusting the settings so the screen wasn't so bright and the volume wasn't so loud, I flicked through various news channels.

I kept the largest Sophie in the house with me in case Rud decided to do something stupid and come back with a gun or something. As I scratched behind his ears and watched television, Sophie watched me.

The news could have been a rerun. Trouble in Yemen, still or again, I wasn't sure. The government was refusing to protect customers against payday loan outfits. The same politicians who couldn't wait to say they cared about the troops refused to protect military families from payday lenders.

Then came the weirdest story of the day. Some church somewhere held a service for automatic weapons. The congregants wore tiaras made of rifle cartridges and got their AR-15s blessed by their minister. I've been around guns all my life. They're weapons or they're tools. They aren't ornaments and they don't need blessings.

Sophie pressed his snout beneath my palm, encouraging me to continue petting.

"Your motivations are transparent, Sophie," I told the dog, but I obliged him.

Maybe I don't understand people very well because they aren't meant to be understood. You'd have to be crazy to understand the people who make it on the news. I have this theory that each brain is so unique, it's like we're all operating in our own personal galaxy. Maybe galaxies drift closer together and influence each other's trajectories, but always at a distance. What's going on in your head is as alien to me as whatever's happening in corner stores on planets orbiting far-off suns. We're made of starlight and dirt, sure, but we're all strangers to each other.

That was on my mind when I heard the crunch of gravel under a car tire. My father wasn't due back for a few days so I pulled on my wraparound sunglasses and peeked out the small window by the front door. A sheriff's deputy stepped out of a cruiser.

"Stay, Sophie. I don't want you getting shot."

I walked out on the porch, waved and smiled, making sure to show my hands were empty.

"Ernest Jack?"

"That's my father," I said. "He's not here right now."

"And who are you?"

"His son."

"You're Ernest Jack Jr., then?"

"People call me Easy. Y'know, like Easy Rawlins?"

"Who?"

"Never mind. What can I do ya for, deputy? You lost? The town's back the way you came."

"I got a disturbing call this morning. Someone reported dogs out here barking all night."

"There's not a soul for miles so I don't know who would complain, even if that were true, which it isn't."

"A little bird told me that a young man matching your description was threatening him with attack dogs when he stopped to ask for directions. Funny, you asked me if I was lost. Do a lot of people stop to ask you for directions?"

I refused to take the bait and get pulled down his line of inquisition. "I know the little bird you're talking about. Did he tell you he was drinking and driving last night? And trespassing?"

"He did not, Ernest."

"You can call me Mr. Jack. And what will I call you when I file the complaint of harassment, police brutality and false arrest?"

"I haven't done any such thing — "

"Does Sheriff Eggers know you're out here?"

"Eggers retired last year."

"Oh. That's too bad. He was likable."

"You can call me Deputy Carstairs."

"So Rud Bench sent you out here? Like an errand boy?"

"You better cool that attitude with me, Mr. Jack."

"And before you get your ass in a twist, I should tell you to smile for the cameras. We've had trouble in the past with people trying to steal our dogs. We loaded up on security, little pinhole cameras record everything."

By the set of his jaw, I could tell that messed with how he thought this confrontation was going to go. He pulled out his phone and began recording me. Maybe he was trying to intimidate me but in fact, I felt safer.

"I heard you were away for a long time," he said. "What brings you back?"

I ignored his question. "Did Rudyard Bench tell you he beats his wife, too?"

"Drinking and driving and wife beating, huh? You throw a lot of mud around, Ernest."

"My mud'll stick. Track down Becky Bench and ask her how she got her shiner."

"I'll ask if she files a complaint."

I guessed he already knew about Becky's domestic situation. Abusers don't stop their abuse. Those stories always seemed to end in divorce, jail, a hospital or a cemetery. "Are we done, Deputy?"

He shrugged. "For now."

"Next time you got a question, maybe you better pass it on to the state troopers. I like those guys. Nice big hats. I like their hats."

He put his phone away. "Ernest?"

"Mr. Jack, you mean."

"Mr. Jack, then. You got a lot of attitude for a guy who's done nothing wrong."

"In my experience, people who are righteous have lots of attitude. The meek don't inherit the Earth, Deputy. They get everything taken from them."

"I'm just sayin' don't bring that attitude when you come into my town."

"I went to school in Lake Orion, Deputy. How long have you been around?"

"A few years. It's my home now."

"Then ask around about me."

"I did. You want to tell me about a stolen mail truck back in the day? Back when Eggers was sheriff? I'm sure you remember the incident. You were pretty much the only suspect."

"Old news. I was a kid when that happened."

"Lots of boys out in the country can drive — "

"Eggers cleared me. Check the file."

"Cases can be reopened is all I'm sayin'."

"When a horse is dead, you don't keep beating it, Deputy."

"When it's a dead boy, we don't let things go so easily. The killer was never found."

"Uh-huh. Have a good day, Deputy Carstairs. If you wanted to be friends," I said, "you got off on the wrong foot."

"Who says I wanted to be friends?"

I looked at him, memorizing his face. I'd be thinking about him for a long time. I'd lose sleep pondering how many ways I might murder him and get away with it. Nobody gets away with murdering a cop so I knew it would remain a fantasy. That knowledge wouldn't allow me to let it go, though.

I asked my mother once if these repetitive thoughts were normal. She took a long time to answer. The sicker she got toward the end, the slower her answers came. I remember the rattle of pills as she touched each prescription bottle by her bedside table. She twisted each one to peer at the labels to figure out which medicine to take next. Finally, my mother told me, "Passing fancies is all that is. Everybody has nasty thoughts, Ernest. Don't worry about it overly much."

I snapped back out of the memory. The deputy had said something and I'd spaced out. "Said?"

"I said, 'I'm wondering if you got away with something under Sheriff Eggers' nose.'"

"Enjoy the wonderment, but no, I didn't kill that guy."

"He was a boy."

"I was younger than he was."

"Do you believe in second chances?" Carstairs asked.

"No."

"Me, neither. When's your dad back?"

"Don't know."

"Tell him to call me." The deputy took off his hat to get back in his cruiser. I thought that was the end of it but he paused to ask, "How's the gun business? Makin' some money?"

"I don't know anything about that."

"That right?"

"That's what I said."

"I've heard a lot of things about you. Nobody likes you around here but nobody said you were an idiot. I hope you're not an idiot on top of everything else."

I shrugged and said nothing.

"You know about civil asset forfeiture? Some things, if I catch a man doing them, I can take his car, his truck, his house, anything of value he might leave after he dies."

"Well, look at that, Deputy Carstairs! Despite holding no cards, you managed to get in the last dig and assert your dominance. You're a real man! If you want to pee on the driveway, go ahead. Dogs do mark territory like that."

Carstairs grinned like a fool and drove away. Dad had said the dog breeding business was slow. When Dad got back, we'd have to have a serious talk. Whatever side hustle he had going on, he'd have to back off until the heat died down.

I went back inside and got on the internet to see what surveillance cameras might cost. We didn't have a single camera. I'd lied about that. Within a few minutes, I found a fairly cheap one online and ordered it to be delivered express

Until then, we had a pack of trained guard dogs. The dogs should have been enough. I sure wish it had been enough.

9

I called Becky a few times but she didn't pick up. Was our hookup just a one-time thing for her? Was getting with me only about revenge on her husband? I didn't know and I felt like a fool chasing her.

I tended to the dogs and worked on drills with them for the afternoon. Most dog training is pretty simple. They do as they're told, you reward them. If they don't do as they're told, they don't get the reward. It's actually easier to train several dogs at a time. When one dog does something right and gets the treat the others don't, the slower ones catch on pretty quick. Add a firm tone to a command and give them lots of positive strokes and belly rubs and just about any decent dog can learn to follow simple orders. I wish some of the soldiers I'd trained with could say the same.

I like the early morning hours and the night so when I was done working with the dogs, I went back in the house, boiled three eggs for dinner, took a shower and had a nap. When I awoke, the phone was ringing according to the code I'd given her.

I was groggy when I picked up. "Becky?"

"No, it's me." My father didn't sound happy but that was normal. "Everything okay?"

"The Sophies are good."

"Anybody come lookin' to buy?"

"Not a one. Sorry."

A few beats of silence on the other end of the line felt like emptiness opening up at my feet. Finally, he said, "I think I'm going to have to extend my business trip. Can you handle things while I'm gone?"

"Of course."

"You'll be needing to buy more dog food soon."

He wasn't wrong. The dogs ate like horses. "I think there's plenty for another few days."

"I might be longer than that. You'll need some money."

"I can take care of that. When are you planning to come back?"

"Don't know yet. Gotta make some more calls."

I couldn't decide how much to tell him over the phone. I decided I had to tell him something. "Deputy Carstairs came by."

"What'd he want?"

"He made some noises about keeping an eye out for you."

"That man's a snake," he said.

"He talked like he knew you."

"That's how I get the business I do. I know people."

"Yeah? And?"

"Paul Carstairs used to hook me up with police departments that needed dogs. Then he wanted to get into the gun business. There's more money in the gun business. Whatever I do, he gets his cut. Just another tax man."

"He didn't mention anything about money."

"So why's he got a hard-on for me? Hey, speaking of hard-ons, you asked if it was Becky calling. Does that have anything to do with him showing up?"

"Could be. Her husband came by, acting sore."

"Jesus, Junior! Rud Bench is a hothead. Worse, he's a lawyer. Worse than that, he's in thick with Carstairs."

"You know that for sure?"

"I still have friends in town. I hear shit."

I doubted my father had friends, per se. I suspected he had

customers who had money to spare to buy weapons, people who shared Dad's suspicion of police.

"Doug Weston owns the golf course," Dad said. "Soon as young Bench moved to town he paid for the memberships over at Timber Lea for the whole police force. He and Carstairs golf together all the time."

The name Doug Weston rang a distant bell. I had a vague idea that I'd gone to school with one of Weston's daughters. She'd been a grade ahead of me. I wouldn't have pegged rich old Mr. Weston for a gun enthusiast but there's no one stereotype for those customers. As a teenager, I'd seen soccer moms get blocked in by bikers in our driveway. They all said they came to see our dogs. The gun deals were made out of sight of the road.

Dad started coughing and it turned into a thick, wet hack.

"You okay? Donny down at the store was asking after you. He sounded concerned for your health."

"You know the problem going to a small town doctor? You always know somebody in the waiting room. Old gossips lean in to listen when you talk to the receptionist or talk to the pharmacist. And Donny's always watching what you buy, commenting every time I buy a goddamn aspirin. What's going on with you and Becky?"

"Nothing, Dad."

"Hope so. You let that one get away in high school. Best to let her find other fish in the sea now."

"Dad — "

"I got a spot on my lung is all, Junior. That and a spot of bad luck and no insurance. I'm just riding it out. We'll have to see where it goes. Could be nothing, could be anything. I can't afford to find out."

"Sorry to hear that."

"Yeah, I was, too. I didn't want the subject of my health to be for public consumption. People look at you different when you're getting old or sick. Might have been my own fault. I talked to a few people about it in the beginning when I was trying to figure out what to do."

I thought I heard a moment of softness and humanity from my father. Then the anger about Carstairs roared back. "You know, it could have been Doug Weston himself who opened his fat mouth to the wrong person. Three can keep a secret long as two are dead. Isn't that the saying?"

"You don't have to keep anything from me, Dad."

"Nothing to be done so no use talking about it. You didn't happen to become a doctor while you were away, did you? No, didn't think so."

"Dad, I'm, uh...."

"About the money," he said.

"I can keep things going for a while. I've got some checks coming and — "

"Listen more, talk less. Then look behind the cherry jam," he said. "If that's not enough, check under the couch."

"How about you come home and use that stash to get some help?"

"It's enough to feed the dogs and a little more. It's not near enough for all the bills. Those bastards can wait. The dogs can't. You know where to find it. I planned ahead a little in case I couldn't make it back as I planned."

If he was using the stash and the decoy stash again, Dad's issues were serious. Obviously, Dad was back in the gun business deeper than I'd suspected. Circumstances were about to get downright dire.

10

"Behind the cherry jam" was code.

After I finished the call with my father, I made a beeline for the basement. I knew where to look because I was a little kid when I helped Dad build the place for the decoy stash. A few preserves sat on a rickety shelf made of old barn wood. The shelf stood in front of an enclosed space about the size of a walk-in closet. The shelf swung out on recessed hinges for quick access to the gun safe hidden behind it.

My father kept a few things in the safe. "If someone ever breaks in looking for guns or money, you bring them here," he told me. "Better to give up a little than to give up everything. Most people settle for a lot less than they can really get. This is to make sure they do."

I wasn't quite ten when my father constructed that hideaway. He wasn't specific about who might break in to take our weapons. He might have been thinking about the criminals he dealt with. He might have been talking about the cops. When I asked, he changed the subject.

I slid the hidden door aside. Dust rose in the stale air, making me cough. After that settled, the darkness was cool and inviting. I'm comfortable in the dark and the ambient light was just enough to make out the shape of the tall gun safe. The last time I'd stepped into this spot was with Becky. Sometimes we slipped into this space to make out.

Small town people talk about teenagers, speculating about the sex they're having (and probably a bit jealous). As Becky and I held hands or kissed on Broadway Street, the local prudes would look on with disapproving eyes. Becky and I had made love in the back of her mother's car, in the old hayloft, on the couch upstairs and down here in the basement. Having sex behind the cherry jam wasn't Becky's favorite place to get half naked but when hormonal urges become more urgent, teenage lust takes over. We'd let go of the reins and let loose here many times.

I yanked the pull chain to the hanging forty watt bulb. The gun safe combination used to be the day and month of my parents' wedding anniversary. I punched in the code 0-8-0-2. The familiar click told me Dad hadn't changed the code. When I pulled open the tall steel cabinet, there weren't any surprises. I found his favorite deer rifle, an old over-and-under 12 gauge and a Colt .45. Nothing exotic. My father probably had legit paperwork for these weapons. This was the decoy stash, after all.

A little gold key hanging by the shotgun opened the ammo drawer at the bottom of the safe. I found a box of rounds for the handgun and a carton of cartridges for the shotgun. A few loose bullets for the rifle rolled around. There were also three envelopes.

I opened the heavy manila envelope first. It'd been opened and closed many times over the years, mostly by me. My father was not sentimental and did not enjoy reminiscing about my mother or family. With few stories passed down to me about our history, I was reduced to staring at old pictures and documents for clues. Though there was nothing new, I had pored over the contents of that envelope as if I was trying to break a secret code.

My grandfather's broken pocket watch and Dad's expired passport fell into my palm first. Then there was the deed to the house, my mother's obituary and an old checkbook to a bank in Seattle. A tiny dime store photo album — my mother's — held a few pictures of distant cousins whom I never see, half of whom I can't even name. A smaller envelope held a lock of my hair from when I was a toddler. Though my hair turned dark brown, I used to be so blonde my hair was almost white. Tucked in with my birth announcement, I found my birth certificate, crisp as the day it was issued. I wonder how many people still put birth announcements in the newspaper. Not nearly as many as used to, surely? I couldn't remember the last time I read much more than a newspaper headline.

My mother held on to my baby teeth in a small yellow envelope. Dad wasn't sentimental but I think he left that little envelope of enamel keepsakes alone because Mom wanted to hold on to them.

What eventually happens to stuff like this? Someone will throw the teeth away someday, but who? If Dad lost the house, there would be an estate sale for the benefit of the creditors. Maybe some auctioneer's assistant would hand these tiny treasures over to me. How long would I hold on to them? Or would they be reduced to oddities in a night table drawer by my deathbed?

I vaguely remembered that after Katharine Hepburn's death there was a huge estate sale. Hollywood memorabilia and, I'm guessing, a lot of pantsuits were snatched up by fans of the great actress. Kate Hepburn led a remarkable life but in the end, what was left? My father would say, "A garage sale is where somebody drags shit down from their attic, sticks it on the lawn to sell it for a pittance so you can drag it off and stick it in your attic."

I put everything back in the manila envelope and tucked it away, careful not to bend it.

The second wrinkled envelope was rolled up in a cylinder and wrapped tightly with a thick elastic band. At first glance, it looked like it held a respectable wad of cash. That was the decoy component. When I unwrapped it, I found a lot of ones, fives, tens and a couple of twenties. It was a little over $200 in cash. Dad was right. That wouldn't pay for much medical care. It wouldn't even go far for buying big bags of dog food, treats and pig ears. If one of the dogs got sick and I had to call the vet, this roll wouldn't do at all.

I left the money where it was and opened the third envelope, as new and pristine as if it was fresh from a stationery store. I found a gold key and a set of car keys on a ring. I recognized the key ring immediately. It was a little John Deere tractor in bright green and yellow. Those were the keys to my father's prized muscle car in the barn.

The little gold key was separate from the ring. Examining it, the key looked quite small and irregular. A white tag was tied to the key by a white string. I recognized my father's careful block printing. He'd labeled the little key: WHERE THERE'S A WILL.

Despite his troubles, my father often said, "Where there's a will, there's a way." Actually, that was my mother's motto. I didn't know my mother's last words to my father so I imagine that's what she whispered to him as she shrank into death on her bed.

After Mom died, Dad often repeated that phrase but he always said it ironically.

I locked the safe again, pulled the chain and stood in the darkness for a few moments. The basement smelled musty but it was quiet and cool.

This land would be worth something but whoever bought this property next would level the house to build anew. Unlike Dad, I was sentimental. I didn't think about this hidden nook as a way to placate a home invader or a symbol of my father's checkered past and paranoia. It was where Becky and I made passionate love in the dark. I wondered where she was now and how long she would wait before returning to her dangerous home with Rud Bench.

I checked my watch, a diver's special with big phosphorus green markers. Still a couple of hours until dusk. I'd wait before I checked my father's real cache.

That choice to rest my eyes and stay out of daylight ended up saving my life. A million tiny choices set our course. The way is never clear until you look backward.

11

"Check under the couch" was code, too. Dad didn't mean the saggy couch in the living room. He meant the dilapidated old sofa in the barn. At dusk, I checked on the dogs to make sure they were fed and watered. They swarmed around my feet, tails wagging. I petted each Sophie to make sure they all got an equal amount of attention.

Dad had piqued my curiosity and as darkness fell, it was time to look for what he'd left for me. "I'll take you guys out for a run around the perimeter later," I told the dogs. "First, I have to check on Dad's stash."

I walked through the dogs. To maintain alpha status with the pack, it's essential for a trainer to walk through them instead of walking around them. They respect the pack hierarchy as long as you don't give in too much. I guess humans are much the same.

One of the German shepherds had a white spot in the middle of his chest. He always seemed to stand at the edge of the pack, the odd one out. Though of a decent size, he was still the runt of the litter. He had to fight for attention as his brothers pushed him aside. On impulse, I let that Sophie come with me.

He didn't heel well and needed reminding that he should stay at my side as I walked the property. A tiny tug on his leash did the job but this Sophie seemed to have a short memory. Or maybe, like me, he suffered the curse of wanderlust.

Just about everybody I'd known from Lake Orion was married and settled down somewhere. Several were already working on their second marriages. I was too curious about what came next to stay in one place for long. That was one of the few ways the military had made me happy. Now I was out. What was next? I wondered if Becky would be interested in getting away with me for a while. I hoped she was finding the exit to her shitty marriage to a bad guy. However, I didn't assume she'd want to hook up with me.

When we broke up, Dad told me bluntly, "A pretty girl like that? She's looking to hitch her wagon to a star. You're more of a stump, Junior."

I didn't join up because Becky dumped me. I made the snap decision to join the Army and get out of Lake Orion because of that conversation with my dad. He called it speaking plain and "just being honest." I called it acting like an asshole.

The barn hadn't been used for hay in a long time. When it wasn't on the road, the barn housed the big Kenworth. It was also the lair for Dad's prized possession, an old dented Barracuda. Heart came out with the song "Barracuda" in 1977. My father scraped together enough cash to buy Plymouth's 1973 model thirdhand soon after that.

I always liked the Barracuda. The dents made it look tougher. There was something about the way the grille came around the headlights that made it seem aggressive. If it had been in better condition, the car might have had more value as a collector's item. Dad kept the V-8 engine humming and took it out for a drive in the summer occasionally. That car was the only extravagance he reserved for himself. The Barracuda was mostly for him to drive. I could tell Dad loved my mother, not because they indulged in displays of affection in my presence, but because he let her drive the Barracuda.

The only time I'd seen my father crank the radio up was when "Barracuda" came on. Mom didn't care for the song but thought "Radar Love" by Golden Earring was the perfect driving song. That

was from 1973, too. It was as if my parents picked their happiest time
— long before the financial troubles and cancer diagnosis — and
tried to make that one year go on and on, 1973 forever.

Beyond the truck bay, the barn housed several smaller rooms.
People farmed this land for a couple of hundred years before my
parents came along. The previous owners kept a couple of oxen. If
someone bought this farm out from under Dad, they'd probably keep
the barn and bulldoze the house. A different barn stood on this same
spot until the roof caved in after a particularly heavy snowfall sometime in the winter of 1962. When the roof gave way, two outside walls
went with it so they rebuilt the whole structure. This barn was built
to replace it in 1963.

I discovered the secret in the barn when I was a kid. Dad told me
it was pretty much the same as most barns with one crucial difference: 1962 happened. That changed everything. That was the year
Americans remembered they weren't safe and war could come
here, too.

At first, I thought he was talking about the storm that had brought
the roof down long ago. "No, no, it was 1962 that made our barn
special," Dad explained.

Beyond the stalls was a big room that once held the plow the oxen
pulled. Dad sold that blade long ago to pay some bills. I don't imagine
he got much for it. Beyond the plow room was a smaller room at the
end of the barn. An array of tools hung from pegboard on the walls.

An old police scanner sat on a small shelf Dad built just for the
device. There are phone apps for that purpose now but Dad had been
listening to radio chatter on emergency frequencies for years. He
received it as a Christmas present from my mother. I remembered the
smell of the plastic as he pulled the scanner out of the box.

Whenever Dad was in his workshop, he left it on.

I asked him why he never played any music while he worked. He
told me, "Can't dance and work at the same time."

Sometimes on summer nights, he brought the scanner out on the
front porch. He and Mom would sit side by side, rarely speaking,
voyeurs to domestic violence calls in Flint, firefighters in Detroit and

all kinds of assorted mayhem that are unleashed on the world when darkness takes its turn.

After Mom got sick, she stopped coming out on the porch to listen to the scanner's unfolding dramas. Dad kept listening to the grim news unfolding in real time. I asked him why he found it so fascinating.

"It's a great big dirty world, Junior," he said finally. "Something bad's always happening somewhere. We got guns so I don't worry much about home invaders and stuff like that. We're basically out in the country and got some space around us. Chances are, trouble won't find us out here ... not if we keep our heads down and stay off the radar. Since your mother was first diagnosed, listenin' to that scanner, it's kind of soothing. I hear about all the problems I don't have."

"Knowing other people are in trouble makes you feel good?"

"Not like that," he said. "Makes me feel like, as long as I have guns, at least there's something I have a say about. Cancer doesn't give you a say. People told your mom to fight it but cancer treatment is about the most passive thing anybody can do. You lay there and take it. Needles go in, you wait in waiting rooms, you get scanned, and on and on it goes with all the doctor appointments. Your mom's friends weighed her down with too much, telling her all the remedies she might try to save herself." He chuckled. "They got so exhausting with all their cures that wouldn't work, your mom got rid of the well-meaning friends and kept the cancer."

"Is that why you like guns, Dad?"

He didn't reply for so long I didn't think he was going to answer me. Finally, he said, "We're just looking to grab some control, son. You're too young to understand. You still feel safe. Sorry to tell you, you're wrong."

He didn't sound sorry, especially when he quoted the Declaration of Independence. "We hold these truths to be self-evident, that all men are created equal, that they are endowed by their creator with certain unalienable rights, that among these are life, liberty and the pursuit of happiness." His was a bitter laugh. "Don't let 'em fool you, boy. We can pursue it but people like us ain't supposed to catch it."

"People like us?"

"Regular people. We're never gonna get on TV unless something really bad happens. You'll see. As you get older, you'll start the hunt for love and riches. Forget those truths they tell you about in school. We hold these values above all others: sex and money. That's the only declaration that can make you feel your oats. Dollars and titties are just the means to an end, what you want to get the feeling you need. We're really looking for safety. Life's a wild ride, kid. Remember when you went on that roller coaster at the county fair? It's for a quick thrill but you still have that safety bar that comes down so you won't fall out. People only think they want excitement. They don't. Don't ask for an exciting life, Junior. Be grateful if you get a boring one. The less happens, the safer you are. That's as close to happiness as I expect to get."

"I don't want to believe that," I told him.

Dad shrugged. "That's because you still believe what they're selling you on TV and at school. Take your mother. Things are pretty exciting for Sophie right now, what with all the treatments and pain. Your mother's on a wild ride and up ahead, the tracks are out. She's about to go flyin' off into space, no safety bar to keep her from falling out. We all fall out someday. It's different when you can see the end coming."

"Jesus, Dad."

"Just being honest as best as I can see it. You're still thinking like a young man. I want you to be safe. Think like an old man so maybe you'll get to be one of them."

Mom had kept her illness secret from me as long as she could. She pretended everything was normal even as doctor visits began to fill the calendar on the fridge door. As she got sicker, Dad spent more time listening to the police scanner. He cleaned his guns obsessively, trying to impose order on the one thing under his power.

Entering his workshop at the end of the barn, it seemed little had changed. Along the wall, a steel table held all the gunsmithing necessities: a deluxe gun screwdriver set, vises, the benchtop belt sander, rifling tools, a brass punch set, Acraglas gel and a Leupold scope ring tool among various other essentials. Dad had sold off a lot of stuff over the years so he wouldn't lose the property. However, the shop looked as clean, neat and complete as it was the day I left for Fort Benning.

Dad didn't think I had it in me to bow to authority, even after I made it all the way through boot camp. Fourteen percent of candidates dropped out of training when I went through. The fact that my father was certain I would be among the dropouts is what kept me in the army. Drill instructors talk about the importance of motivation and persistence. Spite will do.

Besides a lone stool by the table, there was only one other piece of furniture in the workshop. A ragged plaid couch sat to my left. It used to be in the living room in the house but that was so long ago I couldn't remember it there. When Dad said to check under the couch cushions, he meant that I should look under this couch.

I slid the sofa aside and pulled up the little throw rug. The trapdoor wasn't much bigger than the width of my shoulders. When I pulled up the trapdoor, the littlest Sophie stuck his head between my knees to get closer to the black hole at my feet. Curious, the dog sniffed at the rising dust and peered down into blackness. I lifted a heavy Maglite flashlight from the bench and pushed the German shepherd's head out of my way so I could climb down the steep ladder.

The dog whined and looked a little frantic.

"Stay, Sophie. We haven't trained you on climbing ladders, certainly not backward."

Dad had not built this bunker. The previous owners added it to the construction plans for their new barn just as fears of nuclear war were at their height. "They call it the Cuban Missile Crisis now but at least around here, old-timers called it the Cuban Missile Scare," Dad explained. "That's what I mean when I say 1962 built this place."

Reading about it in high school, "crisis" made it seem impersonal. There were plenty of crises: oil, energy, water and whether we'd have bananas, almonds or bees in fifty years. Not many people wanted to admit they got scared.

The bunker that was supposed to save the family from becoming radioactive ash was lined with concrete blocks. It held four bunks. Rough shelves, probably meant for canned food, lined the walls. There were no lights and they hadn't installed plumbing so it seemed to me the previous owners were half-baked survivalists who hadn't thought things through. Assuming they survived the initial blast, life down in this hole would have been pretty grim.

I spotted an electric lantern and switched that on. It cast a dim light so I still had to use the Maglite. I had been down here only a few times. It felt like a tomb. I never took Becky down that ladder to wrestle off our clothes for a quickie away from prying eyes. I didn't know about this room until I was twelve and I never told anyone outside the family about it. My father warned, "I'll take you to the woodshed if beans are spilled." He needn't have threatened me. I understood even then that it could be dangerous for my friends at school to find out the bunker existed. Dad was always worried that his work as a gun dealer might bring what he called "the wrong element" to our door looking to get a bunch of weapons for free. I never even told Becky.

I shone the light around the small room. A small fireproof safe sat on one of the shelves. The shelves were mostly empty except for a small assortment of weapons. Dad didn't seem to have much inventory. Ammo boxes and a black case crowded the small floor space.

I pulled out the shiny gold key. *Where there's a will,* I thought.

The fireproof box's lock opened with a soft click.

12

Dad must have been very sure the bunker remained a secret. The guns had no trigger locks and the little safe was no more than a few pounds. The contents would be safe from fire but not from thieves. If a would-be intruder knew of this place below his workshop, it would be no trick at all to walk off with his weapons and the safe. As far as I knew, the only people who'd known about this hiding place were me, my father and my mother.

Three can keep a secret if two of them are dead.

It bothered me that my brain offered up that tidbit at that particular moment.

As Sophie whined in the bright square above my head, I opened the safe's door. It was an evening for greasy wrinkled envelopes. There was no will bequeathing me the farm. Each envelope was labeled in my father's careful block lettering:

$$$ FOR MEDICAL
$$$ FOR BANK
$$$ FOR TAXES
$$$ FOR DOGS

$$$ FOR CARSTAIRS
$$$ FOR MISC.
$$$ FOR JUNIOR

MOST OF THE envelopes contained little more than a few dollars. The envelope labeled miscellaneous was empty. There was close to a thousand dollars set aside for Paul Carstairs. My eyes went wide when I started counting out the worn bills from the envelope Dad left for me. That envelope contained $12, 248.10.

Tucked in amid the wad of cash was a little picture of my father standing beside me in hip waders holding a fishing reel. Dad never said, "Let's go fishing." He always said, "Let's go wash some worms."

In the photo, I would guess I am seven years old. I'm holding up the first trout I caught. I had forgotten the photo but I guessed my mother was the person holding the camera. I did remember hooking that fish, watching the bob dart down in the water as the trout hit the bait. When the fish was good and hooked, I tried to give the reel over to my father, asking him to take over. He refused. "You can do it yourself, Junior. You're a Jack, aren't you? Be a Jack! Land that fish!"

Those were the only words of pure encouragement I remembered from Dad but when you don't get sugar often, you hold on to the memory when it is doled out.

As nice as the photograph was, it was the inclusion of the dime that brought tears to my eyes. He was scraping money together. I didn't share my father's love of guns. He taught me to shoot and to hunt. I'd used weapons plenty but I didn't love them as he did. I often wished he'd gotten into a side hustle that didn't possess such dangerous potential. If he was so bound and determined to have a profitable illicit business on the side, why not grow weed to make ends meet like so many other farmers in the area did?

I didn't always get along with Dad. My childhood was filled with bickering and not a little fear. I'd inherited his tendency to anger. Sometimes I felt he was so in love with guns for the same reason he used to smoke cigars and a pipe. He was a little too concerned with looking manly. His work as a gunsmith and occasional gunrunner must have made him feel more dangerous. He should have watched a little more Mr. Rogers as a kid and eased up on the old John Wayne movies. However, for all the ways he was ill-equipped as a father figure, he did want the best for me.

This cache of money told me he was trying hard. It also told me what he never would: My father was undoubtedly dying. We weren't the sort of people to visit lawyers and bankers. We wouldn't have the mojo to negotiate debts and draw up wills. We were the sort of people who lose their money and property to lawyers and bankers.

The dog whined again. I ignored Sophie in that moment. Looking back, I understood that the canine heard things I could not. I didn't start running for the ladder until the dogs out in the pens started barking. My first thought was we had after-hours visitors and I had better cover up the entrance to the bunker again.

Then the shooting started. *Pop! Pop! Pop! Pop!*

I jumped back down and retrieved a nickel-plated .38 from Dad's inventory. I stepped into the square of light at the bottom of the ladder to check the load. My father always expected trouble because, as he often said, "Poor folks expect trouble and we're very rarely wrong." He stored his weapons loaded.

Pop! Pop! Pop! Pop!

By the time I got to the top of the ladder the shooting had ceased. I knew it was bad because the dogs had gone silent.

13

The first rule I broke was leaving the trapdoor to the bunker open. Sophie was barking, excited. I hushed him and told him to stay. The German shepherd obeyed but the way he did it, it was as if his hindquarters were on springs. My hold on the dog's will was tenuous. I ordered him to lie down. Again, Sophie complied but the animal did not rest his muzzle on his paws. He was very alert and his tail beat the wooden floor like a drum. I didn't have time to tie him up so I repeated my demand that he stay and headed out the door, not daring to run until I was out of his sight.

The second rule I broke was to hurry outside without taking the time for reconnaissance. My knee ached as I ran. It had been a while since I had tried to run full tilt. I usually took eight extra-strength Tylenol a day when I was more active. I'd only taken a couple that morning. The pain running up my leg and into my thigh reminded me that I should follow doctor's orders and not ration my medication. I took in the cool night air through gritted teeth and rushed forward.

I only slowed my pace when I came around the corner of the barn. An unfamiliar car sat in the driveway. Its nose was pointed toward the road, ready for a quick getaway. The car's engine was running loud with a powerful bass to its rumble. It was too dark to make out the model. My night vision is sharp but mud was smeared over the license plate. A cloud billowed from its dual exhaust.

Slow down, Soldier, I thought. *Somebody's planned ahead and you've got no plan. You're letting the gun in your hand do the thinking.*

I barely knew cars. My father could tell many models of old cars apart but even his expertise failed with modern cars. New models had all gone through the same wind tunnel. Most of them looked alike to me.

I slipped into the shadow of the barn, waiting, listening. I heard nothing but a familiar smell came to me. I sniffed the air. Cedar, balsam, rosemary ... lavender. I knew that smell. It took me a moment to place the memory.

Culver City, I thought. *Holy Cross Cemetery! Drakkar Noir!*

I was supposed to walk a lot as part of my rehabilitation program for my leg. I was so sensitive to noise at that time I couldn't stand to walk city streets. In malls, even the mumbles of crowds bouncing off walls formed an inescapable and irritating drone. Cemeteries are quiet places. The last time I'd caught that heavy scent, I was off to visit the memorial to actor John Candy, one of my mother's favorites. While other families watched classic seasonal movies, our family settled down in front of the TV to watch *Uncle Buck* every Christmas Eve. It was the only movie we all agreed on. I knew that strong cologne from the cab I took to get to Holy Cross.

From the direction of the dog pens, I sensed movement. I raised the .38 and waited for the intruder to come closer. He was carrying a rifle. I heard him change the magazine. I needed him to come close. I could hurt him with the .38 but he'd kill me with the rifle easily.

He was a tall bald man dressed in black. He moved in an unhurried way, scanning ahead. If I moved, he would have spotted me. I slowed my breathing and waited for my moment. When he was no more than a few feet away, I said, "Drop your weapon or I'll drop you."

He stiffened in surprise but he didn't drop the rifle. In situations such as these, I'd learned the hard way that hesitation is the enemy of life. I fired a round at the ground at his feet.

The intruder said, "Okay, buddy, okay." He slowly bent and placed the weapon at his feet.

The way he did it reminded me of an incident in boot camp. Some gomer was on the range, trying out an automatic weapon for the first time. As he pressed the trigger, he apparently expected it to fire in single shot mode. When it kept firing, the idiot turned to the range officer and said, "Sergeant!" as the weapon continued to fire. The rest of us dove out of the line of fire. He might have killed a couple of us but fortunately, his ammo ran out before anyone got perforated.

The sergeant looked cool and relaxed. He approached the recruit and instructed him to turn and place the rifle at his feet. As soon as the weapon was safely on the ground, the sergeant kicked him in the ass as hard as I'd seen anyone get kicked.

"Where'd you serve?" I asked the tall bald man.

"Who says I did?"

I fired another shot. This time the round dug into the dirt closer to his feet.

"Iraq," he said. "Then Afghanistan. Been out a few years."

"You killed my Sophies."

"Huh?"

"The dogs."

"You call them all Sophie?"

"Yeah, I called them all that until you killed them."

"That must have been confusing. Why would you call them all the same name?"

"You have no idea. They're all males. They're all named Sophie for reasons. It's nothing to you."

"Are they transgender or something?" He sounded genuinely curious.

"Why did you kill my dogs?"

"It's a job, man. I need one. For what it's worth, I didn't enjoy it."

"Who sent you?"

In the moment that he hesitated to answer, time seemed to slow. Something about a slight movement of his head made me think he was looking behind me. It occurred to me that I wasn't getting a whiff of Drakkar off the bald man. The man who killed our dogs had not come alone. In the second I managed a half-turn, I glimpsed another intruder with a heavy beard. He rose out of the shadows and clocked me on the right side of the head. I went down hard. The shock was so bad, I didn't feel any pain in my leg.

What's worse than dead, Soldier? Stupid and dead. You're about to die of embarrassment, Easy. Embarrassment and bullets.

Two things saved me from joining the dogs in Valhalla, or whatever comes next.

First, I held on to the .38. I went down but I squeezed off a few shots, hitting nothing.

When I rolled onto my back I looked down the long barrel of a 9mm with a silencer. They should have used that. Silencers are far from silent but if they'd thought to use that to kill the dogs, I would have been blissfully unaware and safe down in my father's bunker.

The second thing that saved me from getting murdered was that the remaining Sophie broke a rule, too. He did not stay put as ordered. The dog raced around the corner snarling. The animal's jaws closed around the forearm of the man with the 9mm.

He shrieked and squeezed off a shot that chunked into the ground beside my head.

I kicked at his legs and caught him inside his left knee. He fell sideways and began screaming for help as he wrestled with Sophie. They moved in a tangle, the dog refusing to give up my assailant's arm.

I made it up to my knees before I felt the cold muzzle of the rifle on my forehead. "Call off the dog, my friend."

He gasped as he felt the muzzle of the .38 dig into his crotch. "Point your cannon somewhere else and I will."

Slowly, he eased the tip of the barrel away and I staggered to my feet. "Sophie! Out!"

I had to say it a couple more times but the German shepherd finally got the idea and let go. The man he'd taken down lay in the grass bleeding. He got on his hands and knees and began cursing as he searched the tall grass for the handgun he'd dropped.

"Go," I said.

The bearded man got to his feet, holding his ruined forearm. "What? That's it?"

"Mexican standoff," the man with the rifle said. "I've got a gun, he's got a gun, you lost yours. Let's get the hell out of here."

Sophie growled. I didn't dare take my eyes off the man with the rifle but by his harsh rumble, I knew the dog didn't appreciate how tenuous the truce was.

"Don't come back!" I said.

"That's it? Really? You gonna let him do us like that?" The wounded man sounded astonished.

"I don't kill unless I get paid. I didn't get paid to kill anybody but a bunch of dogs," the rifleman replied. He backed away slowly. His companion followed him, still cradling his injured arm, still cursing.

They climbed into their car and roared off in a cloud of exhaust and dust. As soon as they got to the end of the driveway, their tires squealed on the pavement of the county road. They left in the direction of Lake Orion and I thought it was pretty damn obvious who sent them.

"Catch you later, assholes," I whispered.

The rifleman was a dog killer but he wasn't an idiot. His pal would definitely have murdered me for free if not for Sophie. Holding my pounding head, I sank down onto my butt in the cool grass in the moon shadows of the barn. Sophie took this as an invitation to lick my face.

"You're a good boy," I told Sophie, "even better than I thought. Thank you."

I didn't want to go back to the dog pens. I knew what I'd find. Still, I had to check in case, by some miracle, there were survivors.

I got to my feet and looked for the intruder's dropped pistol. I didn't see it and told myself I'd find it easily in daylight. There was a higher priority that needed tending to.

As I hefted my .38, I told myself that I was worried my attackers would come back. That wasn't true. They were probably done for the night. The real reason my hands shook, the thing I dreaded most, was that I might have to finish off a mortally wounded dog.

I walked back to the pens, checking the pistol's load as I went. It turned out I'd been in a standoff with no ammunition. I'd fired all the shots I had in the confrontation.

Sometimes lucky will get you through when smart won't do. That's not the way to bet, of course.

14

The last Sophie ran back and forth along the perimeter of the dog enclosure sniffing, whining and barking. No bodies stirred in the pens. My head felt like a pounding drum. I checked each body. They hadn't had a chance.

"C'mon," I said. "I can't do anything more for them tonight. I'll bury them tomorrow but tonight, I've got to rest."

I gathered up a dog dish so the surviving Sophie could have some water and walked back toward the barn. The German shepherd didn't follow me right away. When I glanced back, I imagined the dog was waiting for me to perform some magic trick to bring his brothers back to life. I gave him time, walking slowly. As I reached the corner of the barn, he finally ran to join me.

Back in the barn, I threw the deadbolt on the big door and retreated to my father's workshop. The workshop's sliding metal door had a heavy padlock I could lock from the inside. I would have preferred my bed but the house wasn't as secure as this room. Plus, I had the weapons in the bunker if I needed them.

I sank down into the couch and closed my eyes. Sophie was agitated and paced a long time, not touching his water. Eventually, the dog padded over to rest its head on my hand.

"Don't fall in love with a puppy," Dad had told me once. "Not when I'm going to have to sell them."

As I got older, even though I had to say goodbye, I fell in love with training them. Sometimes we sold the dogs to outfits for serious uses, like patrolling airports or malls. We used to sell quite a few to suburban families, too. The worse the economy got, the more dogs we sold, at least for a while.

One time, we were driving back from Frankenmuth. One of the restaurants there served the best chicken dinner in the state. On the road outside of Flint, we spotted a gray clapboard house. A ripped curtain served as a business sign in the front window: Tattoo Parlor. Beneath that was another sign in red: Out of Business.

My father slowed the car to gaze at the ramshackle house and made a tsk sound.

"What, Dad?"

"You don't see what I see?"

"Bad news for somebody who wants a tattoo?"

He shook his head. "That there signals bad news for everybody. When times are tough, people buy dogs to keep the burglars away."

"That sounds like good news for us."

"To a point," he admitted. "But when a tattoo parlor on the outskirts of Flint goes out of business? Man alive, we are in for a bad time of it. The politicians say they want world peace but what they really need is to make sure everybody gets a decent job. Good jobs, no crime. In a souring economy, people want a watchdog. In a dead economy, they can't afford to feed a dog. Probably can't afford to feed their kids."

My father, the amateur economist who couldn't ever seem to hold on to money, was exactly right. The exodus soon began. Nearly 10,000 homes in Flint emptied out. "They say the recession is over but we'll never catch up. The employment rate is pretty low, but it's all shitty jobs and lots of people have multiple jobs."

I asked my father where all those people went. He didn't know so I looked it up at school. Most people who left Flint weren't coming back.

The drum in my head became a softer metronome as long as I kept my eyes closed and didn't move my head too much. I petted the dog, smoothing his ears back and feeling the soft velvet at the edge of the underside of each ear. "Sorry about your buddies, pal. Can you be the alpha dog for a while? My head hurts too much right now."

The alpha dog theory is actually bullshit. Dogs and their wolf cousins are naturally cooperative. In the wild, there is a hierarchy to a wolf pack. However, they work together much more than the alpha dog myth suggests. One leader emerges as the alpha dog, but that's a phenomenon of animals kept in captivity.

"I think we all must be in captivity," I told Sophie. "That would explain a lot of shitty behavior among humans."

I opened one eye. The dog stared at me. His eyes were so expressive, it seemed he had something to say.

"If you do decide to start talking," I said, "I've probably got a brain bleed and I'm going to die."

The dog looked alert but did not speak.

"Okay, fine, I'll live," I said resentfully. I shut my eyes again but I couldn't sleep. What kind of person shoots a bunch of dogs as if they were fish in a barrel? I thought about the logistics of it and started to get mad again. He wouldn't have stood back and fired at a distance. He put the muzzle of his weapon through each empty diamond in the fence. He would have been close. He would have been looking in their eyes as he squeezed off each round to execute each black and tan beauty.

Still, the guy had walked away. He'd retreated. If he really wanted me dead, all he had to do was wait for his buddy to get in the car. He could have crouched behind the getaway car's engine block and sniped me with his rifle.

No, I thought, *there was no particular malice in the act.*

Like the bald man said, he didn't enjoy killing the dogs. It was just a job to him. I wasn't sure whether that made his actions better or worse but it told me he wasn't completely soulless. That didn't mean I wouldn't kick his ass next time I saw him. Or kill him. I hadn't decided yet.

As for the person who gave him that job? "It would be a shame if something happened to your dogs!" Rud Bench had just stood at the bottom of the steps to the house and said that to my face. I didn't think I needed to call in Sherlock Holmes, the Scooby gang and Batman to figure out who was to blame.

I cursed for a while, pet Sophie and eventually drifted off to sleep. The morning came too quickly and far too bright. It's harder to see the details of a bunch of dead dogs at night. I prefer the comfort of darkness.

When I asked my unit's doctor what was wrong with my eyes, he smirked and said, "According to the tests, there's nothing wrong with your eyes, Lieutenant. It's just that you've seen too much."

15

I knocked on wood for luck. The trouble was the rapping came in odd numbers and I couldn't get it right for some reason.

Maybe it's a concussion, I thought. *Maybe I need to get to a hospital. But I can't afford a hospital. We've got enough bills. Keep knocking.*

To get luck, knock on wood twice, clean and even. If I got too many knuckles in on the knock, I have to knock again, but always in twos. If I accidentally knock three times, that's bad luck. Even numbers are fine except I can't knock six times. Six is very bad. Get that wrong and I have to keep knocking but make sure I get past thirteen because thirteen is a baker's dozen of bad luck.

About the time I figured out I was dreaming, whoever was pounding on the barn door was really whaling on it. It's weird when what's happening in the real world sneaks in and takes over the script of your dreams.

Sophie licked my hand and then my face. I pulled myself up to a sitting position and waited a moment to see if my head would slip from my shoulders and to the floor. That didn't happen so I guessed it was safe to challenge gravity.

The couch was still askew and the trapdoor was open. Reluctantly, I climbed down the ladder. The concrete block walls were cool to the touch. I wanted to stay down in Dad's bunker in the comfort of weapons and darkness. The knocking was farther away but no less insistent. I put the spent .38 back on the shelf and picked up a Ruger. I checked. This handgun was also loaded. I thought about taking it back up but, after a moment's debate, put it back on the shelf. Bad guys don't generally knock. What if it was Deputy Carstairs? It wouldn't do to be strapped if the cop had come back.

I climbed back up, covered the trapdoor with the ragged rug and pushed the couch back into place. Sophie stayed by my side as I popped the lock to the workshop and made my way to the big barn door. The person on the other side of the door had given up. I slid the deadbolt back and, wincing in pain at the bright sunshine, peered out to see Becky making her way back to her Audi.

I told Sophie to stay and began walking toward her, shading my eyes with one hand. When I called after her, Becky whirled and ran to me. She hugged me tight, her mouth at my throat. "You didn't pick up! I've been calling you all morning! Why didn't you answer? I checked the house and it was empty! I looked for you by the pens! The dogs are all dead! It's awful!"

"I know."

"What happened?"

"Had a couple of visitors last night."

"They killed your dogs?"

"It wasn't mass suicide."

"Who did this?"

"Didn't catch their names. Couple strangers, one tall and bald with a rifle. The other was shorter, had a thick beard. He wore a lot of cologne for a guy with a beard. I always thought of that as an after-shave sort of deal."

"Why would someone do that?"

I pulled back, narrowed my eyes against the bright light and stared in her face. "Guess."

Becky's lower lip trembled. "You're thinking it was Rud's doing, aren't you?"

"Aren't you?"

"Did they hurt you?"

"Not as bad as the dogs."

"Oh, Easy! I'm so sorry!"

"You've got nothing to be sorry about. Your piece of shit husband, on the other hand — "

"Let's get you inside. Are you okay?"

"Got a headache but not as bad as last night. Not much could be worse than last night. I don't know what I'm going to tell my dad." I felt stupid as soon as I said it. This wasn't like the time I broke a lamp tossing a ball inside the house. Dad loved the dogs but they were also his legit business. A dog trained for a single purpose could sell for $3,000 at least. Trained up for more than one purpose, each dog could sell for as much as $10,000. That would have put at least a little dent in the medical bills.

I whistled for the remaining Sophie. The German shepherd barreled out toward us as if he'd been waiting for me to give the go-ahead. He circled us and tried to get between Becky and me, barking at her and baring his teeth. His hackles stood up as he planted his feet, prepared to spring.

"Sophie!" I yelled. "Out! Friend!"

The dog looked at me, perhaps confused. I couldn't blame his caution given the events of the night before. I made a chopping motion with my hand as I repeated the command, "Out! Friend!"

The dog returned to his place at my right ankle and sat. He was still nervy, as if the ground was hot under his butt. I petted the dog and invited Becky to do the same after allowing him to sniff her hand.

"Close your fist first," I said.

"Wouldn't that look unfriendly?"

"Never offer an open palm to a dog that's strange to you, not until they get a chance to check you out. Give him a minute to get used to you, then you can pet him. Do that for a bit and Sophie will be your friend for life."

She chuckled. "Like you."

"Like me?"

"I hadn't seen you in years. Never called. We weren't friends on Facebook — "

"I'm not on Facebook."

"You know what I mean. I showed up here the other day and it's like old times, at least between you and me. It's almost like all those years in between didn't happen. I wish that were true."

I rubbed my aching leg. "Me, too."

Sophie soon allowed Becky to run her hand over his head and down his back. She ran her fingers through the German shepherd's fur in slow, languid circles. The dog settled more, his eyes heavy, tail wagging.

"There you go," I said. "Friends."

"You've got the knack, don't you? You haven't been back long but you obviously connected with the dogs right away. Do you think he'd still attack if you told him to?"

I shrugged. "Everybody likes the people who feed them."

"Still a cynic, I see."

"No, I just get dogs." I stooped to join in petting the German Shepherd. "They're easy to get along with and they don't ask much."

"That's you, too, Easy."

"How do you mean?"

"You don't ask much. You know, you could have come away with me to university. You didn't ask. I've spent a lot of time thinking about what might have been lately."

"I couldn't see that working, Becky. Me in town? Waiting tables or bouncing in a bar somewhere while you go off with your college friends? You think that would have worked?"

"You still a snob?"

"Nah, I think you need money for that."

"A reverse snob, then. You thought I'd drop you for some guy who studies macroeconomics and does yoga?"

"We were young. Too young. You went someplace I couldn't follow. That's all."

"And here we are, you with a bunch of dead dogs and me with a husband who is, as you say, a piece of shit."

"It's all scary twists and hairpin turns on a narrow road down the side of a cliff, isn't it? One wrong move and you're fucked."

"And not in a good way." Becky nodded as she stood.

I stopped petting Sophie. The dog whined so I continued. "The last time I talked to my mother, I asked her if she had any regrets. She wasn't specific but she did say, 'We are all traitors to the better people we could have been.' I understand dogs and I understand that. I've made a lot of decisions I regret."

"You got a head fulla demons, Easy?"

"Yeah, but they're good conversationalists. We're on pretty good terms, most of us. Let's get inside. I left my sunglasses in the house last night and this day is killing me."

She gave me a look. "You gonna tell me what's wrong with your eyes? You get migraines or something?"

"Something like that. Got conked on the melon last night. That's the latest headache."

Sophie circled us as we made our way across the yard to the house, alert and lively. He didn't appear to be haunted by the execution of his brothers. To not know you're going to die someday, to be able to release memories of the bad times so easily? What a joy it must be to live life as a dog.

"These two guys I described, the bald and the bearded, do they sound familiar?"

"Lots of bald and bearded guys around, Easy."

"Let's put it this way. If your husband wanted to find a couple of guys willing to kill a bunch of dogs in a pen, how would he do it?"

Deep in thought, she pursed her full lips. I was reminded of how pretty Becky was, how easy it was for her to be beautiful without even trying.

"Well, I guess you could find anybody who'd be willing to do just about anything. The dumb way to do it would be over the internet. If you or I wanted to find a couple of guys to do something awful, I'd go down to a dive bar with a couple of hundred bucks. Maybe I could find someone just pulling up to any bad corner in Flint. For Rud it would be a lot easier. He's a lawyer. He's defended scumbags. He'd probably take a look through his client files and find a couple of guys that way."

"That's what I was thinking."

"Are you going to call the cops in on this?"

"That's not really an option. If I called the police, they'd poke around here as part of their investigation. With Dad's business, imagine what he'd say if he knew I called the cops — "

"A regular person would."

"You know that's not really an option."

"What are you going to do, Easy?"

"You ever see the movie *John Wick*?"

"Sure. The hitman whose dog gets killed so he wipes out the entire Russian mafia single-handedly? I saw it. Kinda silly fun."

"I didn't say it was a documentary. When Rud was here, he said something about how it would be bad if something happened to my dogs. And here we are, a couple days later and I've got dead dogs to bury. They were just about ready to sell, too."

"You taking inspiration from Keanu Reeves?"

"What if I did?"

"I wouldn't blame you. Most people wouldn't. I don't want to know the kind of people who would blame you."

"Good to know," I said. "You got an alarm system at your house?"

"Yes."

"Easy, are you gonna kill my husband?"

"Not sure what I'm going to do yet. Right now all I want is to get inside, rest my eyes and take some Tylenol. What do you want?"

"I want to give you the alarm code to my house and let nature take its course."

16

Doubling up on my painkillers, I told Becky everything that happened the night before. I asked her to go back out to find the handgun the bearded Drakkar Noir guy dropped. Twenty minutes later, she came back empty-handed.

"You sure you looked around the end of the barn?"

"Tall grass around there but, yeah, I searched every inch. I can go back out and look if you like but I'm telling you, it's not there. The guy must have scooped it up when he went on his way."

"Hm. I don't think so but I was trying to look in two directions at once at the time."

"And you'd just sustained a head injury," she said.

"Nah, they must have come back for it while I locked myself in the barn." That idea creeped me out. Yes, I had weapons and two locked doors between me and them. But what if they'd decided to soak the exits with gasoline and burn the barn down with me in it? I might have survived down in the hole for a while but when the structure collapsed I'd have been trapped down there. Maybe I would have died from oxygen deprivation. I'd seen men die in fire. I didn't want to think about that.

Eventually, I fell into a restless sleep. When I awoke around two, I felt much better. Becky was gone. She'd left me a note of sorts scrawled in pencil on a scrap of paper: Fed Sophie, put him in the barn.

When I flipped the paper over I found the address to her house and the alarm code: A-1-4-5-8.

I still had dogs to bury. When I went out to the pen I found that Becky had covered them with a tarp. It takes a lot of time and effort to dig a grave. Burning's easier, but that would have made it too easy on me. I've had a lot of low moments. This was one of those times. These dead dogs were my failure. If I had sent Becky away to deal with her marital problems first, the German shepherds wouldn't be dead. I had been weak. If her husband wasn't such an asshole, he wouldn't have hired those goons to kill the dogs. If Becky and I didn't have all that unfinished business ....

All the ifs built on each other. A few bad choices can add up to a crushing weight.

I didn't blame Becky. I wasn't inclined to blame myself overly much. The sex with Becky had been a comfort for me. I didn't imagine she felt that way about me anymore but for my part, I'd made love. It didn't feel wrong at the time. I didn't want to make it wrong. It was a mistake, certainly but I refused to call it a sin. No, the dogs were dead and I decided that was all on Rud Bench. Anything less was victim-blaming. That Audi-driving, golf-and-country-club bastard had to be made to pay.

By early evening I wasn't quite done digging. As the light ebbed a cool breeze kicked up and made the work go faster. As evening turned to night I was finally able to ditch the sunglasses. Digging is sweaty work and the glasses tended to slide down my nose every few minutes. It was ten by the time I was done. My leg complained a bit. I went back inside the house, showered, popped a couple more Tylenol and iced my knee while I waited for the painkiller to take effect.

It was hard to tell when the pain eased because it was always there. Extra-strength Tylenol took the edge off but I'd decided to live with the pain if I could. Too much of that could destroy a liver. There didn't seem to be any easy answers. I'd known a couple of guys who'd become hooked on Oxycontin. A lieutenant I'd trained with had kicked his Oxy habit but only after he'd gone deaf in one ear.

The worst cautionary tale was a private named Jay. He'd lost everything and wound up on the street. He had approached me as I exited my rehabilitation center in San Diego.

"Hey," he began, "quite a limp you got there. Takin' anything for it? Got any Flexeril? Or how about Oxycotton?"

"Oxycontin, you mean?"

He grinned and called me a noob. When I smiled, he took that as an opening to talk some more. I didn't say much but I had nowhere to be so I listened. Jay scrounged for money and for drugs. "At $50 for a forty-milligram pill," he claimed, "I'm a businessman! With all the wounded vets in San Diego, you might even call me a war profiteer!"

"Growing sector," I said. "How'd you end up out here?"

He looked around and looked bewildered for a second. "Same as how everybody ends up where they do. We all want to be heroes. Didn't you?"

"I guess."

"Sure you did. Ask any little kid what they wanna be when they grow up and they'll tell you straight up: firefighter, cop, doctor, something like that. Later on, we get beaten down and we forget. We give up on bein' heroes and focus on gettin' by. We forget ourselves."

We forget ourselves. Yes, I'd felt that, like a hole in my memory, ever since the IED went off. Ever since the phosphorus grenades ....

"Later on, we grow up a little," Jay continued. "Expectations fall. People — bosses, assholes and even well-meaning friends — they tell us we gotta be realistic. That's when life gets real and real shitty. That's when we tell ourselves that just gettin' by is what makes us heroes. That's how you know you don't matter anymore. A comfortable rut gets to be a shallow grave. Eventually, you get to thinkin', maybe it doesn't matter so much one way or the other what I do, y'know? You hear what I'm sayin', son?"

"No."

"That's 'cuz you already forgot who you was."

Jay carried all his possessions in a battered backpack and smelled like the devil's asshole. His business ventures were not treating him well. He was subsisting. I would have felt worse for him but I wasn't much better off.

I offered to buy him a sandwich at Subway. He smelled so bad we couldn't eat inside the restaurant. I brought his meatball sub out to him on the sidewalk.

Between mouthfuls of meat and bread, Jay enthused about what else I could do for him. "The rush is fast, man, but you gotta know how to do it. Oxy is a time-release pill so you gotta peel off the coating. Some guys chew it or snort it. I like to slam it."

"Slam it? Like doing shots?"

"Nah, noob! You gotta slam it, man. Inject it is what I mean."

I'd considered taking the popular painkiller but it sounded like it might be like taking a chainsaw to a block of butter. I knew myself. If I started and it felt too good, I might not want to stop. Becky was a little like that: Something so good it's dangerous to start.

I saw Jay on the street outside the rehab center on a few more occasions and bought him a sub each time. As far as I know, he's still homeless in San Diego. I don't want to know what Jay has to do to feed an addiction that can cost $300 a day.

The last time I saw Jay, he said, "You know what they call people like me? Oxymorons! But we're all morons about something. We're *omnimorons!*"

We're all morons about something. Fateful words. My father and I might not be much better off than Jay. Dad complained about being broke but he never named a number that would get him out from under his mountain of debt. I told myself he couldn't still owe anything for my mother's long course of treatments. Surely he'd have lost the farm or the collection agencies would have written him off by now. Maybe it was Dad's own medical bills that were holding him under debt's weight.

We never talked about the amount of money it took to keep Mom alive. Right up until the day my mother died, we never spoke about her dying, either. It wasn't hope that made us avoid the subject. Acknowledging reality would have meant that her looming demise was real. We kept on pretending until the day we put her down in the dark, cold ground. Details about money and illness: These were unsafe subjects, never discussed but constantly haunting us.

I decided that it would not be smart to murder Rud Bench. Threats and violence wouldn't solve all our problems. Money would. Rud Bench's money.

Well, a few threats and a little violence did have its place. If he got twice the bruises he'd given Becky, I figured he'd be half as likely to hurt Becky again. Those were better odds than getting the cops involved and threatening him with a piece of paper.

Dad's words came back to me. *You can do it yourself, Junior. You're a Jack, aren't you? Be a Jack! Land that fish!*

17

Before I could go to town, I had to take some kind of weapon. Since the new plan was to avoid killing Becky's husband, I decided to go with a somewhat less lethal option. I pulled out the top drawer of the chest of drawers in my room. I found dress socks, some rolled up ties and a box for a tie pin I'd received for Christmas one year. None had been used. I pulled the drawer out completely and groped along the back of the cabinet until my fingers found the long slim package. After a couple of tugs, it came free with a ripping sound.

The package was wrapped tightly in yellowed packing tape. I used Dad's car keys to slit open one end and tore at the cardboard to get it open. The elasticized belt slipped into my hand as if it was brand new. I hadn't touched it since the end of the summer I entered eighth grade. It didn't look like a weapon. That had always been the point.

At the end of seventh grade, I'd taken my bicycle to get to a pool party at the far edge of town. Victor Down, a junior and a star on the hockey team, had the house to himself. His parents were away for the weekend and his two older brothers, Ronny and Jeff, were home from college. Word got around school that they planned to throw a whalin' party (or as they put it, "Tear it up!") The social event of the year turned out to be life-altering in several dark ways. I got my name that night, too.

I'd arrived at Victor's house looking for friends who told me they were coming, too. They did not show. Our school wasn't that big so all the faces were familiar. I stood by the pool, watched the crowd and sipped a Coke slowly, trying to make it last. If no one from my classes showed up, I planned to slip away. I was only graduating from seventh grade. I did not realize I was a guppy entering shark-infested waters.

Small farms aren't normally long on green paper no matter how tall the corn grows. Victor's house was on a family farm but they seemed to have big money. The Jack family never cracked the cash knack. I had no idea how the Downs got rich. I wondered if they were one of those families who sold weed. Kids at school said marijuana operations were everywhere in Oakland County. We called it Toke-land County then. Maybe the kids around here still did.

Perhaps the Downs decided to retire to Lake Orion to get away from the high life. Some people associate rural living with authen-ticity as if the height of the buildings and how close they're shoved together determines how big an asshole you are.

"Hey, son. You lost? You look lost."

I turned and found myself face-to-face with Victor. He held a Heineken in his hand and wore a smirk on his face that might have been surgically implanted. I don't remember him having any other facial expression.

Until that moment, I'd only had one interaction with him. He'd cut in front of me in line at a water fountain at school once. He hadn't even spared me a glance. It was if I didn't exist. To Victor Down, I was a ghost.

"Whatchoo doin' round here, son?"

"Hey," I said. I didn't like being called son. I had one father and I didn't like the way he said it, either. It sounded particularly conde-scending coming from a boy only a few years older than me.

Victor looked me up and down like I was some kind of exotic bug he'd never seen before. I went back to sipping my Coke.

"You ever go camping, son?"

"Uh ... no," I said. "Went to a Boy Scout Jubilee once."

For some reason, Victor set out to embarrass me. Because he could, I guess. He laughed harshly and a little too loud, making sure to attract the attention of everyone nearby. I could feel my scalp heating up. I hoped my cheeks weren't flushing red. I wished I'd stayed home.

He mocked me in a high, goofy voice, "'Boy Scout Jubilee,' he says!" He looked around to make sure everyone was paying attention. They were. "Jesus, gay or what?"

Victor's brothers pushed through the crowd to watch their little brother pick on a smaller kid. Ronny and Jeff must have been drunk before the party started. They laughed like hyenas. Jeff, the oldest by three years, even drooled a bit.

I gave a theatrical sigh. I was embarrassed and a bit frightened but I tried to make like I was bored. "Jesus, gay or what?" I said to Victor in the same high, goofy voice he'd used on me. "For me, the answer is what. For Jesus? I can't speak for Jesus. He did hang out with a lot of dudes but he hung out with prostitutes, too. Don't know about the lepers."

My puny attempt at a joke got a laugh from some girl I couldn't see. Hoping that was the end of it, I turned to leave. Victor had sixty pounds on me, easily. He grabbed my shoulder and spun me around. "You sure you didn't go to camp, Ernest?"

"No, I did not go to camp."

"How 'bout jail? Didja go to jail?"

That's when I figured out what he was doing. *Ernest Goes to Camp. Ernest Goes to Jail.* I'd only seen one of those movies but I'd heard about them all since I was in elementary school. Not many kids are named Ernest.

"No, I didn't go to camp or to jail," I told Victor evenly. "I didn't save Christmas, either."

My growth spurt hadn't hit yet. Victor was broad and, even in his bare feet, four inches taller than me. He blocked my view but I heard that same laugh from the invisible girl. That gave me a little boost of confidence but Victor was a big hockey goon. Any self-assuredness I'd mustered quickly began to go cold in his looming shadow.

"Whatsamatter, Ernest? Scared Stupid?" Another Ernest movie name-checked. An actor named Jim Varney had starred in a bunch of those movies. I worried Victor had looked up all of their names and was determined to shame me with my name until he'd gone through the whole list.

"I'm not scared," I said. "I'm bored. Lame party."

At this, his brothers crowed.

"You little shit," Victor said. "I know who you are. Your dad raises dogs on the other side of town. I thought you were lost. You're off your leash! Hey! Who here invited Dog-Faced Boy?"

That worried me. That sounded like a nickname that could stick. A bad nickname at school can follow a person for life.

"Dog-faced Boy! Your name's Jack, isn't it?" Victor continued, playing to the crowd. "Anybody see his brother Jerk around here? They're the Off brothers!"

The crowd bayed like hounds treeing a raccoon. Except for that one invisible girl who laughed at my sorry jokes, I hated them all. I wanted them all to die in a fire. I wanted all of Lake Orion to get sucked up into a spaceship and probed with dildos made of alien diseases, barbed wire and hot sauce.

"Hey!" A girl's voice came out of the dark. "Take it easy on him! His mom's sick."

He looked at me. "That true, Jack Off? I heard your mommy's sick? She got fleas? Shouldn't be surprised. You're dog breeders, right? Poor doggies. She shouldn'ta fucked those dogs, son!"

I planted my feet and pushed Victor in the center of his chest hard. He stepped back a couple of feet and teetered on the edge of the pool for a second before regaining his balance.

He laughed louder this time. It was a mean laugh. Without words, he told me again that I didn't matter. I was nothing to him, less than nothing.

I didn't have the weight or muscle to push him into the pool. Still, I darted forward and did what I'd seen my father's dogs do hundreds of times. As loud as I could, I barked in his face. I was about to bite his nose when, taken by surprise, he fell backward into the pool.

The crowd was stunned and in that moment of silence, I dropped, "That was easy."

The crowd roared. They laughed. Even Jeff and Ronny howled their approval.

The girl who laughed at my jokes started up a chant, "Easy! Easy! Easy!" That girl was Becky Cleeshaw.

I took a bow. That sealed the deal. No one would remember the Dog-faced Boy. All anyone remembered was my new name.

Pissed and a little drunk, Victor hauled himself out of the pool and began to chase me around the pool. The crowd cheered as I rounded the diving board and ran as hard as I could.

You know how lifeguards say, "No running?" There's a good reason for that. Embedded in concrete at the side of the pool was a small metal loop. It was meant for the rope that separated the shallow end from the deep. On our second race around the pool, Victor almost had me. I was sure if he'd caught me, he would have beat the living shit out of me. Instead, he managed to get his left big toe caught in that small loop.

Later, some kids claimed they'd heard the snap of bone. All I heard was his scream. Running at full tilt, catching his toe and then falling forward, he hurt himself in a permanent way. He thought he was bound for a career in the NHL. It turns out that the big toe is essential for balance. His aspirations for a pro hockey career broke then. What was left of his toe hung by a few shreds of skin.

Someone screamed. Jeff and Ronny sprinted to their brother but, after a minute's drunken fascination with his injury, their eyes turned to me. A couple of girls who'd been swimming threw up in the pool.

Becky appeared by my side. "We'll go call an ambulance!" She pulled me away and we ran into the house. She got hold of my hand and kept pulling. "C'mon! C'mon!"

"What about calling the ambulance?" I asked.

"Nah. Fuck that guy. C'mon, Easy!"

We didn't make it official until the Christmas dance the following year, but I think that was the moment Becky Cleeshaw became my girlfriend. She didn't like the terms boyfriend and girlfriend though. She said they made us sound like little kids, playing at something.

"What should we call each other, then?" I asked.

"I'm your Becky and you're my Easy. If anybody asks, don't tell them I'm your girlfriend. Say I'm your girl-*fiend*."

If that were the end of the story, you could call it a happy ending. Happy endings are for books and movies, not for people like me. People like me are usually the useful tools, the background characters, the extras lurking around the edges of someone else's happy ending. Stories that end happily aren't finished.

18

Victor's parents spoke to my parents about the bully's surprise amputation. Dean and Marie Down suggested we should pay half of their son's medical bills. Given his shattered aspirations for a professional hockey career, Dean told my dad that we were lucky they didn't sue. "This isn't just a boys-will-be-boys situation," he insisted.

I wasn't present for the conversation but my father reported he'd made several salient points for the Down family's edification:

1. Underage children had been served alcohol in their home so "don't go bringing the law into your goat orgy."

2. The party had lacked proper adult supervision. Though Victor's older brothers might have technically qualified as adults, they failed the intelligence test. Dad suggested Ronny and Jeff had only been present to "get high school girls drunk and cruise underage tail."

3. Their youngest had been verbally abusive to me at a fragile time given my mother's medical issues.

4. It would have been a boys-will-be-boys situation if their son hadn't chased me with the intent to do me grievous bodily harm.

5. The bully doesn't get to be the victim just because he loses.

6. Dad had seen Victor skate. He wasn't ever going to be in the NHL unless he learned how to drive a Zamboni.

7. If Dean or Marie Down ever showed up at our house again, they'd get torn apart by dogs in an unfortunate accident that would make the amputation of a toe look like a church picnic. My father did concede that, given the pain of their fool son's spontaneous self-inflicted amputation, the Jack family would kindly forego the need for Victor to apologize. Apparently, the negotiations grew heated after that because my father closed with the following points.

8. Dean Down was an asshole. Dad said he couldn't even pronounce the name of the town correctly. Mr. Down called it, "*Oh-rye-un*," emphasis on the *rye*. (Everybody in Michigan knows it's "*Or-iun*," emphasis on the *or*.)

9. Marie agreed with her husband so she was also an asshole.

10. They'd given birth to a trio of dirty assholes.

THERE WAS PROBABLY MORE but that's the summary of the top ten.

Dean and Marie decided to let sleeping dogs lie but Becky informed me that ugly rumors were circulating through Lake Orion that summer. Victor Down was bent on vengeance.

He was on crutches for a while so I had time to stew on my imminent demise. At first, I carried three flat rocks in my pockets at all times. Convinced all three Down brothers would come for me, I hoped I'd be able to nail them between the eyes. I was David, they were Goliath. However, I didn't have a slingshot. In the back of a martial arts magazine, I found an ad for a belt that concealed a short blade in the belt buckle. It was designed so the handle would pop into my palm. The triangular blade fit neatly between my second and third fingers. The ad read: Surprise your attackers with a punch that has a knife in it!

I paid extra for express delivery, checking the mail all through July and spending a good part of the time terrified. When my new knife arrived in the mail, it lasted two days before I chipped the blade on a tree trunk. Later that afternoon, the blade separated from the handle completely. I managed to cut a gash in the space between my fingers with the dull blade.

My father found me in the barn, crying on the couch. He stood in the doorway for what seemed a long time looking down at my bloody hand. Not only was the belt broken, I'd paid too much for it. Slowly, Dad came over and took the broken blade and handle from me. "Just cheap monkey metal," he observed.

I wiped the tears from my eyes. "Victor and his brothers will come for me, Dad."

"You think?"

"Victor can't play hockey anymore but he's still a goon. Beating people up was all he was good for. I'm afraid to go into town. If I step off our property, Ronny and Jeff are gonna drag me into the woods. As soon as Victor's off his crutches — "

"So you bought a knife."

"Can I have a gun?"

"You plan to shoot 'em?"

"I'll just scare them off."

"Trying to scare the shit outta somebody is often how bigger trouble starts. A lot of people die that way."

"Then you tell me what to do."

Ever the pragmatist, Dad replied, "Most people don't die from stab wounds. Let's start from there as a backup plan." He took the belt, the blade and the handle to his workbench and set about making me a better, sharper and stronger knife.

"Your mother tells me you asked about going to another school."

"Or getting homeschooled, yeah. I only feel safe here because of the dogs."

"I'll have a talk with the Downs again — "

"Yeah, 'cause that went so well last time."

"I have a feeling it will all come out in the wash," he said. "This summer will be a cooling off period for you and the Downs boys."

"His toe isn't going to grow back, Dad."

My father tilted his head back and forth as if weighing what to say. Finally, he said, "You never know, Junior. Victor might have a come-to-Jesus moment."

"He's gonna send me to meet Jesus."

"We won't let that happen, Junior. That, I can promise."

"How can you promise that?"

"Because we're willing to do whatever it takes 'cuz that's what it takes."

19

I wore the repaired belt buckle knife for the rest of that summer but I didn't go into town. Ronny and Jeff drove by the house slowly a few times to remind me they hadn't forgotten their vendetta. I was sure Victor was plotting a horrible revenge. They eyeballed me and gave me the finger. The message was clear: The Downs boys would come for me.

That was the summer of no sleep. I had a repeated nightmare that woke me screaming. I'd wake up tied to the bed with Ronny and Jeff sitting on me. Victor would stand at the end of the bed, grinning down at me. His smirk was back. He held tinsnips in one hand, eager to clip off my big toes for good measure and my dick for a bonus.

I was terrified of going back to school, certain that Victor would corner me in a locker room or pull me into a closet.

Then all my troubles suddenly went away. Someone was willing to do whatever it takes 'cuz that's what it takes."

Late on the eve of Labor Day, someone stole a mail truck. Richard Tatum was our mail carrier. Against regulations, he frequently used the postal truck as his private vehicle. He always left it in his front driveway, not three miles from our front door.

The thief parked the truck down the road from the Downs farm.

Jeff was out of town at the time. Ronny drove Victor back from a party at the lake in a little Honda Civic. The driver of the stolen mail truck sideswiped their car and forced Ronny and Victor off the road. The car rolled and crashed down an embankment. They might have been okay if it hadn't rained so hard earlier that weekend. The shoulder was soft and the irrigation ditch was deep. The Honda landed on a tilt. Victor's window was down and he hadn't worn a seat belt.

Ronny woke up in a panic, looked to his right and found his brother had drowned. Unconsciousness plus seven or eight inches of water was enough.

By the time Sheriff Eggers showed up at our front door with questions, Victor was in a coma at Orion-Oxford Urgent Care.

I remember sitting on my parents' bed, my father to my left and my dying mother to my right. Between questions, we listened to my mother's wheeze.

Sophie Jack, exhausted and pale, looked Sheriff Eggers dead in the eye. and said, "My son had nothing to do with that accident — "

"It wasn't an accident, Mrs. Jack."

"Were the keys to the truck left in the ignition?"

"They were, as a matter of fact. How'd you know that?"

"Because that would make the postal truck easy to steal. I've seen Richard Tatum take that truck to the grocery store and leave the engine running in the winter. He thinks since it's government gas, it doesn't cost anything. Sounds to me like some kids took it for a joyride and things went off the rails."

"Off the road in a ditch," the sheriff said. "We found the truck banged up on the side of the road near Bald Mountain."

"Then look for somebody over there 'cuz there's nobody here but us chickens."

The sheriff barely looked at me but I thought his gaze lingered over my father's face for a long time. "Where were you, Ernest?"

My mother didn't give Dad a chance to answer. "He was right here with me, holding my hair while I threw up in the toilet all night, Sheriff. The first few minutes is productive. After that, he has to keep bringing me water so I can vomit liquid. The dry heaves hurt bad."

This was the one and only time I'd heard my mother talk frankly about her illness or of dying and she would never speak of it again.

"Sorry for your trouble, ma'am." The cop finally looked at me, probing for a weak link. "Can you shed any light on where you were last night, Ernie?"

"Easy," I said. "People call me Easy now."

"Okay, fine. How about it, Easy?"

"I fed the dogs after supper, went up to my room, read a little and slept a little. School starts tomorrow. I didn't sleep well but I heard my parents. They were up through the night. I heard Mom throwing up."

He gave a slow nod. "Okay, folks. You should know, this isn't over. There will be an investigation."

"You better hurry, Sheriff. I'm dying and I'd hate to leave without you solving the mystery so I can thank whoever killed that awful boy."

"Loose talk, Mrs. Jack."

"S'cuse me, Sheriff, but dying slow has given me some perspective. Everybody dies someday. Nobody gets saved and that kid wasn't ever going to cure cancer. Not everybody is of equal value. Far as I'm concerned, accident or not, somebody did the world a favor. Don't lecture me about loose talk. I'm finding the process of dying quite liberating."

Her demise was almost a year away then. However, as if to demonstrate how close the reaper was, Mom broke into a series of wet coughs. She waved him away, too tired to talk anymore. She fell back on her sweaty pillow and Eggers retreated. She was still coughing as he left. She stopped coughing as soon as we heard the front door close behind him.

Victor Down did indeed have his come-to-Jesus moment. While my father cooked bacon and eggs for my mother and me, the phone rang. Someone from town told Dad that my tormentor was dead. My return to school was delayed a couple of days. Ronny left town to go back to college somewhere back east after the funeral.

Soon after that, I took off that mail order belt buckle knife Dad had fixed for me. I put it in the long slim cardboard box and taped it to the back of my dresser behind the top drawer. I never thought I'd have need of it again.

I never told anyone that my parents did not stay home the night Victor and Ronny were run off the road. Dad had taken care of my mother just as she described on many long nights. That night, Dad had taken her for a drive. He'd soon returned. I heard the phone ring around 1 a.m. He left in the Barracuda and brought her back by 1:30. I had no doubt my mother had killed Victor Down. I never thanked her for defending me. We never spoke of it. We pretended it didn't happen. I wanted to ask her if she'd meant to scare, injure or kill Victor. Mom probably wanted to deliver a brushback pitch to scare him off my ass.

Holding the knife concealed in the belt buckle again, I was off to scare the shit out of somebody. Trying to scare the shit outta somebody is often how bigger trouble starts.

I was a string bean when I was in high school. However, the long belt was elasticized. After a little fuss, I managed to adjust it to its new length. The knife slipped in and out of its short sheath easily. I could still smell a trace of oil on the blade. The blade's edge was just as sharp as the day my father made it.

You can do it yourself, Junior. Remember who you are! You're a Jack, aren't you? Be a Jack! Land that fish!

I planned to throw another brushback pitch. We learn nothing.

20

Before Becky sent me off to have a chat with her husband, her words reminded me of Dad. *When you see Rud, remember who you are, Easy. Be yourself and everything will work out for the best. Everything is going to get fixed, I know it.*

Remember who you are, Easy!

Accelerating down the highway on a noble mission to deal with that asshole, I was feeling more like my old self. I loved the growl of the Barracuda's engine as I barreled down the road toward Lake Orion. I heard somewhere that the revs of a muscle car's engine actually boost testosterone. At that moment, I thought I could almost feel it. The road was so empty it could have been the end of the world. I sped and then sped up some more. My heart raced. Stretch out, baby! Stretch out and run!

There is exhilaration in noble causes and sudden acceleration. I was off to solve a problem. I liked that feeling. So many problems have no clear resolution and no easy way out. As I made my way toward Rud Bench, I felt like I was taking control. I'd fix things for Dad and for Becky. It was going to work out okay for everybody, except maybe for Rud.

That confident feeling slipped a little as the glare of oncoming traffic hit me. Headlights felt like pressure at the back of my eyes, like uncaring fingers pressing into my brain. I slipped on the yellow sunglasses I used for driving at night and slowed down. Close to town, I kept the speedometer just a couple miles over the speed limit. Hands at ten and two, I leaned forward a little, trying to look like a respectable citizen. Driving too slow would attract attention as much as speeding. The key to being left alone in public places is acting like you belong, pretending you have somewhere important to be.

I circled the block once to case the house. It was a two-story home with a three-car garage. The front of the house was lit with spotlights in that way that only owners of nice houses think to do. Nobody lights up their doublewide trailer as if to say, "Hey! Take in the glory of the poverty!" It was easy to imagine Becky living in a house like that. She'd always been bound for great things. If Rud wasn't such a bad guy, she would never have sought me out. She would have stayed in her nice house with the big backyard with plenty of room for a pool, cabana and a big stainless steel barbecue for entertaining friends and colleagues.

It was hard to figure a guy like Rud. He had Becky and a profession that would have set him up for life. Becky was smart and beautiful, destined for a life of security and comfort. Her parents had died young in a car accident and had left her enough money for college. She wasn't an heiress to a huge fortune but with her brains, she didn't need a nest egg. She had seed money to invest in her life. To keep her happy, all Rud had to do was not be a dick.

I was convinced personalities spring from nature, not nurture. I'd seen it with dogs, how their personalities seemed to be ordained from birth. And humans? An asshole can't hide his assholery for long. We're born to be the people we are. I was born to be poor and Becky was, one way or another, always going to be safe, insulated from bullshit. At least she would be after I had a talk with Rud about his behavior. I planned to give him what one of my sergeants used to call "A right good spanking." (Though he was from Georgia, he thought it was hilarious to train us to death while shouting in a plummy English accent. It was pretty funny the first time.)

I parked two blocks away on a busy side street. It wouldn't do to park in a residential area in an old car with a big rumbly engine. The neighborhood was too upscale for me to go unnoticed by nosy, defensive neighbors peering out between Venetian blinds.

The key to the back door was where Becky told me I'd find it, under a potted plant on the back porch. The key turned easily but the door creaked and squeaked. I entered and left the back door open slightly in case I needed a quick exit. The keypad on the wall was right where Becky told me it was, too. I used a knuckle to punch in the code and went off to find the living room. Houses like these don't have living rooms, though. The great get "great" rooms. (Becky was right. I was a bit of a reverse snob.)

In one of those Chili Palmer movies, somebody sneaks into a house at night and turns on the TV. That was my plan. Turn it on, turn it up and lure Rud downstairs. Whether he showed up in his tighty-whities or pajamas, I'd have the psychological advantage. Maybe I'd spin around in a revolving chair like a Bond villain, catch him by surprise before I gave him the talk about how his goons nearly killed me and how they killed Dad's dogs. I figured he owed us $60,000, plus an extra $40,000 for pain and suffering. If he bucked too hard, I'd come down $10,000 or so. Either way, I'd get compensation and he'd back off Becky.

If Rud got too hot about it, I'd stab him in the hand. Nobody talks about hand wounds but they're a huge pain in the ass, particularly when you need to do something as simple as wiping your ass. If you get stabbed in the hand, every moment you're awake is a constant reminder of whatever you did to get stabbed.

When Dad got back, I told myself, we'd be in a better place. Maybe I could get him off the road, pay some bills and buy him some better medical care.

It seemed everything was going well until I got to the hard part. I smelled Drakkar Noir again.

21

I whirled, searching the dim room. Too late, I heard the click of the hammer on a revolver getting pulled back.

It was the guy with the beard who had hit me on the back of the head the night before. And goddamnit if he didn't spin around in a chair before he leaned forward to switch on a table lamp. "Hello, Mr. Jack," he whispered. "Please keep your voice down. Mr. Bench is sleeping upstairs. We do not wish to disturb him."

"Hi," I said. "Did you order pizza? That'll be $25, plus tip if you like."

"But you don't have a pizza, Mr. Jack."

"Musta left it in the car. No anchovies, right? Nobody likes anchovies. That shouldn't even be a thing. Wait here, I'll go get it."

"Siddown." He gestured with a little silver pistol toward a couch.

I sat. "How'd you know I was coming?"

"We killed your dogs," the man said, "and you're you. Of course, we knew you'd come. We know about you. You have a reputation."

"Who from?"

He gestured with his weapon in vague little circles. "You know. People."

"Around here? That's mostly undeserved. Where's your friend? The dog killer?"

"He has the day shift. I have the night. You can call me Andre."

"Okay, Andre. What do you want?"

"I want what everyone wants."

"Ice Capades tickets?"

"Money, Mr. Jack. Do you have any?"

I thought of the $12,000 my father had scraped together for my escape to a better life. Staring down the barrel of that little pistol, any life would be better than this. "I've got a little set aside for a rainy day, sure. Me ant, you grasshopper."

The bearded man smiled and glanced down at his gun. "This isn't just any rainy day. It's typhoon season. How much?"

"Ten thousand," I offered.

"Not nearly enough. To live, you have to beat what I'm already being paid. Try again."

"I can get you $12,000."

"You cave too quickly."

"Guns pointed my way must make me antsy."

"It gets worse, Mr. Jack. If you could give me $12,000, you should have offered your maximum bid first."

"Twelve and the keys to a boss muscle car?"

"This is insulting. Am I not scary enough? Should I shoot you in the ankles and knees before moving on to the main event?"

"You're plenty scary, Andre, but negotiations aren't my strong suit. I don't deal with car salesmen well, either."

He smiled. "The amount you offer is not enough to save your life."

"Is it enough to buy me some time?"

"How's that?"

I cleared my throat, thinking hard. I had to get this right because, in the dim light, his weapon looked like a small caliber pistol, a .22. To kill me, he'd probably empty the pistol into me and it might take a little time and a lot of pain to die. To live, I needed to make his greed work for me.

Greed isn't working for me, so far, I thought. *If I'd come for vengeance, I wouldn't have brought a knife to a gunfight.*

"If $12,000 isn't nearly enough," I began, "I can't pay you what I don't have. But wouldn't you rather have $12,000 on top of what you're already getting paid?"

"I have an understanding with my employer."

It was my turn to smile. "Don't get all noble on me now. You already told me you were for sale."

"Touché, fuckbag."

"Let me live and you get the $12,000. Plus, you wouldn't have to split it with the day shift dude."

"If I let you go, you could disappear. My employer would be disappointed. No, I think I better kill you now. Besides, you piss me off. I've been dying to kill you since you hit me."

"You'll be leaving $12,000 in its hiding place and you'll never get it."

He tilted his head to the side. "You're saying it's not in the bank?"

"Ill-gotten gains," I said. "No way to launder it. It's off the books and, like I said, in a hole."

He stood. Still smiling, he put a finger to his lips and came closer. He placed the muzzle in the center of my forehead. "Where is the money, Mr. Jack? This can go easy or it can go hard — "

"Easy," I said, barely a whisper at all.

"What?" Andre leaned forward a little.

"I'm Easy. I just remembered who I am." I reached up quickly with my right hand and grabbed the slide on the little semi-automatic so he couldn't put a hole in my head. He started to pull back. With him standing and me sitting, he could wrench the gun away in a second and start shooting. I kicked out with my good leg and connected with his left knee. It was more of a push than a kick but it brought his upper body forward. My left hand closed on the belt buckle knife. I thrust the blade up into his neck and twisted it savagely as I pulled him down toward me.

Through gritted teeth I echoed his words, "Dying to kill me."

My father was right about stabbings. Statistically, very few people die from stab wounds, especially compared to gunshots. Contrary to what you may have seen on television, most inmates who get shivved in prison survive the attack. A short blade usually won't kill unless you know what you're doing. I knew what I was doing.

As Andre fell forward, I kept my hand on his gun. Even with the arteries and veins in the neck open like a faucet, he had a little fight left in him. It didn't last long, of course. Soon his jaw opened and closed as if he was a fish suddenly up in the air, flopping and dying on a dock.

You're a Jack! Land that fish!

Andre went limp and all his weight came down on me. As I struggled to push him off, a light popped on upstairs. Slippery with blood, I shoved Andre to the side. He fell to the couch face first, then to the floor with a loud thump. Killing and dying is not a quiet business.

In the cast of the table lamp, Andre looked up at me. He looked alert for a few seconds. I saw no accusation or anger in his face, only confusion. It was as if he'd gotten off at the wrong bus stop, disoriented, realizing his mistake too late as the bus pulled away. The light behind his eyes died. Andre's jaw went slack.

I heard Rud Bench call, "What's going on down there?"

Before he could rush downstairs, guns blazing, I got to my feet and hurried back the way I'd come, out the back door and into the night. The darkness welcomed me, as cool as stepping into a pool at an oasis after suffering the desert heat.

I realized I still held my little knife in one hand and Andre's pistol in the other. I hadn't planned to take anything with me. I was only here for Becky and to collect a fat check for a pile of dead dogs.

It was just as well. Leaving weapons behind at a crime scene would not do.

22

Covered in blood, I steamed away to get back to the car. How many cameras had I passed on my way into town? In Baghdad, we used a very successful strategy to track down bombers. Drones flew above the city twenty-four hours a day taking pictures continuously. When an IED went off, we'd go to the recordings and work backward, tracing the tangos back to their homes. Fortunately, Lake Orion is pretty small. I racked my brains but I doubted the Barracuda had been caught on camera unless I'd passed an ATM machine by the 7-Eleven.

What was I thinking when I took the Barracuda into town, anyway? The car was too unusual. Even its rumbly V-8 engine might stick in someone's mind.

Oh, right. I didn't sneak into that house with the intention of killing anyone. It just worked out that way. I imagine most guys in prison and on death row say something similar.

As soon as I was back in the car the second-guessing continued. What if I pushed the car down the street a bit before hitting the ignition? I'd be quieter and farther from the crime scene but I'd be too memorable if someone looked out and saw me pushing.

I'm out of practice dealing with danger, I thought. *Distance and time. I need distance and time.*

I took a few deep breaths and looked around. The street seemed as dead as Andre. After my heartbeat slowed a little, I drove away trying to regain the detached calm I'd felt as I'd driven into Lake Orion. I'd had a plan. It's easier to be confident and relaxed before the battle plan meets the battlefield.

I took a circuitous route out of town, sticking to side streets as much as possible before getting on the only road that would take me home. The first problem was the weapons but that was also the easiest to solve. I stripped the gun as I drove, fumbling a little because fresh blood is slick and clammy, sweaty palms aren't much help, either. As I paused at a stop sign I glanced down into my lap and realized the pistol was a little Ruger, ten rounds. A nice little gun, easy to conceal. It would have been a nice addition to my father's collection after the serial number was filed off. Instead, I parked by Elkhorn Lake and tossed it in, bullets and all. I wouldn't be tied to Andre or whatever murders he might have committed with that Ruger.

What about fibers, numb-nuts? You didn't go into that house in a hazmat suit. How many hairs had I shed? How many skin cells had I left behind as I struggled with Andre? What would I tell the cops when they showed up at my door? That the sun was in my eyes?

One disastrous all-encompassing fire at a time, Easy.

I walked along the shore for a while before taking off my mail order belt. The day I put it on for the first time, I'd called it Orion's belt. Very briefly, I felt like a superhero. As soon as I slipped that cheap little knife out of its concealed sheath and held it in my hand for the first time, I felt like Batman.

But safety is an illusion.

The knife Dad had so carefully fixed for me made barely a splash when I hucked it into the lake. I walked on a little farther before balling up the belt and buckle and chucking it, too. It made an unsatisfying splash not far away. It's hard to let go, to leave things from the past behind.

Next came my turn. I waded into the cold water and stripped. I tried to get the worst of the blood off, doing my best to wash and wring out my clothes. I scrubbed at my face and hair to make sure there was no blood there. Then I took a mouthful of lake water, gargled with it and spit it out. I was a little concerned Andre might have given me hepatitis or something, but maybe I'd get giardiasis from the lake instead. Tonight was all kinds of fucked up.

I hate it when a plan doesn't come together. The last time things went this badly, phosphorus grenades and IEDs were involved.

For a terrible moment, I thought I heard voices nearby. I bent my knees, trying to make myself small so the water came up to my upper lip. Listening intently, I strained my hearing to its limit. What would I have done if someone did discover me out here? I might chalk up the late night skinny-dipping alone to skunk attack, general weirdness or my PTSD. I had a diagnosis and prescriptions. I could establish that much. However, someone would find it a weird coincidence I was splashing around in Elkhorn Lake on the same night a guy got killed in town. Death by murder was not a common occurrence in the Lake Orion Charter Township.

Then there was the question of why the seat of my car was covered in blood that didn't belong to me. I didn't feel bad about Andre. I didn't murder him. I killed him. It was self-defense. Proving that distinction to a jury would be a much more difficult problem.

Two girls laughed. The noise seemed to be coming from across the lake. I searched the darkness as I began to escape toward the shore. A light popped on across the lake and I heard a loud splash. Sound does odd things across the water at night. A boy and a girl were talking. I might not have been the only person skinny-dipping in Lake Elkhorn that night, probably for vastly different reasons.

I couldn't make out the bass notes in what the boy said but the girl's higher voice carried. "Whatever happened to Avril Lavigne?" she asked.

I waded back to shore as quickly as I could without splashing and stumbled back toward the car. I'd get blood on me again, but this cold bath was a start. By now, the police would be crawling over the crime scene and asking Rud Bench a lot of questions about the corpse on his floor. How long would it take him to point them toward the guy he was pissed at for sleeping with his wife?

Becky was special and Rud was a bastard. She and I had a lot of history together. Still, I had to ask myself if she was worth a trip to prison. Even if that didn't happen, lawyers meant more debt. As great as Becky was, I'd jumped back into trouble as soon as I hit town. What if I'd stayed in San Diego and enjoyed the beach? It wasn't hard to find companionship anymore, not in the age of Tinder and God knew how many other dating apps. Loneliness was no excuse.

But you didn't do it for the money, really. You did it for love. You're too easy, Easy.

I put my shoes back on but nothing else. As I made my way back to the car, the arms of pine branches reached out of the dark to scrape along my bare torso with spiny fingers.

One of my counselors back at the VA in San Diego once asked if I believed in God. I remember looking around the sharing circle at the guys in wheelchairs and the guys who wore prosthetics. No one who'd gone to war escaped without bearing horrible scars, visible or invisible. There were a few guys who talked tough but the tougher they talked, the less I believed them. Either they hadn't done much or they'd done so much they had to believe crazy to make crazy feel normal. When people tried too hard to convince me how righteous they were, it felt like they were trying to convince themselves.

"I don't know about God," I told the counselor. "I don't see much evidence in this room."

"What about the flowers?" an airman piped up.

"Uh ... *whut*?" There were no flowers in that room.

"The designs of the flowers, I mean. How can you explain all the beauty and symmetry in the world without God?"

"How can you explain dengue fever, child brain cancer or the fact that we're all sitting around this circle?"

"Man's fault! That's all man's fault!" A freckle-faced woman who'd worked in the Chemical Corps bounced in her seat, eager to show me the error of my ways. I've found many believers can't wait to show you're a dumbass and they've got the Big-T Truth on lockdown.

"Man's fault?" I asked. "Really? Sorry, but did you cook up cancer and dengue fever in your basement? I sure didn't."

"If you don't put your faith in God," she insisted, "you've put your faith in man and in yourself! How's that working for you?"

I didn't want to argue and I didn't want to argue anyone out of their beliefs if it gave them comfort. I shrugged.

"The bad things are a result of our sin!" the freckle-faced woman explained.

"Okay," I said. "You're right."

I hoped they'd move on but the counselor made the mistake of pressing me. "The way you say that, I have a hard time believing you. This is a safe space but it's also supposed to be an honest space."

"Uh-huh."

"We're just trying to help. Maybe believing in something bigger than you, believing in a larger plan — "

"I do believe in God," I said evenly. "It's just that He's such a bastard. I mean, look at us!"

My observation did not go over well in the sharing circle. I did a lot less sharing after that.

Climbing back into the Barracuda, shivering and sitting my bare ass in blood, I took that as more evidence for my beliefs. I had sinned. Neither God nor Man was going to let up on me anytime soon.

I turned the heat up to maximum, cranked the fan high and turned the Barracuda toward home. There was still plenty to do.

23

I talked to Jesus many times, usually in a bar in Germany. He was a military policeman and his last name was Diaz. Everybody called him Jesus, as in "Gee-zuzz." He took pains to correct them every time. "Hay-soose! It's pronounced Hay-soose!"

Jesus Diaz was a funny guy with the gift of gab who shared my obsession with movies. He also told me a few stories about the dubious joys of being a cop within the military. "Chasing down AWOL GIs is pretty easy work. They always go straight home or to a girlfriend's place."

That was a good lesson on how not to get caught. I didn't make the mistake of parking the Barracuda in the barn. Deputy Carstairs could impound it for evidence of my guilt. I took the car down a bumpy old logging road. Branches closed in on both sides and scraped at the paint. Dad would have been pissed about that. I wasn't worried about putting another scratch in one of the car's old dents. A mile and a half back in the woods I found a good spot to pull in among the trees.

In the movies, commandos covered vehicles with branches to conceal them from prying eyes. Unless I had a team to help me find enough branches to hide the big bulk of a 1973 Barracuda, that didn't seem practical. I left it where it was and hoped it would be fine beside the logging road until I could come back to clean it up.

Pondering Jesus' words about where chases always seem to end, I considered my next move. Was my best course of action to simply grab the money Dad set aside for me and escape to America's backroads? Or would the cops pick me up as I hitchhiked out of town?

No, I decided. *If you run, dogs give chase.* Leaving abruptly would make me look guilty. I had to stay and clean up my mess.

I put my damp clothes back on. The chills hit me again but eased as I began to heat up from jogging. The moon was almost full so I usually had enough light to see by. When the foliage closed in too much, I tripped and fell several times. By the time the house and barn came into view, I was about ready to amputate my left leg. The nerves screamed at me to slow down and remember I was gimped up.

Sometimes in the depths of her illness, someone would ask my mother how she felt. "How do you think I am? I'm *gibbled!* I'm broken! I'm a walking corpse! And how's by you?" Then she would stare at them them, daring them to complain or say anything at all. Mom liked the word *gibbled.* It threw people off as she went on the attack.

Anticipating a hot shower and a change of clothes, I started to feel a bit of hope as I walked in behind the barn. Then I spotted the Audi in the driveway parked beside the house. In the dark, I couldn't tell if it was Becky's car or if Rud and his dog-killing henchman had come back for vengeance.

Overseas, we called all the bad guys the same thing: tangos. Henchmen sounded more sophisticated somehow. We didn't make such distinctions in Afghanistan but back home in Michigan, criminals and killers fell into several categories. On American soil, bad guys could be crazy or mean thugs. Mass shooters were often diagnosed by journalists as mentally deranged or desperate. If the bad guy was some shade of brown, that's when he got the label of terrorist.

It's not that I thought Rud Bench was some kind of evil genius. He wasn't Lex Luthor sneaking kryptonite into Superman's Cheerios. But Becky's husband had money to spare. People with money rarely go to jail. Guys like me who go up against guys like Rud wound up in jail all the time.

In a few ways, my life in the military was simpler. The bad guys pretty much looked alike and talked alike. We had clear rules of engagement and there were no degrees of guilt. The bad guys had to die so we could go home. That was our clear never-ending mission, impossible to ever complete, doomed to failure. I believed in that mission for a while. As more guys I knew got hit or hurt, my belief ebbed away to nothing.

I went to the barn to retrieve a weapon, determined to bring a gun to a gunfight this time. Halfway way down the ladder into the bunker a floorboard creaked above me. Someone had followed me into the barn and stood in my father's shop. I'd pulled the couch out. The trapdoor was open. I figured I had just seconds before whoever it was looked down and shot me in the face.

Who would it be? Becky's shitty husband? Deputy Carstairs? The most likely candidate would be the man who killed my dogs. He hadn't been paid to kill me before. Since I killed Andre, he might have convinced Rud to take the upsell. For the premium package, maybe he'd shoot me and dump me in the woods or a lake. Or maybe the bald man would just kill me for free.

I'd known guys who bragged they'd kill anybody for a case of beer. It would be sloppy and they'd probably get caught but they'd do it. Life is cheap everywhere, even when we pretend it's not.

A shadow fell on the square of light beneath the trapdoor. My hand closed on a Smith & Wesson Bodyguard 380. I swung the semi-automatic around, ready to fire.

Becky.

I almost pulled the trigger.

"I can't believe you never told me about this neat little hiding place! I guess we all have secrets, huh?"

24

I stuffed the handgun into the back of my pants and started back up the ladder. "You never saw this, Becky."

"I didn't?"

"For your own protection."

"Why?"

"This is Dad's business. Aren't things complicated enough with you and Rud?"

She looked me up and down. "You okay? You look like you've been through the wringer."

"That's ironic since I'm all wet."

"I heard the Barracuda rumble by, like, forty minutes ago? How far did you park it in the back of the beyond? Did you get stuck in the mud on that old logging road?"

I ignored her questions and closed the trapdoor. Then I flipped the rug over it and shoved the couch back in place. I couldn't believe I'd kept the bunker secret since I was a little kid and now I'd messed up. "You never saw that."

She nodded and gave me a sullen look.

"Swear!"

"Fuck! Shit! Damn!"

"I'm not kidding around, Becky. Swear you never saw that."

"Okay, I swear I never saw whatever we're not talking about."

"Good, it's for your protection."

"So you said. Speaking of my safety, what the hell happened at my house? I got a call from Rud. He was close to hysterical. What went wrong? He told me there was a dead guy in our living room. At first, I thought he meant it was you."

"Close, but not quite. Where were you when Rud called?"

"I've been staying with Dolores."

"A friend?"

"A good friend. You remember Dolores? She was a year behind us in school."

"No."

"Button nose? Big boobs? She does my hair. She went by DD back in the day."

That sounded vaguely familiar, but I had much more significant concerns. "Get back to the part where Rud called you. The dead guy — "

"Dead guy. Right. Rud said there was a dead guy on the living room floor covered in blood. He heard somebody run out the back." She smiled. "He didn't see you."

"What else?"

"He's called the cops."

"I guess that's what people do. Anything else?"

"He's blaming you. I said that was impossible because I've been with you all night."

"Was Dolores with you when you were on the phone at her place?"

"Nope! That's the beauty part. She was out."

"It's the middle of the night. Where is she?"

"Dolores likes to dance. She and a couple of her girlfriends went to a house party in Troy."

"Why didn't you go?"

"I like Dolores. I don't like her girlfriends. I can say I was with you all night. Nobody can say I wasn't. You should have heard Rud's voice.

He was shaking and screaming at the same time. I've never heard him so rattled. It was great."

"Not really the point right now, Becky."

"You don't understand. It was ... it was a great thing to hear him sound scared for a change. You have no idea the hell he's put me through."

I took a breath and tried to clear my mind for a moment. My brain ached and my skull felt like it was stuffed full of wet cotton.

"Focus. Rud called you on your cell, right?"

"Yeah. That's when I started trying to get hold of you. When you didn't phone me back, I figured I better get my ass over here. If I'm going to be your alibi, maybe we better have sex, too."

That's when it occurred to me she was at least a little drunk. I leaned forward and sniffed. Her breath was fruity. "Wine?"

"Wine coolers. No big deal."

"When did you get them?"

"On the way over here, at Hillside."

"Then you're on camera somewhere. There will be a time stamp on the recording."

"So what? Who's to say I wasn't here and just popped over to Hillside to buy wine coolers? That doesn't screw up your alibi."

"Hillside isn't the closest place to get wine coolers."

She seemed disoriented. She'd had the equation worked out in her head and solved for X, and I'd come along and informed her this wasn't a math exam. It was a history exam and she had all her facts wrong.

"The story won't hold together."

"Sure it will. I can lie convincingly. I already told Rud I was with you."

"You also said he was hysterical. When the cops ask, just tell them you came over about now and found me at the house acting normal and not standing here in wet clothes."

Her face clouded and she gave me a slow nod. "We better get over to the house then."

I didn't realize how intoxicated she was until she moved. Limping after her, I craved Tylenol 3s. Extra strength Tylenol wasn't going to cut it tonight. My knee spoke in the language of pain. It told me that this would be a day and night lost to medication, hot baths and ice packs.

"Easy? You didn't say. Who was the dead guy?"

"Andre. No last name. Beard. Liked strong cologne. Ring a bell?"

She teared up. "Strong cologne? That guy's name wasn't Andre."

"What — "

"I know a guy who fits that description. Never figured why a guy with a beard that thick wore so much aftershave."

"I thought that, too."

"My theory is that he was trying to cover up B.O. It has to be Micah."

"Who?"

"A client of Rud's. He came by the house to go golfing with Rud. Paul Carstairs drove him."

"Any idea where he's from or why he was a client?"

"I think he's from Detroit, maybe?"

"Was from Detroit. Past tense."

"I don't know anything more about him."

"But you're sure it was this Micah?"

"Put that cologne together with the beard, it's gotta be him."

"And he's a buddy of Carstairs. Great."

"You gonna tell me what went wrong?"

I wanted to tell her about the fight, blow by blow. However, the less she knew, the less acting she'd have to do when the police showed up.

25

Someone pounded on my front door just before eight the next morning. Sophie barked. Becky was still asleep as I crept out of bed. We'd had a busy night. Becky took my soiled clothes and buried them in the woods. A long hot shower got the last of the blood off me. It took a while longer for the heat to soak back into my body.

As the pounding on the front door continued, I pulled on a fresh shirt and jeans, breathing deep. If they took me in for questioning, I'd play dumb, get a lawyer and stall. If Becky held up her end and all went well, I'd make bail. Depending on what a lawyer told me, I'd stay and fight or run away. As I limped downstairs, I prepared my baffled look.

Take it slow, I told myself. *Don't assume cops are telling the truth when they say they've got you screwed to the wall.*

The door shook with the pounding and that drove the German shepherd to bark even more furiously. "Sophie!" I yelled. "Stand down and wait for further orders!"

The dog looked back over his shoulder at me for a moment and resumed barking. Nobody listens to me.

"Who is it?" I called.

"Police! We need to speak with you, Mr. Jack!"

We? I didn't recognize that voice. It wasn't Deputy Carstairs.

"Sure! Just a second!"

"Right now!" That was Carstairs. He'd brought a friend. That made sense. It was a murder investigation.

"I just don't want you to shoot my dog! Let me put him downstairs! Gimme a sec!"

I heard Carstairs say something about how I'd said that last time he was here, too. No one could blame me on that score. Cops had a history of shooting watchdogs, even if the canine was a yappy little Shitzu. I got Sophie out of the room and down into the basement where he'd be safe.

When I opened the door, a man in a brown sports coat stood beside Paul Carstairs. The guy looked friendly enough but the snap on the deputy's holster was undone and his hand was on his belt, ready for a quick draw.

The guy in the sports coat introduced himself as he flashed his badge. "Detective Jerry Buck."

"I've never met a detective before. Shouldn't you be in a trench coat?"

"That would be a little too on the nose," Buck said.

"I watch reruns of Columbo sometimes," I said.

Buck looked too young to get the reference. He wasn't what I pictured when I thought of the words "Michigan detective." Between his curly hair and bushy eyebrows, he didn't look like he'd carry the name Jerry Buck, either. His vibe was more Young Rabbi.

"You already know Deputy Carstairs," Buck said.

"We've met," I said. "We're not close."

Buck allowed a small grin as the deputy's expression darkened. I wondered if they were starting in on the good cop/bad cop routine early.

"Can we come in?" Buck asked.

"My girlfriend's sleeping. How about we talk on the porch?" The hour was early and the sky was so gray, I didn't have to wear my sunglasses. That was probably a good thing. Without my usual wincing in sunlight, I might pass for normal.

Staying outside on the porch didn't seem to bother Buck but Carstairs had steel in his voice. "You don't seem surprised to see us."

"I'm surprised you weren't here earlier," I said. "I guess you fellas have been up all night."

The detective's bushy eyebrows shot high. "What have you heard?"

"Just what Becky told me."

"Becky Bench?"

"Same."

"She's the girlfriend sleeping?"

"That's right."

"You know she's married to Rud Bench," Carstairs said. It wasn't a question. He was just letting the detective know I had loose morals.

"Well, if you're here to arrest her for adultery, I'll go wake her up. Is that still a crime in this state? I'm not clear on what my responsibilities are when some piece of shit abuses his wife and drives her out of her home into the arms of a cool, understanding and peaceful man who would never hurt her."

Carstairs rolled his eyes. "You done?"

I made a show of considering his question. "No, I think that about covers it."

"About last night, what did Mrs. Bench tell you, Mr. Jack?" Buck asked.

"Her husband called her to say there was a dead guy in their living room."

"And what did you say to that?" Carstairs said.

"I said I thought that was unusual."

The deputy did not look happy with me but I thought Buck looked at least a little amused. That might have been his mask, though. I imagined interrogating suspects required a good poker face.

"Then what happened?" Carstairs inquired.

"Not much to tell. Becky came over here from her friend's place and stayed the night. Her friend was out and she didn't want to be alone."

"So she needed comforting and you provided it," Carstairs said.

"You're implying we had sex last night. We did not. Images of dead guys and bloody living rooms do not contribute to a romantic tableau, Deputy. Maybe that sort of thing would turn your crank. It did nothing for us."

I scored a grin from Young Rabbi that time. Still, he stayed on point. "She didn't go home to check on the place? Doesn't that sound a bit odd to you?"

I furrowed my brow. "Her house was a crime scene. I told her you guys wouldn't even let her in the door. We discussed it. Becky was pretty upset, as you'd expect. She almost decided to head home but by then she'd had a bit too much to drink. She went to bed and has been snoring a little ever since."

"And where were you last night?" Carstairs asked.

I thought I caught a flash of annoyance on Buck's face. Maybe my whereabouts was on his list of questions but he hadn't wanted to get there quite so quickly.

"I've been right here since Sunday," I said.

"You weren't over in Lake Orion murdering a man in Rud's living room?" Carstairs asked.

"Nope."

"You didn't go over there looking to make trouble with Rud?"

"I was under the impression he was out to make trouble for me," I said. "Somebody shot my dogs. Don't know who but I suspected it was Rud's doing."

"Somebody shot your dogs and you didn't report it?" Buck asked.

"Figured I'd wait until my father got back from his business trip. He knows the worth and would have all the paperwork for the insurance and whatnot. Besides, when you were here last time, you made it clear I shouldn't show my face in town, Deputy."

Carstairs tried to laugh that off. "You thought the man whose wife you were sleeping with shot your dogs? You didn't report it and you didn't go over there to confront him, either?"

"They're my dad's dogs and it's his business. If I wanted to make trouble with Rud, he'd be dead. But it's not Rud Bench who's dead, right? If I was mad enough at somebody to shoot them, I can't imagine mistaking one guy for another. Unless Rud had a twin brother — "

"No one said anything about shooting anyone," Buck said.

I gave him puppy dog eyes and shrugged. "Oh," I said. "I just assumed." It was the only line I'd actually planned on to cast doubt that I was the culprit. With that line delivered, it was time to shut this interview down.

"Since I don't have anything more to tell you — "

"What time did you go to pick up Becky?" Carstairs pressed.

I pointed to the Audi in the driveway. "I haven't been off the property in days," I said. "She drove here last night, sometime around... nine, I think? Not sure."

The detective pulled out a notebook and wrote something down.

"We'll need to talk to Becky," Carstairs said. "Her husband needs her."

Becky appeared behind the screen door. "Did Rud hurt somebody?"

Way to throw your husband under the bus, Becky!

Carstairs didn't look pleased to see her at that moment. "Didn't see you there."

"I'm Detective Buck, Mrs. Bench. Why would you think your husband hurt somebody?"

"Because he's hurt me."

"Can you come down to my office and help us hash this out?" Buck asked.

"I don't mind as long as I don't have to be alone with Rud. We're separated. He can get nasty when he's agitated. He sounded crazy when he called me last night raving about all the blood in the living room."

Becky went with Bench to the police cruiser. Carstairs lingered a moment. "Don't leave town. We'll surely have more questions for you." When he was sure Young Rabbi was out of earshot, he added, "Your father isn't coming back until we get the deal done."

"Huh?"

"Someone is going to visit you tonight to talk business. No bullshit, understand?"

"What business is that?

"The no bullshit business."

"Is there such an animal?"

"This business is big business so don't fuck around. If the deal doesn't get done, you'll end up in prison fast. I can make that happen. Right now Buck is focused on Becky and Rud. It wouldn't take much pressure at all to steer the bulldozer right over you. Cooperate and I might be able to keep you out of jail."

"Where's my dad?"

"Safe, long as I get my cut and you do as you're told."

That was going to be a problem. I didn't like doing as I was told.

26

Dad didn't call and Becky didn't, either. I'd learned in the military to not worry about the things I couldn't control. At least I learned that's what I was supposed to do. But that was like telling somebody not to think of pink elephants.

Now you're picturing pink elephants.

I see you struggling to get your hands out of those zip ties. Please stop being stupid. Even if you could free your hands, what do you think you'd accomplish before I cracked your skull? I'm the one with the shotgun. Just shut up and keep walking. You know the old joke? How far can a dog run into the woods? Halfway. Then he starts running out of the woods. Just keep walking. I'll tell you when to stop.

Now, where was I? Oh, right ...

I failed to stop worrying about Becky. However, the Army taught me that work can push a lot of worry out of the way. I had business to take care of in the woods: the Barracuda.

I watched the woods and the road for a long time. Satisfied that I was alone and it was safe, I took a pail and some cleaning supplies down the logging road. There was a tiny creek nearby which gave me some water to work with. I'd parked the Barracuda in the dark and the stream wasn't as close as I thought it was. I had to do a lot of walking back and forth over uneven ground.

I popped a couple of Tylenol and got down to work. The floor mats had to come out first. I washed them in the creek. That was the easy part. The trouble with cleaning all traces of blood out of car upholstery is the crevices. A car isn't a linoleum floor. I couldn't scrub everything down with vinegar and dowse it with bleach. Forensics would find traces of Micah's blood in its present state. If I cleaned the car too thoroughly, that would appear suspicious, also. Something about the Young Rabbi's bright eyes told me he was smart enough to look beyond what was in front of him. He'd look for what wasn't there, too.

After hanging the floor mats over the branch of a tree and a few trips back and forth from the creek, I began to realize how stuck I was. A headache hit me hard. It could have been residual pain from being brained in the back of the head two nights before. As the sun climbed to its zenith, bright sunlight burned off the gray of the early morning. The pulse of the ache behind my eyes might have been that, too.

Sweat made my sunglasses slide down my nose as I worked. I kept to the shade of the trees as much as I could. Back in San Diego, a VA doctor told me that if I was going to live like a vampire, I better start taking Vitamin D supplements. "Staying out of the sun, you will avoid wrinkles and skin cancer. You still need Vitamin D for lots of reasons, not least because without it you may experience more bone pain and chronic pain."

As the twinges in my leg grew to a gnawing ache I decided the best I could do for the Barracuda was to vacuum it at a garage. I'd clean it up just enough so I could take it to a car detailer. Once it was perfect, I'd eat some Cheetos in it. My getaway car couldn't look too pristine. I'd have to figure out the safest ratio of orange crumbs to clean so as not to arouse suspicion. It's not like there's a chart for this sort of thing.

When I'd got the ratio just right ... somehow ... I'd put the car back in the barn. I'd put the dust cover over it and hope for the best.

"Oh, that car, Detective Buck, sir? My dad doesn't like me driving his car much. I just took it for an oil change in Detroit."

That might sound plausible but I'd have to take the Barracuda on a long road trip. I'd have to find some far-flung detailer, an out of the way shop and pay in cash.

Criminal enterprises are such hard work. Living legit is easier. It's a wonder anybody tries anything shady.

I could blame my predicament on DNA and social obligation. My parents saved me from the Down brothers so I couldn't leave Dad to his fate. We believe we are in control but, all the time, invisible forces are doing their thing, pulling and pushing. Sometimes the powers working on me make me feel like taffy.

And then there was Becky. I wanted to be her hero, to be hers. That's not DNA so maybe it's hormones and tricks of the brain trying to make us bond and reproduce.

The invisible forces at work make me think I was right about God. If He really cared about what I do, you wouldn't be walking into the woods with a shotgun in your back.

Watch your step. We'll stick to the path a bit longer before you get lost in the woods.

27

I left the Barracuda in the woods and hiked back to the house. When I got there, the Audi was gone. If Becky had returned from her interview with the Young Rabbi, she hadn't left a note. I looked at the dirt in the driveway and noticed the tracks of a double set of tires.

Tow truck, I thought. Becky's Audi was no doubt on its way to a forensics lab somewhere. The Young Rabbi did not waste time looking for clues.

I checked the barn. It was locked up, just as I'd left it. I fed Sophie and let the dog have the run of the property. Sitting on the porch in my father's rocking chair, I left the front door ajar to listen for the phone. The German shepherd ran around. I was a little jealous of how he moved with such ease and energy.

After a while, I pulled the stool out of the living room. Propped up, I rubbed my left leg from the painful spot just above my knee down to the ankle. That didn't do much for me so I tried heat on my kneecap. That felt good without feeling much better. I switched to an ice pack. That dulled the pain a bit more.

I still had a little portable ultrasound wand in my pack but, somehow between the West Coast and Michigan, I'd lost the charging cord. I suspected someone at a bus station swiped it, probably thinking it was a cell phone charger. No matter. Ultrasound never did seem to do much for me. Physiotherapists had given me exercises to strengthen my legs and ease my pain. However, I'd slacked off on doing my physio homework since I'd been home. Mostly I needed sleep and rest.

Worry pushed sleep back for a long time. I was stuck thinking about my pink elephants. Where were Dad and Becky? What was happening with the murder investigation?

Loyalty commits us to strange paths. I bristled at taking orders but it's how I'm made. A dog will love you no matter what you do. That's why everyone loves dogs.

As the sun bent low in the sky, the pink light woke me. Sometime in the afternoon, I'd finally succumbed to a dreamless sleep. When I looked down, Sophie was at my feet on sentry duty. The dog looked up at me as if to say, "It's about time."

"Hey, Sophie."

The dog got up and licked my hand.

"Gross," I said.

The dog didn't seem to mind.

When the phone finally rang, I rushed to get up. Too long in one position, I'd stiffened up. I limped to the living room as Sophie stayed at my heels, eager and interested as if thinking, *What next, boss?*

"Dunno, Sophie."

"Easy?"

Becky! Finally! "Where are you?"

"I'm at Dolores' place."

"How'd it go with the cops?"

"Fine. That was the easy part. I shouldn't say anything much over the phone but, suffice to say, I lawyered up."

"You've been gone since early this morning, though — "

"It was a lot of hurry up and wait. They asked me a few basic questions, no issues. Then I called a lawyer and there was a lot of waiting around. I couldn't get anybody from Rud's firm because they're representing him. We had to wait for a lawyer from out of town to show. Dolores knew somebody. Anyway, I agreed to let the cops take my car for some tests to rule out that I was there last night. That couldn't do any harm."

"You said the cops were the easy part. What was the hard part?"

"I saw Rud briefly. He's still freaking out. He's saying it was you but he's convinced Buck thinks he did it."

"I thought your husband was tight with the cops."

"He thought so, too, but Detective Buck isn't from Lake Orion. Rud never got a chance to suck up to him. The thing that's tripping everybody up is Rud claims he didn't know Micah was there. Turns out the dead man's last name is Burmanthol, by the way."

Micah Burmanthol? That sounded like the name of a doctor or an accountant, not a killer for hire. It was odd to know the name of the man I'd killed. In the past, I had typically not known the names of my targets. Names give personhood. I didn't feel bad exactly. The kill was righteous. However, I did wonder if there was a Mrs. Burmanthol somewhere. Did they have kids? And what were the many variables that had fallen into place to bring us face to face over a gun and a knife?

I checked the grass by the barn again to look for the dead man's handgun. The cops were looking hard at Rud now. I had a suspicion they'd be looking at me as soon as Paul Carstairs got what he wanted out of me. If a search turned up any connection between Burmanthol and me — the dropped gun, for instance — the Young Rabbi would be all over me.

I even checked the dog pens in case Sophie had picked it up and stowed it away. German shepherds don't tend to be diggers. I doubted the dog had buried the weapon. The goons must have come back that night to retrieve the gun. I wanted to believe that but, in a murder case, one hanging thread can make a noose.

28

To loosen up, I did the exercises my physiotherapist prescribed. After I got tired, I sat on the porch with an ice pack on my knee wrapped with a Snoopy beach towel. I recognized it from my childhood. Mom got it for me at Walmart from the time before I knew what chemotherapy was.

As I waited for villains to show, frogs sang their repetitive song to mark their territory and call for mates. The noise male toads and frogs make at night is meant to warn other males away. To me, it sounded no more threatening than the beeping sound a truck makes when it backs up. If there were lyrics to the amphibian chorus, I couldn't figure them out. Only the sharp snap of the bug zapper at the end of the porch interrupted their singing.

Long after dark, my company finally arrived. They came in a black minivan with a dent in the fender under the left headlight. Dad had done business with some pretty tough-looking characters before. I pictured a couple of bikers showing up, maybe emissaries of the Highway Men or the Outlaws. The American Motorcycle Association said that only one percent of the bikers you see on the road are involved in organized criminal enterprises. I expected One

Percenters. Instead, a fiftyish woman wearing a blue blazer, a blouse with a puffy collar and a dark skirt stepped out in shoes with low heels. With her pleasant face and curly blonde hair, she looked like a real estate agent or one of those nuns who had dumped the stereotypical habit.

A handsome man who appeared to be of mixed European and Asian descent stepped out of the driver's side door. He wore a buzz cut in front and ponytail in back. I could grate cheese on those high, sharp cheekbones. He looked young enough to be her son and sufficiently symmetrical to be a model. He wasn't tall but he was thick through the chest and shoulders in a way that suggested he could handle himself in a tussle. In the light cast by the porch light, he crossed his arms so his fists puffed up his biceps. He stared my way as he leaned his back against the hood of the vehicle. He had a handgun in his belt, holstered forward on his hip as if it was more for a display of potential lethality. I decided that goon's nickname would be Buzz.

"Mr. Jack? Ernest Jack Jr.?" The woman strode toward the porch, extending her hand for me to shake way too early. "So sorry for the late hour. It's been a busy day full of complications and implications."

I ignored her outstretched hand and didn't move from my seat. "I'm Easy."

"Pardon me?"

"My name. It's Easy. Easy Jack."

"Easy." She finally dropped her hand and ran it through her hair as if that was what she meant to do all along. "I like that name. You're my first Easy. I hope you're also easy to deal with."

"I don't know about that yet." I suddenly felt rude. Should I stand, shake her hand and offer her tea? We didn't have any tea and this was bad business so I stayed put.

She glanced at the bulk of my wrapped knee. "What's going on there?"

"Fell from my horse. Polo accident ... water polo. The horse drowned."

"Mm-kay ... " She cleared her throat. "I've been in discussions with Ernest Jack Sr.," she continued. "He's proved to be stubborn about a few things I hope we can iron out."

"Sounds like him."

She looked around. "You have a lovely porch, Easy. May I sit?"

I tilted my head toward the empty chair to my left. She turned it so she could face me before sitting down and smoothing her skirt.

It wasn't that her nervous energy charmed me so much as it threw me off. I knew how to deal with aggression. I hadn't expected a diplomatic approach.

"Who am I dealing with?" I asked.

"Me. That's more than you need to know. I believe in being as honest as possible or necessary."

"As possible and necessary. I guess a lot of people work that way."

"You're a dog handler," she said. "You know dogs. Me, too. I have a lovely pair of Corgis. For the purposes of this conversation, you can think of me as the one who holds your leash. You're my new Corgi."

"Woof."

"It would be better if more people understood their place in the world. I think it's especially important in business, especially, *especially* when agreeing on a partnership."

"That's an extra dose of especially."

"So you know I mean it."

"I got a bad deal on a used car once," I said. "The salesman called me 'sir' a lot. Doesn't mean he meant it."

"These are dark and desperate times, Easy. I understand your skepticism — "

"You also use my name a lot, like you got that out of a multilevel marketing seminar on how to close a deal. Just tell me, where's my father?"

Her face hardened. "We have him. He's not being especially cooperative. I think you will be more cooperative. As we speak, your usefulness is keeping you out of jail."

"I need to talk to him — "

"That won't be possible until we can proceed with delivery of the items your father was hired to procure."

I nodded toward the one I called Buzz. "What if I get my dogs to tear your friend apart? Would that change your mind?" I was down to one dog but they didn't need to know that.

Except they already knew.

A man at the end of the porch cleared his throat. In the purple glow of the bug zapper, I saw that he held a rifle. He wasn't the dog killer but he had one of those grim faces that suggest he'd enjoy a sandwich after he shot me. Casual murder wouldn't bother his digestion. The guy must have walked in from the road before the minivan pulled into our driveway. If I still had a pack of dogs, they might have warned me. He looked like a standard issue sent-from-Central-Casting bad guy except for the unfortunate little tuft of hair below his lower lip.

"Hi," I said to the rifleman. "Rockin' that soul patch hard, huh? Haven't seen one of those in a few years. You gonna bring that look back? Good luck! It'll be an uphill battle but I respect your great struggle, comrade. You gonna try to get the words gnarly and tubular back in style, too?"

The man looked sour but said nothing.

The woman let out a long-suffering sigh. "That's Mr. Ramone."

"Hi, Ramone! Nice rifle."

"Mr. Jack, Mr. Ramone is quite a skilled bodyguard. In addition to being a pilot, he has a short temper. I sometimes find that aspect of his character useful. To keep things clean and neat, I rarely unleash him in full fury."

"You talk pretty. And his mom must be real proud."

The goon's face was stone.

"Mr. Ramone never leaves my side."

"No trick to that. First thing I teach my dogs is to heel, too."

She cleared her throat. "Don't be that way, Mr. Jack. Shall we turn back to the subject at hand?"

"Sure. Didn't mean to be gauche in my lady's esteemed presence."

She held my gaze, making sure she had my full attention. When she spoke again, the woman who held my leash took a cold and stiff tone. I'd been screamed at by drill instructors. That didn't bother me.

What disturbed me was that her smile did not fade as she threatened me. "I have your father chained up. You have one dog left. You're not in a position to deliver ultimatums. You need to understand that. Or do I need to bring you to heel?"

"Fine. What guns was Dad supposed to deliver?"

"Not guns, Mr. Jack. I'm here about other material."

"Other — "

"Don't play stupid. You've got yourself in trouble with the local police. A man is dead and I'm told there is forensic evidence that could implicate you."

As soon as she said it, I knew in my bones what she was talking about. Rud Bench and Carstairs knew Micah Burmanthol. Dad owed Carstairs money and Rud hated me because of Becky. By taking away the dog business, the cop was pushing to get his cut out of this side hustle. But my father did not want to complete the shady deal for some reason. Maybe Dad couldn't deliver what they wanted. Perhaps someone had tried to change the terms. I wasn't playing stupid. I really didn't know.

I guessed they had me on Burmanthol's handgun. Suppose a partial print of mine was on the missing pistol from the night they killed the dogs? Such damning evidence could send me away for a long time. Even if I could win a court battle, the circumstantial evidence alone would put me in an orange jumpsuit for a year or two. A long time would pass before I even got to stand in a court to plead self-defense. Between the wait and the appeals, the pain would stretch out for years. Even if I won in the end, I'd lose years. I'd lose Becky.

The woman checked her watch and got up from the chair to stand over me. "Family is everything, Easy. Family is why I do what I do."

"And what is it that you do, exactly?"

"By day? Real estate."

Nailed it, I thought. "Neato," I said.

"By night I deal with logistics that advance my day job."

"Logistics. What does that mean for you exactly?"

"It means I talk to little people like you who have no idea they're up to their necks in deep shit." Her pleasant expression didn't change an iota as she said this. "Do take me seriously, Mr. Jack. I'm a naturally friendly person until it's time to be less friendly. People have underestimated me in the past. Their graves are unmarked and the bodies will never be found. We don't want any more complications. This has to be dealt with quietly and my patience is not a forever thing. You need to understand that. Get me my goods or you will drown in a world of shit."

I believed her.

"Ta-ta!" She smiled and waved. As she hit the bottom step, she paused as if she'd just remembered something. "You killed a man. We know it. That's all the leverage I need. Your father is just icing on the cake. You're lucky to be on the supply side of my equation."

"My dad better be in good shape when this is done or I will be coming for you."

She laughed. "No. You won't."

The man at the end of the porch clacked the bolt on his rifle and pointed it at my feet.

"Your father is not a well man, Easy. In fact, I was worried he wouldn't survive questioning. But enough of that. I want to deal with this matter quietly, no more complications. Let's try to keep this friendly and professional," she said.

When people talk about keeping anything friendly and professional, does that ever work out?

"Are you at least gonna tell me what I'm looking for?" I asked.

"Your father said you'd know where to look. Go fix his mess. Someone will be in touch within forty-eight hours. After that, the homicide detective will take you into custody." She smiled wider and tipped her head toward the man with the rifle. "That, or Mr. Ramone will come calling."

The man with the rifle smiled broadly.

"I will have your father call you. I'm not a monster, Easy, but I am very focused on my goals."

Every infamous monster in the history of the world was probably pretty focused. Hitler was a fussy guy who liked reading cowboy novels and loved his dogs. Still, pretty focused. And a monster.

The woman looked back and gave me that same empty, arid smile. "Be a good boy, Easy. Go fetch!"

Once she and her goons were gone I called Sophie. The dog pushed the screen door open with his nose. "Thanks for the backup, buddy. Woulda been better if you could operate a machine gun, though." I scratched the dog behind the ears for some time before pulling my piece out of the wrap around my knee. It was the little Smith & Wesson Bodyguard 380. The steel was chilled from being nestled by the ice pack. It wasn't a heavy handgun but I found the cold weight of it in my hand comforting. I had the feeling the weapon might get some use if I managed to stay out of jail. As soon as I gave that woman and Deputy Carstairs what they wanted, I'd be dead or in jail.

After their taillights disappeared down the drive, I got up and limped into the house. Despite the ice pack, the bad knee was at its most painful. I stood at the table and stretched my hamstrings while I pecked at the keyboard.

The little surveillance camera had arrived that afternoon and I'd installed it right away. Most of the images I'd caught from the porch were too dark to be useful but there was one good shot. As the woman had mounted the stairs, the light by the front door had illuminated her face.

After uploading the image, I used Google to do a reverse image search. I found her at the bottom of the first page of search results under visually similar images. I found a match with a picture of her shaking hands with the governor of Florida. I'd been visited by a billionaire. America's fiber optic heiress, Mazie Lane, was the mistress who held my leash, my neck in a choke chain.

If I'd had audio on the security camera, I'd have some evidence for the Young Rabbi. Evidence wouldn't really matter, though. They had my father tied to a chair in a basement somewhere. Rich people rarely go to jail, no way, no how. Mazie Lane had the kind of money that can easily make little obstacles like me disappear. This would never see the inside of a courtroom.

Being rich is the closest anyone gets to being a god. Mazie Lane looked like a vengeful god.

29

The phone rang the next morning at six. It was Dad. "Junior? Looks like we've been drafted."

He didn't talk like a scared kidnapping victim. He only seemed annoyed. I tried not to sound like the frightened target of a crooked cop and a blackmail scheme. "You okay, Dad?"

"Fair to middlin'."

"Have you got a gun to your head right now?"

"In a manner of speaking, yeah. I hear they've got your tit in a wringer. They're treating me pretty well, though. They expect me to keel over any minute so they're playing nice. Can't very well push you around if I'm dead, huh?" He gave a prolonged, grinding cough that reminded me that my father wasn't at his best. In the years I'd been away, he'd transformed into an old man prematurely. If he were my age, I could easily imagine him looking for a way to overpower his captors and getting away. But this wasn't a movie and Dad wasn't the man I remembered from childhood.

"What do you want me to do, Dad?"

"It's not what I want you to do. It's what these people want."

Someone in the background said something I couldn't quite hear.

All I could make out was that it was a male voice. I wondered if it was Buzz or maybe the hired gun who'd killed our dogs.

"'There's a Hole at the Bottom of the Sea.' You remember that kid's song? You learned it at Sunday school before your mom gave up on church. Remember?"

The way he spoke, with a similar cadence, I could hear the lyrics to the song in my head again.

"What am I going to find in the hole, Dad?"

"In a hole, in a case, you'll find the key. In the black case with the blue dot, you'll find instructions for what to do to get what they want. The people I'm with will call you."

The same muffled voice said something and Dad said. "Forty-eight hours from last night is what I'm told. No more."

More muffled talking followed and there was more than one person in the room.

"Son? I'm a soldier. We do what good soldiers do, right? It's in the recruitment pamphlet. Where there's a will."

"Going to get it might be a problem," I replied. "The cops told me not to leave town. If they show up looking for me — "

Muffled voices shot back and forth in angry tones. Someone had covered the phone well so I couldn't make out anything useful. This went on for almost a minute. My father didn't appear to be part of that exchange.

Finally, a familiar voice came on the phone. "I can guarantee you the police will not be paying you a visit. If you screw up the delivery, I will nail you to a cross, crucify and burn you. Understand?"

"Yes, Deputy Carstairs. Tell Dad that I'll do what good soldiers do."

The line went dead. I thought what an unfortunate phrase that is. There was a good chance my father would be dead soon, too. He said he was a soldier. That wasn't true. He was in a battle now but he had never enlisted and fought no war. I remembered our conversation from my first day back: Good soldiers don't just follow orders. They sacrifice.

"It's in the recruitment pamphlet," I'd told him.

And, where there's a will? I wasn't sure if that was a clever allusion to the money he'd left me in the bunker or one last note of irony, Dad's way of saying goodbye.

I looked over at Sophie. The dog gazed back with adoring eyes. I wished Becky looked at me with that kind of adoration. Nobody can compete with a dog for worshipful looks.

"C'mon, Sophie. The bad guys want to play hide and seek. Dad wants me to run away while he sacrifices himself. Let's play seek and destroy."

30

Sophie trotted by my side as I limped to the barn. As I descended the ladder into the bunker, the Maglite in my hand yielded a circle of light. The dog stayed by the trapdoor, watching and whining. "Don't stress. Let me do the worrying," I told him. "You should be chill. You're a dog. You don't even know what time it is. Only humans can anticipate their own deaths. You're a lucky guy even if you do carry a girl's name."

On my previous visit, I'd focused on the envelopes of money and the small assortment of weapons on the shelves. Now I turned my attention to the black cases. I'd assumed they were all ammo boxes. There were several piled up against the wall. On closer examination, I found that one was different. The case looked big enough to hold a typewriter. Under the handle, I found a small blue sticker.

I popped the clasps and discovered a big manila envelope atop more than a dozen thin layers of plastic explosive. People usually picture a brick of Semtex when they think of a bomb. The explosive material can be produced in sheets, too.

A cell phone was duct taped to a mechanical detonator and strapped with a zip tie to the underside of the lid. The mechanism was simple but it looked like it would be effective. In blue ink, the bomb maker had written the cell phone number on the underside of the lid. It would be easy to put the two components together and make a working explosive.

Dad had never had a problem dealing in guns and prescription drugs from Canada to make ends meet. He'd always drawn the line at heavier ordnance, though. Making bombs was not within his expertise as far as I knew.

Rather than peer at the contents in the beam of a flashlight, I went up the ladder. I placed the couch over the trapdoor and sat to examine the contents of the envelope.

I found a letter in my father's tight scrawl.

JUNIOR,

YOU'RE READING this so I've messed up. Paul Carstairs made me find explosives and smuggle them. It was that or go to jail for some side deals he was part of his own self. That cop is a filthy blackmailer. I had no idea that getting prescription drugs from Canada for some old friends in need would put me this far under the outhouse.

According to the man I met in Saskatoon, this particular batch of blow 'em up was manufactured in Poland. Remember how we sometimes trained bomb detection dogs before you left? There was a chemical that slowly evaporated from explosives so the dogs could pick up the scent. This explosive is old enough that it doesn't have a taggant like that. It's hard to detect and it's flexible enough to line a laptop or a printer. There's more than enough in the shipment to take out something massive. I don't know what Carstairs has planned but it can't be good. They could make a shaped charge and put it anywhere.

There are bigger fish than Paul Carstairs involved. I thought about calling the FBI but the Feds aren't going to side with a smuggler with shady connections. I could flip on Paul but I'd still lose my home and do jail time. The rules aren't made for people like us. I see no way out and jail's no way to live. Don't worry about me. I'm about done with my life, anyway.

Take the money I've left for you. Take it all and the Barracuda and lose yourself. I always wanted to wander down Route 66. You might try that. I hear the beaches in California are great. Mexico might be better.

Something I never told you about your mother. At the end, she was gasping for air through the pain. Her lungs were filling up. Her heart was closing up shop. Despite all that, her last words were, "This sucks. Where there's a will, there's always some asshole asking you to pay the toll."

I loved your mother for that. Your mother loved you more than I did (but in my defense, I've known you longer. Haha!)

I'm taking the easy way out. We Jacks don't seem to be long on the right kind of luck, but I do wish that for you, Junior. Even though you don't use it much, I'm proud you carry my name around.

Dad

PS ASK KERRY ROBAR from down the road to take care of the dogs. I love dogs because of all the animals, they're the most innocent. Hope I come back as a dog.

DAD WAS A PLANNER. His letter was my ticket out of obligation. He was right about the Jack family being short of luck. "Not long on luck, nor brains, neither," as my mother would say.

Not much luck, but we did have heart and spite.

My father was ready to die so I'd have a forty-eight hour head start. Love that strong commits a person. That's the strange paradox of sacrifice born of love. Now that my father had given me leave to run for my life, I had a higher obligation to try to save him. There was no way I could walk away.

"Time to kick Fate in the teeth, Dad," I said.

I didn't have a plan yet. However, I did have a good dog, lethal weapons and experience using them. As I petted the German shepherd's big head, I told him, "We're going to help Dad take the Easy way out." The dog looked up at me with a quizzical expression. German shepherds are smart and loyal. They're shit at understanding puns but they are good dogs.

"Hey, Sophie," I wondered aloud. "Dad held back one case. I wonder how many of these cases he managed to smuggle in the old Kenworth? What's so big that it needs that much explosive? They aren't trying to blow up a person. This case alone would do the job and then some. What is Mazie Lane up to?"

The dog wasn't any help with questions, either.

I hauled the case up the ladder and buried it by the pens where the dogs were buried. After further consideration, I did the same with the rest of the weapons and ammunition that Dad had hidden in the bunker. I trusted Becky with the secret of the bunker. However, Dad was very sick. If his captors became impatient or if I missed the deadline, I needed to make sure they had nothing they could use against me.

31

I needed transportation. The Barracuda was too memorable. I left it in the woods. Nobody goes to war on a ten-speed either so I called Becky. She showed up in her Audi within an hour.

I pulled on my sunglasses and went out to meet her in the driveway. She ran to me, threw her arms around me and kissed me deeply.

"How you holding up?" I asked.

"My living room is a mess."

"Sorry to hear that."

"Paul let me through to my bedroom just long enough to pick up a few clothes. A deputy was with me the whole time, writing down what I took from my own home and photographing it. I think they think I had something to do with Micah's death."

"Intimidation tactics. Don't worry about it. They don't have anything on you."

"That detective, Jerry Buck? He questioned Rud a long time, too. Paul says he's grilling him about past clients. He seems convinced there's an angle there."

"Has Rud got a lot of enemies?"

"He doesn't have a lot of friends. Besides, there's always a shady client who's pissed about his legal bills. Everybody is the villain in somebody's story.

"What's your husband telling you?"

"We're not talking to each other much. He still thinks you did it but since I told him I was with you, he's not so sure."

"Death makes strange bedfellows, doesn't it?"

She gave me a hard look. "How's that?"

"Carstairs hates my guts but he's in my corner, too."

"I don't get it."

"Deputy Carstairs has other things for me to do, things I can't do in an interrogation room."

"What's that about?"

"Stuff to do with my dad."

"Where is he?"

"Million dollar question. Carstairs knows but he's not saying."

"He's using you for something? Do you want me to talk to him?"

"Absolutely not. I'll take care of it. That's why I need your car."

She handed me the keys to the Audi without hesitation. "Bring it back with a full tank."

"Yes, Boss."

She kissed me again, longer and warmer this time. "Can you take care of Sophie while I'm doing things?"

"I guess so. As long as Sophie can get along with Dolores' cat."

"Do you want to stay here? Sophie's got all she needs and I thought you might want to — "

"Play house with you? No offense, but you're too far out of town for my taste. I need to live within walking distance of the coffee shop."

"Sad."

"Shut up!"

"Shut me up." I pulled her to me and kissed her again.

A little red Toyota pulled in behind Becky's Audi. A tall woman stepped out from the driver's seat. Her bleached blonde hair wasn't '70s big but it was '80s tall.

"Friend of yours?" I asked.

Becky turned and waved. "Dolores! Remember Easy?"

"Yeah. You were ahead of me in school." She stood back by her car, arms crossed and pouty. Dolores had a harsh case of Resting Bitch Face. "We all knew about Easy Jack, though."

"We?"

She shrugged. "You know."

"I do?"

Dolores waved in a vague gesture. "After the thing that happened with the Down family. If I was Becky's friend back in the day, I would have told her to stay away from you."

"D," Becky said. "You said you'd be cool."

"I am cool. It's just that a lot of people said it had to be the dad or the son who ran Victor and his brother off the road. No matter what the cops said — "

"I remember the whispers. I was just a kid, Dolores. The hit and run was never solved."

"Yeah. All that came of it was the mailman made sure to lock up his truck after that."

"At least there's that," I said.

"After Down died it died down," she said. "We said that a lot behind your back and under your nose. Down died so it died down."

"Kind of clever in a sick way," I said. "What ever happened with Victor's family, anyway?"

"The parents sold the farm and moved to Florida a few years ago. The brothers moved away. Ronny was in and out of jail for drug and assault charges. Lives in Saginaw now, I think. Heard he cleaned up and works at a Muffler Man. Jeff got a job with that haunted house in Pontiac."

"The one Becky and I went to in senior year for Halloween? What was it called? Realm of Darkness?"

"Nah, the other one that's in an old parking garage. It's huge. Em ... Erebus."

I don't know why, haunted house attractions are thick on the ground in Michigan. Our license plates should read: The Scare Me State.

"Jeff became a puppeteer there."

"Really?"

"The Down brothers aren't the assholes they used to be. They've reformed. Too bad Victor never got a chance to grow up and grow out of being an asshole."

The way Dolores looked at me with narrowed eyes seemed like a challenge. It was as if she was sure those asshole brothers had changed for the better but reform was out of my reach.

"Huh. You seem very much in the know, Dolores."

"In the know and in the flow," she said. "I work at a salon. Lake Orion's not that big. I hear stuff all the time."

"What's the gossip on the murder in town?"

"That you're back from the wars and all mysterious and whatnot. Soon as you reappear, suddenly somebody else dies. Rud's an asshole for knocking Becks around but you've got history around here. Even if you didn't do anything, you look like the type that could."

"What type is that?"

"Whatever you are, I guess."

"Another whisper campaign."

"Nah, we're talking about you pretty loud." She smiled. "I've yelled about you over the sound of a hair dryer."

"Great," I said.

"You remember Kent Godwin?" she asked.

"He was in my homeroom class senior year, yeah."

"Do you remember sucker punching him just before grad? In his graduation pictures, you can see his nose is broken."

"First, I didn't sucker punch him. He started the fight. I ended it. Second, he's not just a loser. He's a sore loser."

"Not how he tells it, Easy."

"Did he say what the beef was about?"

She'd plucked her eyebrows until they were too thin but what she had left knitted together. She shook her head.

"Becky and I had just broken up and Kent was a jerk about it. He'd set his sights on Becky and told me he was next in line. He thanked me for 'breaking her in.'"

"Gross."

"Things got heated but he's the one who started swinging first. Kent's not a good guy. What's he doing now?"

"He worked in parking enforcement for a while but he liked giving out tickets a bit much for people around here to tolerate. Store owners said he was bad for business."

"That fits."

"I don't know what Kent's doing now. I see him walking around the village a lot."

"Looks like I should have stayed in Lake Orion just so I could defend my name. I didn't know I was convicted in absentia."

"All of Lake Orion has been wondering about Victor Down's death for years. Your dad's got a reputation. When he was a drinker —"

"Dad drank a lot and got into trouble a few times around the time my mother was either dead or dying."

"Even your mother, God rest her soul."

"What about her?" I asked.

"My mom remembers her as a good person but she had a temper."

"Everybody has a temper."

"Not like the Jack family."

This wasn't exactly news but it occurred to me that when I thought of my mother, I almost always pictured her on her deathbed. By then, she didn't have much energy left in her to be angry at anyone except God for killing her.

"There's a guy down in Mississippi who went to jail for tying his girlfriend to a tree," Dolores told me. "They had an argument so he left her there to die. They found her body a year and a half later. The poor woman had to be identified by her dental records. Can you imagine dying like that? The thirst? The hunger? Screaming yourself hoarse, wet and cold and knowing you've been left to die?"

"Why are you telling me this, Dolores?"

"The guy who did all that? If that murderer was from Lake Orion and listened to the rumors, he'd wonder about you."

"Wonder about me?"

"Like, nervous. Hiding behind those big sunglasses, what's that dude's story? Is he dangerous? Whatever you are, Becky's been through enough. I hoped she'd have gotten through her bad boy stage by now —

Becky looked furious. "D!"

"Cool, so this has been fun ... catching up," Dolores deadpanned.

"Glad I could give my hometown so much entertainment," I said. "Don't you people have TVs?"

"Dolores is going to drive me back," Becky said. "D, is it cool with you if we take care of Easy's dog for a bit? He's a cutie!"

"You fall too easily for cuties," Dolores said.

"Sorry, Easy," Becky said. "She isn't altogether wrong about that part. I do fall for cuties." She kissed me on the cheek sweetly before turning back to Dolores. "He isn't weird — "

"Broken, then?"

"You don't know Easy like I know Easy. You should see him when he's around his dogs. He's got a quiet, relaxed energy around them."

"Great," Dolores said. "Your boyfriend's part wolf. You know what happens to guys like him under a full moon, right?"

"Thanks for the car, Becky," I said. "Next time you come out to the country, maybe leave Captain Platinum behind? She acts like her diaper's wet."

"Nice," Dolores said. "About keeping the dog, how long is 'a bit' going to be exactly?"

"Just a couple of days," I replied.

Dolores nodded and said, "Fine," but she clearly meant, "Fuck."

Less than two days to deliver the explosives, I thought.

Mazie Lane and Carstairs would use me as long as I was necessary to their plan. Then they'd kill us off to snip off any loose ends. If Dolores was right, it seemed that Lake Orion would not miss us.

32

I drove into town and this time I came strapped for battle. The little Smith and Wesson in my pocket was a comfort. At the same time, I knew that if I was forced to use it, I'd already failed.

As the Audi hummed down the highway, I thought of Mazie Lane's confident smile. I'd never met a billionaire before and I had to admit I was impressed. She hadn't bothered to give me a false name as Micah had. When she told me she was in real estate, I pictured her selling fancy homes in Grosse Pointe or Okemos. Her business was on a far grander scale than that, something that inexplicably required illicit explosives.

A quick search on the internet had revealed Mazie Lane had come from money. Not content to be an heiress to a fiber optics fortune, she was working on making her fourth billion dollars. An investor with substantial commercial real estate projects, she owned malls in Chicago, Orlando and Los Angeles and an emerald mine in South Africa. A well-known patron of the arts, Lane donated to both political parties. I'd read somewhere that if a billionaire dropped $10,000, they'd actually lose money if they bothered to stop and pick it up. Compared to how most of us lived, she may as well have been an alien.

What project could be so important that she would bother coming out to the sticks to speak to me in person? I was just trying to get my father back but the stakes had to be very high for her, too.

After picking up a couple of coffees at Abeantogo on West Flint Street, I headed over to Deputy Carstairs' neighborhood. Cops don't list their addresses anywhere. If they did, they'd have sand in their gas tanks a few times a year. However, Becky knew where Paul Carstairs lived and that he lived alone.

I slid past the house first. It was an unremarkable two-story house on Shadbolt East, what some people would call "a charmer." The humble home seemed about right for a cop's salary. If Carstairs had a stash of ill-gotten gains, he was smart enough to stay low-key and off the IRS's radar. Maybe Paul Carstairs planned to retire young and leave rural Michigan behind. Someone as slick as Mazie Lane might pay a minion by setting up an offshore account with a friendly bank. The Caymans, maybe. That's where I'd go if I were him.

I parked down the street and took both coffees with me. If challenged by a nosy neighbor, I'd say I was waiting for Paul on his back deck. What burglar would bring two beverages to a break and enter? My heartbeat kicked up its pace a notch as I approached the house. Soon I was up the driveway and behind the house, unchallenged. There were lights with motion detectors but I didn't spot any cameras.

Fortunately for me, the deputy valued privacy. His backyard was screened on each side by a high hedge. I could hear kids next door splashing around in a swimming pool but I couldn't see them. I found two doors at the rear of the house. The first was a sturdy door to the basement at the bottom of a short set of steps. The second was a sliding glass door off the small patio with a weathered picnic table and a shiny aluminum barbecue.

I ducked out of sight in the stairwell. I set the coffee cups down by the back door and searched for a hidden key. Almost everybody's got a hidden key. Finding nothing, I guessed that Carstairs might have hidden his spare key out front. I wasn't about to hang out on the front step to look for it, though. Too much exposure.

Next, I checked the sliding door. Locked. However, it was an old house. As I pulled on the handle I noticed a little play in the track. I grabbed the handle with both hands, braced my feet and lifted the door, wiggling it up and down until the door slid out of the top track. The spring in the door's lock popped and I was inside. It was harder to push the door aside than it had been to defeat the lock.

I've picked up a lot of random skills. Some of that knowledge came from my military training. This trick I got from dating Becky. Finding my way around a locked sliding glass door was how I kept her from getting grounded when she arrived home after curfew. We'd gone parking and lost track of time. I missed those carefree days and those sweaty summer nights in the back of her mom's car.

Of course, my teenage years were not carefree. Mom died. Dad was drunk with grief, vodka and beer. Still, I was dating Becky then. I was oblivious to the town's suspicions and hatred toward my family and me. With her in my life, everything was okay. Better than okay. Love and lust makes the world go away.

As soon as I was inside Carstairs' house, I lifted the glass door back into its track so it slid properly. That done, I turned around and spotted a motion detector on the wall flashing red.

A slow beeping came from the front of the house. I raced as quickly as I could toward the front door. The beeping sped up as I entered the front hallway. A keypad sat beside the phone on a small table. On a shelf under the table sat a device about the size of a Kleenex box. As the beeps sounded more rapidly, I figured the siren would sound at any second. After that, someone from a dispatch office would call through the box demanding my password. I reached down behind the table and unplugged the landline connection. The annoying beeping stopped. Someone from the security company could call. They'd just get a busy signal or no answer.

Alarm systems such as these might scare off an ordinary thief looking to pawn a stolen TV. I was here to save my father.

I listened carefully. The house was silent. I smelled something familiar, an earthy aroma. Then I heard it. Nails on a linoleum floor. A dog came running. It was a little pug. His whole body wasn't much bigger than Sophie's head but he came at me barking and growling as soon as he spotted me. I'd often seen yappy little dogs come hard at much bigger canines. All dogs have a bit of the wolf in them. Smaller dogs are often fearless, oblivious to how small they are.

"Hey!" I said, not loud, but firm.

The dog stopped barking but kept growling, ready to bite.

"Buddy! Aren't you the fierce one?" Careful not to look the pug directly in the eyes, I knelt slowly. The dog braced its front feet and lowered its head, ready to jump. I dug a dog treat out of my pocket. Since my return to home, I always had some with me. They were shaped like little bones as if canines cared about the aesthetics of their food. I tossed the first treat in front of the dog gently and waited. Cautiously, the dog sniffed at my peace offering.

"It's okay," I soothed. "You can have it. Life is short and so are you. Enjoy yourself."

The dog snapped up the snack and chewed loudly. I feel sorry for pugs. They are well-known for their breathing problems. The breed also suffers proptosis way too often (otherwise known as, holy shit, my dog's eyeball just popped out!)

I snapped the next treat in two and held it out. As the dog advanced, I placed it on the floor in front of me. The dog didn't hesitate to pounce on the food this time.

When he was done, I held out my fist for him to sniff. "You're home alone all day, aren't you? Poor guy. You need a friend. You don't have to be scared of me, buddy."

Expecting another treat, the dog continued to sniff my fist. I slowly opened it to reveal the other half. It's no good to lie to a dog. They don't respect people who fool them. It may be fun to pretend to throw a ball and watch the dog search for it. Good dog trainers never recommend that sort of play. Dogs respect pecking order. They respond to love, not lies. I ran my hand over the pug's little head gently and soon he pressed into my palm. Dogs give love. They love to be loved and they are without guile.

After a moment or two of petting, I asked my new friend, "You wanna show me around? I'm looking for my dad. He's about 5'10", obsessed with all the money he doesn't have and I think he's dying of something or other. I'm trying to bring him home safe. Have you seen him?"

Carrying the pug around, I searched the house quickly. My father was not chained to the furnace in the basement. So much for easy solutions.

33

Searching Carstairs' home as quickly as I could, I was playing Sherlock but I had no idea what I was looking for. The deputy's messy desk seemed like my best hope. I turned on the desktop computer and tried to be patient as it slowly booted up. The little pug allowed me to hold him in my arms. I guess we both found that comforting.

As I waited for the old computer to come to life, my mind was on the alarm system. If Carstairs was the careful sort, he would have set up more numbers for the alarm company to call in sequence. He might be on his way, lights and sirens blaring. On the other hand, the mess of paperwork and books across his desktop suggested he might be the type to let details slide.

I went through the desk. He used household bills as bookmarks. I found a utility bill marking a picture book of Florida. Old utility bills wouldn't help me. I discovered he'd used his latest credit card bill as a bookmark in a heavy picture book about the Florida Keys. I went through the items on the VISA bill but found no incriminating line item. No airline ticket to Brazil. No rental of a storage container that might, for instance, hold a kidnap victim.

I went through more drawers and found nothing that would lead me to Dad. In the bottom drawer, I found a set of handcuffs and a key. Reasoning that they might be useful, I pocketed both.

The screen on the computer finally brightened and I was prompted for a password. I looked around for a book of passwords. Nothing. No password, no joy. Detectives in those old noir pulp novels seemed to find clues easily: a notebook detailing the plans for the crime, a ledger with the names of co-conspirators or a nightclub matchbook with a scrawled phone number on it. Cracking wise, cracking cases and saving the day was inevitable in those stories. For me, nothing was a sure thing except Becky, the love of dogs and leg pain that would follow me the rest of my life. And "the rest of my life" might not be a long time.

I looked the pug in the face. "I don't suppose you know the password, do you, pupper?"

The little dog looked up at me with his big bug eyes for a solemn moment before nestling into my chest and wiggling his little bum. He was happy, sweet and useless to my endeavors in espionage.

"You are good company, I'll give you that," I said. "People who don't have problems tend to shit all over the notion but I could use an emotional support animal like you. Do you think you could get along with my friend Sophie? You know, in case something happens to your master?" The dog didn't disagree so I told him I'd come back for him if worse turned to worst for Paul Carstairs.

That's when the cop showed up, gun drawn. "You here looking for your dad? Stupid! I generally stay at arm's length. Gotta maintain plausible deniability. This was supposed to go smooth. You're screwing everything up, Easy."

I looked down the barrel of his weapon. I'd been in this position before. No one gets used to it. I remembered every time a gun had been pointed at me in perfect detail. You never know when your luck will run out or which day will be your last.

34

"Hi, Paul. Sweet pug. What's his name?"

"Edmond."

"A pug named Edmond. Nice. I couldn't decide. He looked like a Steve or a Pedro to me."

"You were supposed to go get something. Why aren't you doing that?"

I checked my watch. "I'll get it for you before the deadline."

He raised his pistol and pointed it at my head. "I told her she was giving you too much time to think."

"What was the calculus there?" I asked.

"I wasn't going to store the stuff for her somewhere. I don't want to be within a mile of this deal when it goes down."

"Yeah, you're the middle man. Leave the dirty work for us minions," I said.

"I like to think of myself as a facilitator or a broker. I wanted the stuff out of Michigan quick so I could get paid. However, Miss Lane had important business elsewhere. When she comes back, she'll have the right sized plane for the job. It's not a small load to haul. And now I find you're using the time to screw around."

"With my father's life on the line? Why would I do that?"

"Because you think you're clever."

"You're the one with the gun. I'm holding a pug. Why would I think I'm clever?"

He seemed to consider this. Then he motioned for me to get out of his chair. "You take anything?"

"Nah, but Edmond has stolen my heart."

"Put the dog down."

I did as I was told and placed Edmond on the floor gently.

"Anyone know you're here?"

I shrugged.

"Where's the stuff?"

I shrugged again.

"Did you send someone to go get it?"

"That would be telling. I'm not a tattler."

"It must be someone you can trust with your father's life. You didn't bring Becky in on this did you?"

"No. I'm keeping Becky out of this. She has enough trouble with that lousy husband of hers."

He smiled but he didn't lower his weapon. "At least we can agree on that."

"Why don't you put that thing away? You need me to bring you the package. You aren't going to shoot me in your own house."

"What are you doing in my home, Easy? Stop being coy. You know what Miss Lane's after."

"But I don't know why. I want to know what she's up to before I hand over the explosives. Dad doesn't want to give them to her so why should I?"

"Because if you don't, there'll be one less Ernest Jack in the world."

"Then two less, I imagine."

"That depends on how useful you prove to be."

"As soon as I deliver, you'll be coming after me for the dead man in Rud Bench's living room."

"His name was Micah Burmanthol. Say it."

"Michael Bum-something."

"Becky talks about you like you're some kind of hero. I wonder if that's true — "

"I'm sure you'll get around to making your point. Take your time. I'm comfortable."

"Somebody's gotta go down for the murder of Micah Burmanthol. If it's not you, it could be Becky."

"You think the Young Rabbi will go for that?"

"Who?"

"Detective Buck, I mean."

Carstairs shrugged. "These things are malleable. Maybe evidence gets lost, maybe it's found. It doesn't take much to steer an investigation in a certain direction."

I stared at the deputy for what felt like a long time. "You got the gun, man. Sounds like you're holding all the cards, too."

"Ernest Sr. made a deal."

"Coerced by you."

"He is a transporter who didn't deliver. He opened the cases and started thinking. He wasn't paid to think. Wasn't his business any more than it's yours."

I said nothing.

"C'mere," he said. "Time you got on your horse and galloped away in a cloud of horse shit. Don't come back here. Don't let me see you again until you've got what we need. Understand me, Easy?"

"Sure do!" I tried to sound cheerful.

On the way out the door, Carstairs hit me on the side of the head. It wasn't the sort of strike meant to knock me cold. It was what my father would call "a cuff." My mother would have said, "got your ears boxed." I stumbled down his front steps but managed to stay upright.

"Just so you know where you are in the pecking order," Carstairs said, "you're my bitch."

I held the side of my head and looked back at him, searching for something sharp and pithy to say. Nothing came to mind. This was the second time he showed me that smug smile. I didn't like it. Edmond needed a new home, one without an asshole for a master. If not for the revolver in the deputy's hand and the fact that he was a cop, I might have reached for my own weapon. Instead, all I could do was stare and mean-mug him.

"Miss Mazie is not going to like you coming around here, either. Don't be a hero. I wouldn't advise you tell anybody else. Haven't you gotten enough people covered in blood and shit already?"

"Thanks for the advice."

"You want to save Becky? Once our business is done, turn yourself in for the murder."

"She's my alibi."

"She'll recant when you confess. The DA will go easy on her when I get her to testify that you threatened her life if she didn't back up your story."

"She wouldn't do that to me. We've got history."

"You better convince her then. You may last longer in jail than you would on the outside. We both know you were there. You killed Micah Burmanthol. You'll get more leniency if you confess. It's your choice. Would you like to be an old man when you get out of jail or a very little old man when you get parole?"

"Any other options?"

"Dead before the end of the week." He shut the door.

I passed his police cruiser as I walked back down his driveway toward the street. I wondered if I'd end up in the back seat or the trunk of that car.

35

I drove around for a while, trying to sort out a plan and finding nothing. Where were the bad guys holding Dad? They had all the power. Eventually, I found myself walking into Paddling's. I hadn't eaten all day and I needed to refuel.

Late afternoon was not the bar's busiest time. I was the only customer. The guy behind the bar looked like he was in his early twenties. He had such a high forehead, I guessed he'd give up on his hairline in another year or two and shave himself bald. He was a handsome fellow who could carry that off. He wore a plain white shirt and an expression that said he'd rather be just about anywhere else.

Grateful for the darkness in the bar, I took off my sunglasses. In daylight, even when wearing shades, I always felt tension around my eyes. I wasn't sure anymore if it was a genuine reaction to sunlight or if squinting had merely become a habit.

I sat at the bar and asked for coffee, eggs and bacon with rye toast. Without moving from where he stood, he yelled my order to a woman in the kitchen. He poured my coffee and planted himself in front of me, apparently eager for conversation. That level of assertiveness could only spring from aggression, loneliness or gregariousness bordering on missionary zeal. That's about what it takes for me to chat with a stranger. I gave in and asked his name.

"Chandler. William, sir." He grinned wide and offered his hand as if this was a job interview. We shook.

"Chandler, William or William Chandler? What's your first name, last name situation. Or is it Sir William of Chandler? Have you been knighted? I'm confused."

"Billy Chandler. People call me Billy. Ain't nobody calls me sir."

"Is Mr. Paddling not working today?"

"Mike's got a hernia. You know Mike?"

"Not really. My dad used to drink here a lot when he was a big drinker. He said Mike made the best Irish car bombs. Is the boss getting his hernia looked at?"

"Nah, he's upstairs lying on his couch waiting for it to get worse. Occasionally he comes down to complain about it."

Either Mike Paddling was scared of doctors or he had to worry about medical bills, too. That dilemma sounded a little too familiar. I needed to change the subject.

I couldn't place his accent and told him so. "Where you from, Billy?"

"You're hearing the musical lilt of a transplant from New Orleans. My parents' influence. After Hurricane Katrina, my whole family packed up and moved as far away from the Gulf Coast as they could. The money ran out when we got to Lake Orion. You know this used to be a resort town? They had a roller coaster here once upon a time. Man, I would have loved to see that."

"Venice of the Middle West," I said.

"How's that again?"

"That's what they used to call it. My dad remembers when they had trains burning through here all the time. Lake Orion went from a resort town to the place people drive from to get to somewhere else."

"You a local? I didn't have you pegged for a local. Haven't seen you around here."

"Used to be. Been away for a few years."

It feels like a hundred years, I thought.

"You came back. There was your mistake, man."

I couldn't disagree. "You don't like Lake Orion, I take it?"

Billy made a seesaw motion with both hands and grinned. "It's okay, but all the action is somewhere else. I'm saving up to go to Hollywood. I'm an actor at heart."

The woman in the kitchen must have been listening to every word. She yelled, "You're an actor who hasn't acted in anything yet!"

"What difference does that make?" Billy shot back. I sensed no irritation in his voice. He was just that sunny.

"What difference does that make?" the woman echoed. "See, that's the sort of self-delusion that can carry you all the way to the top. You don't have a dime but you've got confidence. With that attitude, you'll be a Scientologist in no time."

The woman emerged from the kitchen laughing. She was an African-American woman with a pretty, freckled face. She placed my plate of eggs, bacon and rye in front of me. She looked me in the eyes but she spoke to Billy. "You keep on putting your tips in your piggy bank, baby. At the rate you're saving? You'll be auditioning for the movies in no time. Hope you like old man bulky sweaters because you'll be playing somebody's grandfather."

I took a sip of coffee and winced dramatically.

"Coffee too hot?" she asked.

"Ooh, no. I just tasted something bitter. Tastes like dream killer."

They both laughed good-naturedly.

"Go on," Billy told her. "You just don't want me to leave! You want me to stick around so you can scrub my back in the shower." She took a dish towel from her shoulder and used it to snap him in the ass before retreating to the kitchen. He watched her as she sashayed away.

"That's Mike's niece," Billy told me. Then he leaned back and called after her. "Amy, if you're nice, I'll take you with me!"

"I don't follow anybody," she said. "You want to be my man, you gotta follow after me."

Billy turned back to me and lowered his voice so she couldn't hear him. "Truth is, I'd probably be on a Greyhound already but the one sweet thing Los Angeles does not have is her."

I'd seen a lot in the years I was away. In my absence, my father had aged considerably. By becoming jaded and cynical, I'd aged too fast, as well. Looking at the light in their eyes and the easy banter between them, I remembered that same sweetness between Becky and me.

I knew she married a wealthy young lawyer before I returned to Lake Orion. Still, I came back hoping to see her again. If I'd stayed away, I wouldn't have stabbed some fool to death in her living room.

The sad truth was, if Becky weren't in Lake Orion, I probably would have swung by the home just to say hi to Dad for one weekend. Then I would have kept on going. They say everybody should see Miami Beach once before global warming sweeps it away forever. But Becky didn't live in Miami.

If my superior officers could see me now, they'd kick my ass for my lack of planning.

36

Billy interrupted my thoughts and I was glad of it. "What's your handle, son?"

Usually when anyone called me "son" I bristled. There was something about this guy's easy manner that allowed me to relax. "Easy, Jack," I told him.

His forehead furrowed. "And you? Is that, uh ... ?"

"First name, Easy. Last name, Jack."

"Easy. Cool."

"I once thought so, too."

"You having a bad day, Easy?"

"If you said that you would not be a liar."

"Money problems?"

I let out a laugh. "What? Can you smell it on me?"

"'Cuz who doesn't have money issues?"

I smiled. "You're not wrong." The eggs were touching the hash. I nudged the food around the plate so no component of the meal touched another. That was bad luck and I'd had enough of bad luck.

"You know what I do about my money problems?" Billy leaned in as if he was about to share a secret of the universe before crowing, "Powerball!"

Amy let out a derisive laugh from the kitchen. "Ha!"

"I know!" Billy said. "People shit all over the lottery but let me educate you both on how much sense it makes." He began ticking off points on his fingers. "First, people say the lottery is a tax on the poor. Well, shit, I'm poor and I pay my taxes. Why not get a little motivation to keep on living? It doesn't make sense for rich people to play the lottery but it makes perfect sense for folks like us to scratch them scratch tickets till they bleed. I scratch 'em like a bad rash."

The bacon was crispy, the way I liked it. However, I soon became distracted by Billy as he warmed to his subject. He'd given so much thought to winning the Powerball, I wondered if this was a piece he'd written and performed for auditions.

"They say you got better odds getting hit by lightning. I don't think so! How often do you hear of somebody getting hit by lightning? Not often. How many people do you hear of winning the lottery? Every week somebody's pulled the golden ticket to the chocolate factory somewhere!"

Billy clapped his hands and rubbed them together, excited. "People say winning the lottery ruins people's lives but ain't nobody givin' the money back, am I right?"

"Right," I agreed.

"They say you lose your friends. Shit, buy new ones and make 'em prettier and nicer. You got mo' money problems? S'better than no money problems any day of the week!"

"Damn right," I said.

"And who are these people sayin' the lottery is bad? It gives money to charity, does it not?"

"It does."

"The people sayin' I shouldn't invest in the Powerball are just a bunch of sore losers. What do they know about getting rich? And how else is the average person supposed to dream? If I ever get out of this place, I'm going to be an actor. What do most people have to hold on to for hope? Nothin'. Lot of people 'round here? Their greatest aspirations are for fried chicken and dyin' in their sleep."

Amy came back out of the kitchen, her hands on her hips. "Suppose you did win Powerball. What would you do with that money?"

"I'd be stingy enough that I'd never run out of joy. I'd be generous enough that even you would follow me west to the promised land."

She chuckled. "Crazy."

"That's not crazy. That's the start. You win the Powerball, you got power and you're a baller. I'd romance a string of women — "

"Billy!" For a moment, Amy made a face like she was outraged but then broke into smiles and chuckles.

"I'd romance a string of women," Billy added, "but always come back to you."

"With STIs," she said.

"When you got Powerball STIs, you're feeling so good they go away without penicillin. After I got tired from too much sex — "

"Twenty seconds later," she teased.

"*Ahem!* After I got tired from all the sex there is to be had *everywhere*, I'd try all kinds of drugs and see if they'd open my mind to the universe. DMT, cocaine, gasoline, DDT and roach spray!"

Amy and I both broke out into full-throated laughing at that.

"When I get my Powerball money, I'll help the poor, save orphans from here to Thailand and find out what it's like to do heroin on the moon! 'Cuz, baby, when you got money, you got everything."

We clapped. Billy bowed.

That's how my epiphany struck. *When you got money, you got everything. Everything. And everything to lose.*

Since coming to Lake Orion, I'd had people try to intimidate me. They'd killed a pack of good dogs. Micah Burmanthol attempted to kill me. Carstairs was ready to frame me for murder unless I did as I was told.

I had been looking at the situation all wrong. A billionaire heiress had climbed into a minivan to drive out for a face-to-face conversation with lil' ole me. I didn't know any billionaires or anyone who knew any billionaires. And yet, Mazie Lane, heiress to a fiber optics fortune and crazy wealthy investor, had come to me. Whatever investment she was protecting had to be huge if she was bothering to deal with me in person.

Maybe more important, that afternoon I'd broken into the home of a cop. Deputy Carstairs had not shot me. He hadn't tried to beat the shit out of me. He'd barely even touched me.

I could threaten them with the one thing they feared: losing everything. I began to feel something good rise in my chest. Call it what you want. Power? Hope? Whatever it was, I was fed up with bad luck. It was time to make some of the right kind of luck.

Amy told Billy his speech was worth another back scrub in the shower. Watching Amy kiss Billy was like looking into a magic mirror. I envisioned what I wanted to see: Becky kissing me when all this was over. I saw myself walking free. Dad was safe and getting proper medical care. I imagined all our bills were paid and we had no worries about bill collectors.

When all this was over, Becky and I could have a future together. I could make that happen. I wasn't new to this game. Sure, I had a limp and bright light pushed into the back of my eye sockets like thick fingers. But once a Ranger, always a Ranger. A lot had been taken from me, but a bum knee and headaches didn't change who I was at my core. Rangers lead the way.

I looked into the dark cup of coffee and saw my shadow. I'd lost the man I'd been in Afghanistan. Coming home, I would find myself.

Don't forget who you are, Easy. Not again.

37

D eputy Paul Carstairs had been where my father was. Wherever Dad was being held, it couldn't be far. I was still on the hook for murder, but I would slip off Mazie Lane's leash if I could find my father.

I had to make a couple of stops to pick up some supplies. Dealing with customer service and getting chargers for the devices took a good chunk of the afternoon and evening. When I drove back to Carstairs' place, it was dark. I parked down the street, shut off my lights and hunkered down to wait, my new cell phone at the ready. If anyone came up to the car to ask what I was doing there, I'd tell them I was waiting for a call. Michigan doesn't have a law against using a cell phone while driving but it was a reasonable defense against questions. I scanned the street for movement. The neighborhood was quiet and dead as a cemetery.

I hadn't smoked since Afghanistan. My craving for a nicotine buzz roared back with a vengeance. I chewed gum for a while but stopped when I realized I was too nervy, chewing too furiously. Spasms were an occasional side effect of my medication. If my jaw got sore, it might lock up. I stuck a toothpick between my teeth, slowed my breath and waited for my heartbeat to steady before I got out of the car.

Carstairs' cop car wasn't in the driveway anymore. His Toyota looked like a lot of cars on the road. If Carstairs went for a drive, he'd be easy to lose. I had to hang back because he might know Becky's car, too. If I followed him for long, he'd spot me. Fortunately, it's a lot easier to tail somebody now than it was in old gangster movies. I'd bought a GPS tracker bundled with a magnetic case. It was on sale for less than a hundred bucks. The reviews on the website were full of boyfriends crowing about how they'd "caught the cheating bitch." Several women reported they were on the way to divorce court thanks to the device's usefulness in catching husbands with their pants down.

The street lights were on and I hunched a little as I passed under one of the bright lamps. I suddenly wished Sophie was with me. Nobody looks twice at anyone walking a dog and if they do, they only look at the dog.

I paused in the shadows at the edge of the deputy's property and listened intently. The night was warm and his windows were open. I heard the faint sound of a television. I hoped Carstairs had been rattled enough by my sudden appearance in his home that he was wondering how I got in without breaking anything. Since I'd taken the time to lift the screen door into its track, he must have stewed about my point of entry. Had he found the coffee cups by the back door? Maybe he'd think I wasn't working alone.

Good. Don't feel safe, Deputy. Maybe you'll make a mistake.

I turned up Carstairs' driveway. As soon as I got around to the front of his Toyota I was shielded from prying eyes. I got down on my good knee first, leaning on the car for support. My physiotherapists in San Diego had made me practice getting up and down through many therapy sessions. They'd worked on deepening my squats and easing the pain. I didn't hear it but I was sure I could feel a creak run through the left knee joint as I sank onto the driveway.

Only after my back was on the cool pavement did it occur to me I might have leaned on the car too hard. I could have set off the car alarm. I'd been careless but sometimes lucky cancels out stupid. No alarm sounded.

Just as the instructions promised, I installed the tracker under Carstair's car in less than a minute. Pairing the device with the new phone took much longer. The cell phone was cheap and unfamiliar. However, I had time. Carstairs didn't leave his house until well after one in the morning. I waited a moment to study the GPS display on my phone before following him at a distance. I didn't have to keep eyes on him. Satellites did the work.

The deputy drove out of town. For a moment I thought he might be heading to my father's house. I began to sweat. If he was going to search the house and barn, would I wait patiently while he tore the place apart? Or would it be best to flip the game board over and appear just like he had, gun in hand? Detective Buck would lock me up forever if I killed a cop in my own house. One dead man could be self-defense. Two dead men could be considered the unfortunate start to a dangerous habit.

To my relief, Carstairs turned his car toward I-75 South. There'd be no confrontation in my father's home tonight. But how long before I'd pull out the pistol in my pocket in anger? This game went far beyond one angry asshole husband. I wondered how Becky was doing and when I would see her again. Soon? Her lips were full and her kisses were soft. I wanted to hold her and be held. If I had Becky and darkness and the ability to be left the hell alone by everyone else, I thought I could be okay. That's all anybody really wants, isn't it? I thought of Billy and Amy and how comfortable they were with each other, no complications but a few unfulfilled dreams they were working on.

I'll get that for Becky and me, I thought. Or die trying.

I didn't want to end up in court. I could easily imagine how that would go. All of Lake Orion would be against me and all the old rumors around Victor Down's death would regain high velocity.

I could picture the trial in my mind, too. The prosecutor would ask the Young Rabbi to get hold of my service records. The military might not declassify the details of my missions but they'd probably let my health records go public. Questions would be raised about my eyes. Doctors can't see a headache on an x-ray. They'd bring in experts saying there was no physical reason why sunlight felt to me like the burn of a phosphorus grenade. The prosecutor would paint me as a PTSD case gone bad.

They'd never understand the comfort, the safety I feel when I'm out of the light. In darkness, we are just shapes. All the ugly details are redacted.

I hate when civilians make assumptions about veterans. We aren't a bunch of crazed killers just because we served. Most guys I knew from Group spent a lot of time frustrated and scared. They weren't dangerous. They were bored. Most of them valued peace and tranquility more since they were discharged. Getting back to what passes for a normal life is a difficult adjustment. A guy from Group put it succinctly: Once you drive an Abrams tank down a city street, you've got no patience for L.A.'s traffic jams.

Sometimes it's mundane little details that get to you, like you're always looking for trouble even when there's nothing to see. In war, constant heightened awareness keeps you alive. That same state is a curse when you come home to work behind the counter at BestBuy. Hypervigilance is exhausting.

Carstairs passed the Detroit Arsenal Tank Plant in Warren, Michigan and I thought again of the guy who wanted to express his road rage with a tank. They used to build Abrams tanks there. Funny how the universe serves up such coincidences occasionally.

We once had a Jungian therapist in Group. "When we encounter strange little coincidences," he said, "that's the universe winking at us. Nature sends us hints and signs. We need to sit up and pay attention because these tiny synchronicities mean something that is important to the course of our lives."

He seemed better suited to bullshitting people in academia. That woo-woo stuff didn't fly so well with my circle. I'd witnessed a village full of kids suffering birth defects. Their parents lived in a debris field of depleted uranium shards from spent ordnance. Truth has consequences and, after spending time in that sad village, I started asking the universe for clearer signals. Winks and nods and hints won't do. The Jungian didn't last long with the VA. He moved on to a private practice, probably to deal with the anxieties of wine moms and hipster dads.

I think there's a simpler solution to the problem of evil. The reasons bad things happen is bad people do bad things. It's guys like me — the person I used to be, the man I hoped to be again — who stops them.

Stopping evil often worked on a small scale. Our efforts never seemed to translate to success in the big picture. Non-combatants still went through the meat grinder. Villages full of kids with twisted chromosomes stayed stuck in their genetic tangle.

When things went bad with my team and I was wounded, I stopped being the guy that goes on missions to kick evil in the crotch.

You're tracking a dirty cop, a kidnapper, through the darkness, a small voice in my head said.

"You're going to be that guy again," I told myself aloud. *Maybe. Just maybe.*

Driving through Warren's nearly empty streets, I began to relax. Forty minutes after he left Lake Orion, Carstairs pulled into a parking lot at the Ram's Horn, a restaurant on Dequindre Road.

I rolled up and parked across the street from the restaurant. Carstairs had backed into a parking spot beside a van, as if he was ready for a quick getaway — or maybe ready to give chase at a moment's notice. He was careful. That was bad for me.

Though disappointed the deputy hadn't led me straight to my father, my spirits rose when I spotted who he was there to meet. The bodyguard I'd nicknamed Buzz sat in an ill-chosen booth in the front window of the Ram's Horn. He wore white headphones in his ears and was subtly bobbing his head to a beat. Buzz had already begun digging into a stack of pancakes as Carstairs strode in.

The deputy gestured to the rear of the restaurant and Buzz shook his head, still chewing, unwilling to move. The goon slowly took out one headphone and gestured to the seat opposite him. The way the deputy stood, tall and tense, told me he was pissed off. Buzz was much less careful than Paul Carstairs. That was good.

Reluctantly, Carstairs sat across from Buzz. From where I sat, I guessed he was on a rant about me. I'd meant to find my father or gather information when I broke into the deputy's house. I'd failed at that but it was apparent I succeeded in stirring up the hornet's nest in the dirty cop's brain.

A smarter person would have been nervous. Watching Carstairs talk to Buzz so animatedly, his right index finger stabbing the air as he made his points, I began to smile.

38

Buzz ate and occasionally gave a 'Whaddaya gonna do?' kind of shrug. Carstairs must have figured out he was making himself memorable by making a scene. He settled down when the waitress came around with a refill for their coffees.

I didn't know what to do until I noticed the minivan parked on the other side of the deputy's car. The van had a dent in the fender under the left headlight. It was undoubtedly Buzz's ride, the same vehicle he'd used to deliver Mazie Lane to my door to issue her divine ultimatum.

I made sure to keep the vehicles between the deputy and me to stay out of his line of sight. I couldn't get at the GPS tracker at the front of his car without being spotted. However, my toothpick fit into the air valve on the minivan's right rear tire nicely. I broke it off so it was not easy to spot. The hiss of escaping air was soft. As soon as the deed was done, I took a quick picture of the minivan's rear license plate and retreated to my car across the street.

Carstairs' meeting with Lane's chauffeur didn't last much longer than that. Soon the deputy drove away. I watched his progress using the GPS tracker. He was headed straight back to Lake Orion. The game was down to Buzz and me now.

When he came out of the Ram's Horn, he looked like he was in a hurry. Maybe his talk with Carstairs had lit a fire under him. I guessed his destination might be my father's farm. Maybe his assignment was to search the place or beat the shit out of me. Probably both. I was wrong. Buzz jumped in the van and headed south on the 53 before turning west on to the nearly empty freeway.

He and I needed to have a chat. I didn't mind following him a little closer. Buzz managed to put several miles behind him before he noticed the pull of the dying tire. When he turned on to the shoulder, I wasn't more than fifty yards behind him. I parked the Audi just ahead of him so the van blocked the view of drivers who might whiz past.

Buzz cursed as he crouched to inspect his deflated tire. He barely spared me a glance as I came out of the dark. "It's okay! The situation is well in hand and under control! Thanks for stopping but I got this!"

He didn't look up until I was a few feet away. Then he stared into the muzzle of my pistol, transfixed. "Ooh ... hey, dude." I hadn't heard him speak when he brought Mazie Lane to the farm. His voice was so deep, it was almost metallic and undoubtedly comical. He wasn't that big but he rumbled like an old tank engine. I wondered if he was pushing it or if that was his natural voice.

"What's with the gat, my man? I ain't got much but a few bucks but you can have it all. We'll call it a charitable donation to the NRA, m'kay? Take my shitbox van, too, if you don't mind three out of four good tires."

I remembered a Bible verse one of my drill instructors often quoted and decided to set the mood. "Vengeance is Mine and recompense. Their foot shall slip in due time for the day of their calamity is at hand and the things to come hasten upon them."

A passing car whizzed by and, for a few seconds, I wasn't just a silhouette holding a gun anymore. Buzz tore his gaze away from the business end of my handgun to look up. Only then did he seem to recognize me and understood. "Oh, shit. My dong's caught in the zipper, isn't it?"

"Yup."

"Hey, so you know, I'm just the hired help. I don't know anything that could be useful to you."

"Convince me."

"You should get back in your car and do whatever the boss lady said to do. That would help."

"That all you got?"

"Unless you want to help me change this tire. I guess I don't have to guess how this particular bugaboo came to happenstance, huh? T'wasn't no accidental occurrence, was it? You got a lot of nerve, walkin' around messin' with a man's vehicle. Nerve and balls. You're the Nervy Balls Man. In the Old West, they'd shoot you for interfering with a cowboy's horse, Mr. Nervy Balls."

"Stand up slow and put your hands on the side of the van, cowboy. Assume the position."

He obliged. I told him to lean more, putting his feet farther back before I kicked his feet wider. I kept the gun on him as I patted him down.

"Look at you, movin' with confidence toward your objectives and life goals, makin' your dreams come true."

He jumped a little when I patted down his crotch. "Whoo-wee! Lotta guys shy away from being so thorough! That there's one professional roust, Chief! I'm thinking you should ask first and maybe buy me dinner before you get so handsy. I haven't had sex in hours and I gotta say that was intense and intimate."

"You want me to search you again?"

"Hey, I'm not a machine. Let me have my refractory period. Did you used to be a TSA guy or a cop or something?"

"Bagram."

"Huh?"

"Bagram Air Base, searching for suicide bombers."

"Soldier, huh?"

"What did they tell you about me?" I asked.

"They? Who's they?"

"Paul Carstairs and Mazie Lane."

"Who's that now?"

"You just had coffee with him. Don't be difficult."

He started to shake his head. I dug the gun's muzzle into the spot between his shoulder blades. His back muscles tightened but a little encouragement loosened his mouth.

"The boss lady didn't tell me shit. The deputy, on the other hand? He's surely and sorely pissed at you. You messed with my vehicle so I can see you're the sort of person who does not appreciate the boundaries set by social convention. Messing with my ride is one thing but you intruded on a man's castle, too. You crossed the moat and invaded that cop's environs, Soldier Boy. That was a domicile, a 'B fuckin' E,' in the parlance of Mr. Carstairs. He's one crude motherfucker when he wants to be, I must say. My dear old mother would faint dead away at his abusive language."

Buzz had a pen, a wallet, a lighter, a bent joint, a phone and his keys in his pockets. I opened the passenger door of the van and waved him inside before taking a seat behind him. I was a bit startled to discover an infant's car seat in the seat to my left.

"Put on your seat belt, Cowboy. Then put both hands on the dashboard. Mess around and this will be a very short conversation."

"Yessir, Soldier Boy. You got the gun, after all. I know my place in the world."

39

I poked through his wallet and found his driver's license. "I notice it takes you a long time to arrive at a point ... Mr. Wells."

"Please call me Joshua," he replied. "I was named after the biblical Joshua, warrior of the faith, administrative assistant and helper monkey to Moses. The man for whom I am named lived to 110 years of age. I was kind of hoping to emulate him in that regard, Soldier Boy. So, you know, if it's not too much trouble, I'd appreciate it if you would take your finger off the trigger lest you perforate me by accident."

"It is a terrible thing to hurt someone by accident. When I do it, I usually mean to."

"Not sure that's much comfort to a fella in my compromised position."

"Anybody ever tell you you're full of shit?" I asked.

"Frequently, sometimes at high volume. Fulla shit up to the eyeballs and yet so short of stature. You gotta respect my fecal capacity, am I right?"

"Slow down with the speed of delivery. I prefer quality over quantity — "

"Lemme give you both, Soldier Boy. My mother is a schoolteacher. She calls me loquacious. I hardly spoke for the first five years of my life. She says now that she might have encouraged me too much. I started talkin' a blue streak on my fifth birthday and haven't shut up since. Men envy me my mouth. The ladies sure do love it, though."

He couldn't see my smile in the dark but I had to admit, I liked him. He was cool under pressure, no begging or blubbering.

"I can't be your helper monkey, Soldier Boy," Wells said. "Carstairs is the king. You're wasting your time talking to a lowly peasant. High mucky mucks do not socialize with the help."

"Where'd you pick up Mazie Lane?"

"Carstairs' house. He was bitching about it. He wants his deal done but he doesn't want to anywhere nearby when the sausage gets made. Doesn't want to get any on him."

"You picked her up at the deputy's house. Where'd she come from?"

"Mr. Carstairs picked her up at some airfield she owns."

"She has her own airport?"

"From what I hear, I wouldn't call it an airport, exactly." He shrugged. "All I know is the lady's used to traveling in comfort. Even though I washed the van, vacuumed it out and took out Renatta Jean's car seat. Miss Mazie still wrinkled her nose when I showed up in my van to take her to your place."

"What about the guy with her? The one with the rifle?"

"He was not a chatty fellow. I only found out his name was Ramone when y'all were conversing on your own front porch. He didn't talk to me, only whispered to Miss Mazie. Come to think of it, he might not have even been an English speaker for all I know. I heard him grunt once. Mighta been a French grunt, coulda been a Russian grunt. I'm not up on my European grunts."

I leaned forward and put the gun to his head as I held his cell phone in front of him. "Open it. Move slow. Don't make me nervous."

"Ain't nothing to be nervous about, Chief. As I said, you got the gun." Slowly, Wells took one hand off the dashboard and offered his right thumb. The device read his thumbprint. The screen brightened.

Once he put both hands on the dashboard again, I sat back and scrolled through his texts and contacts. He had a long contact list. I didn't know where to begin. I scanned his recent texts and found one that said, "Arriving now. Pull around to the front and pick us up." Judging by the date, that had to be Mazie Lane.

"Chief? You looking for the number of a good dentist? My dentist is good. I have a feeling you're going to need her once the deputy comes for you."

"Shut up a minute."

"I got a word game on my phone that's pretty good."

I kicked the back of his seat hard. Joshua went quiet.

Another text from a blocked number: Pick up Ms. Lane at 8. That probably would have been Paul Carstairs. None of this was helping me find my father.

"What do you do for a living, Joshua?"

"A little bit of this and a little bit of that."

"You've got a kid. How do you buy baby food?"

"I used to be a locksmith but I'm no longer bonded."

I read between the lines. "You used your skills — "

"For a criminal enterprise, according to the state of Michigan. I was just trying to retrieve some property I considered to be rightfully mine. My ex-wife disagrees on that point and the judge sided with her. I thought we'd get back together after I got out of prison. Turns out, we only got together long enough to procreate my daughter. My baby's name is Renatta Jean and that little angel is the only thing I don't regret. What I'm saying is, don't you put a hole in me tonight, please. Only God can judge. It's bad karma to play judge, jury and executioner."

"The jury's still out on you, Joshua. Answer my questions and this could go okay. Not great but okay."

"Getting' late, Chief. Ask away! I'll do my best to accommodate."

"What do you do now?"

"Sell a few trees. Big biz 'round here and the farmer's get a better cut from me than they do if they deal with the syndicate. The locals benefit from some local representation and I'm a good salesman. I hustle. Still and all, barely pays."

"I hear that. So what else you got going on to pay those baby bills?"

"Odd jobs help me get by."

"Like whatever Carstairs tells you to do."

Wells gave a short nod. "There is that. A man's gotta provide. Me and the ex don't see eye to eye anymore but my little girl is an innocent party. Gotta feed and care for her. I gotta stay on the happy side of the law. I've done a few things for Mr. Carstairs for a year or so. I do what I'm told and he gives me some leeway when I fall behind on the payments. I always come through with the child support because, hey, my baby girl is the apple of my pancake. The alimony payments are tougher. I do what I can. A man's gotta provide but he's also gotta prioritize."

I heard what I took for real regret in his tone.

"Sometimes I can't make ends meet," Joshua admitted. "The ex is a powerful woman with a tornado's personality. When that storm rolls in, she can get pissed all the way off. Mr. Carstairs pours oil on the waters by throwing me some dough from time to time. It is what it is. We're all whores for somebody."

"Tell me again exactly what you do for him."

"Move boxes. For a man of my skills and talents, lifting heavy shit is kind of a tragedy. My forte is actually online gaming, computer hacking and selling weed. I'd drive for Uber but I hate dealing with drunks. Still and all, a jerk's gotta do what a jerk's gotta do."

A jerk's gotta do what a jerk's gotta do.

Scrolling through Joshua's phone, I found something that wasn't there. Our farm had a red mailbox at the end of the driveway with the Jack name on it in white letters. Beneath that, Dad's sign read: Sophie's Choice Alsatians. It was hard to see in the dark. Mazie Lane had arrived at my doorstep late at night. Sometimes what you're looking for isn't there. Sometimes that means something.

I checked my captive's GPS app. The farm was not listed in the app's history. He'd chauffeured the heiress to the farm without the help of satellites. "How many times have you been out to my house before, Joshua?"

"A few," he admitted.

"You moved guns for Carstairs?"

"Like I said, I move boxes. I don't peek at the Christmas presents. That would ruin the surprise. Look, Soldier Boy, I'm not UPS. Got no tracking numbers for you, just so you understand."

"You know my father."

"I saw the gentleman once or twice, sure, rockin' his ass on the porch."

"Where did you take the shipments?"

"Usually to an Arby's parking lot in Pontiac at three in the a of the m. Hey, did you know Arby's is like RB? As in, the name of the place is short for roast beef?"

"I did not know that, Joshua. Thanks." I pressed the gun muzzle just behind his ear. One thing you can say for a gun to the head, it makes one focus. "You've met my father. Tell me where he is."

"I'd tell you where to look if I knew. I barely know your dad. Probably couldn't pick him out of a lineup."

"More bullshit."

"True, I swear. Mostly I dealt with the other gentleman."

"Who?"

"No names in the smuggling biz, cuz. Aliases, right? Everything's on a need to know and Mr. Carstairs made it clear I did not need to know. I stay in my lane."

"Describe him. The guy you dealt with."

"I don't know, y'know?"

"Try."

"Middle-aged, fat, balding. Regular white guy but whiter, like super pale. Always in a lumberjack jacket, even in summer, as I recall. You know the kind of jacket I mean? That red plaid that means you're a down-to-earth sort who might do some hunting but life is really all about the beer? He's got the face of a guy who's missed the train."

"Anything else about his face? Can you describe him more than that?"

"I don't know, like millions of other white guys. The only thing that sets him apart is his eyes."

"What about his eyes?"

"The dude's got really heavy eyelids, like he's always in the middle of getting blown."

"Was he driving the eighteen-wheeler that carried the shipments?"

"Sure. Where do you think I got the boxes from?"

Sleepy Rollie.

Dad had told me the driver who'd taken over his runs was on a long haul to Denver with air conditioners. I hoped Rollie was back from his trip. I still didn't know where Dad was but I had a pretty good idea where to find his ransom.

40

That left the problem of Mr. Joshua Wells. What to do with him? He was interested to know, as well. "What you got planned for me, Boss? It's late and I just had a lot of hotcakes but if you'd like to retire to a bar for a few snifters of brandy, we could pretend we're totally different people and see where the night leads us. I'm not fussy."

"You're an interesting person, Joshua."

"When you're short on opportunities and money, you gotta be long on personality."

"That is so."

"What are your skills, Mr. Jack?"

"Until lately, it had to do with pulling triggers and whatnot."

"Since I don't have anything useful for you, maybe you're thinking of whatnotting me right here. I remind you, sir, I am a proud father. Though I may be long on bullshit, you don't want my little girl growing up without her daddy. Her mother is hot as a glowing frying pan but my baby will need guidance. Don't disappear me, dude."

I sighed and offered him his bent joint. He nodded his assent and I stuck it in his mouth. I used his lighter to get him going.

Wells took a deep drag into his lungs and held it as long as he could for full effect. When he let a cloud out on his exhale, he coughed lightly. "Thanks, Mr. Jack. You're a gent ... unless this is my last ciggy, a blindfold-at-dawn sort of thing. If it's that, I retract my gratitude. Let he who is without sin cast the first stone and leave stoners the hell alone."

I stayed silent, hoping to jar loose some factoid that might help me further. I considered trying to use Joshua's life to save my father. He might be a useful bargaining chip against Carstairs but his life meant nothing to Mazie Lane. I discarded that notion.

"Deputy Carstairs told me something about your father that I found interesting. It's an Arby's stands for roast beef sort of detail. Would you like to hear it?"

If he was trying to charm me, that wouldn't be a factor in any tactical decision. Besides, I liked him already. I let him talk.

"Carstairs told me one time that your father named all his dogs with the same name."

"Yep."

"Doesn't that confuse the dogs?"

"Not as much as you'd think. You call one dog's name and they all pay attention. They're also smart enough to know if you're talking to them individually as long as your tone and attention are right. Besides, Dad sold most of them before they got old. He didn't train them all forever. The training is ongoing. They each have to bond with a new handler anyway."

"I get it. But you know who else named all his dogs the same? Robert Durst."

"The guy from Limp Bizkit?"

Wells laughed. "Nah, dude, nah! You've got your Dursts in a twist. That's Fred Durst. No, Robert Durst is some rich real estate guy. They say he killed three people. Last I heard he was convicted of dismembering a dude but skated on the murder charge."

"They were sure he cut somebody up but let him slide on the murder charge?"

"Rich people and the justice system, man. They don't mix."

It was almost eerie how his words echoed my thoughts. I was sure

Mazie Lane was safe from prosecution. Whatever happened, she'd lawyer up and I'd be long dead before any judge's gavel banged. The Jungian would have called it another synchronicity.

"Durst's little brother said he had a bunch of Alaskan malamute huskies, He called them all Igor. They all died quick. His brother suspected he was killing the dogs, practicing to kill his wife and get rid of the body."

"Three things," I said. "First, Dad calls all the dogs Sophie because he misses my dead mother."

"That's sweet, Mr. Jack. Sorry 'bout that." He did not sound insincere.

"Second, huskies aren't malamutes. There are Alaskan malamutes, Alaskan huskies and Siberian huskies."

Joshua took another long drag on the small joint. "This lecture doesn't end with a gunshot and me dead, does it? I got a doctor's appointment next week and I'm hoping for good news. Don't mess up my test results."

"Do you like dogs?" I asked.

"I do. Had a basenji when I was a kid. Weird little thing. They don't bark. Did you know that? They don't bark, they yodel. God's got a sense of humor, makin' a dog that doesn't bark. Dug under the back fence and got run over and I cried like a bitch for days. Poor little dog. Got him as a stray but I guess lots of us have that urge, you know?"

"What urge?"

"To dig under the fence, get out and run."

"Do dogs like you, Joshua?"

"They do." That's all I needed to know.

"Put your hands behind your head."

He did as he was told. I snapped Carstairs' cuffs on his wrists, careful to loop the short chain around the seat belt so he couldn't pull his hands forward. I used the baby blanket in the car seat to wipe my fingerprints off the handcuffs.

"Okay," I said.

"Okay, what?"

I got out and, while pulling his seat belt back, slammed the sliding door on the belt. That pinned him to his seat. I rolled down his window to give him some fresh air.

He gasped. "That's pretty tight, man. I can barely breathe."

"You'll be fine. Just don't struggle or the belt will get too tight."

"*Sonofabitch.*"

"Chill. We're parting as friends."

"Oh? Are we?"

"I'm not killing you, am I?"

"That's a point in your favor. Seems a friend would let me go but fair enough."

"Friendly acquaintances then. I was never here. You got robbed. Someone will come along and turn you loose eventually. It'll be light in a couple of hours."

"Carstairs won't buy that. He'll know it was you. What should I really tell him? Not a lot of job opportunities around here, Mr. Jack."

"I have a feeling Carstairs won't be in the picture much longer."

"God willing, sure, but I can't remember when God was on my side."

"That boss lady you drove isn't from around here," I said. "A dirty cop is involved. Explosives have made their way across an international border and probably across the state lines. You know what that equation adds up to, don't you?"

"Looks like a corkscrew dick," Joshua said. "Feels like I'm on the receiving end of a corkscrew dick."

"That's how it looks and feels. To me, it sounds like the FBI will show up at some point in full battle rattle."

"Tastes like *shee-it,*" he added.

"If you can't go legit, at least stick to the weed business," I suggested.

"So I'm out of another job."

"What are you? Twenty-two?"

"Twenty-five, next month."

"Twenty-five. You've got time. People lose jobs, Joshua. Find something else. You've got the gift of gab. Clean yourself up, steal a nice suit and go sell cars or something."

"They don't hire ex-cons. Nobody does."

I took the last of the joint from his lips and took a drag. "Do I look like a career counselor to you?"

"You do not, sir."

"Good. Stop whining."

"You look like the soldier boy who just bogarted the last of my weed."

I sighed. "You're an ex-con, right?"

"Asked and answered and so stipulated, counsel."

"Ex means former. You want a new script? Flip it. Lie on your resume like everybody else. A bachelor's degree is never farther away than a computer with a graphics program and a good printer. With a little luck, by the time you're caught, they won't want to let you go."

Despite his discomfort, he smiled. "What'll I tell the deputy?"

"Nothing. Ghost him. This will be over soon."

I left Joshua Wells by the side of the road, cuffed and trapped by his seat belt. He was the best friend I'd made since getting out of the military. I left the key to the handcuffs on the dashboard in front of him. The odds were in his favor that some Good Samaritan would come along and set him free.

I didn't really expect him to try to sell cars for a living while there was still money to be made from Carstairs. I suppose I was so optimistic about Becky, a little hope spilled over into deciding what to do with a career criminal. That was mostly stupid but I liked that motor-mouth too much to execute him. Joshua Wells was just another citizen caught in the trap.

41

I couldn't find any listing for Rollie on my phone so I had to backtrack to Dad's house to look for his phone number or address. As I turned into the driveway, I spotted Dolores' car parked by the house. Becky waited for me on the porch. Sophie bounded off the porch to meet me as I stepped out the car, tail wagging. I bent to pet the dog and gave him a hug before climbing the steps.

Becky sat in my dad's old chair with her knees pulled to her chest to stay warm in the cool night air.

"You're up late," I said.

"So late, it's getting early. Dawn in an hour or so. I was worried about you. I wasn't sure you'd come back."

"I'm fine. Just came back to find something."

"Are you going to get some sleep?"

"No time. I feel good, though. I used to have to stay up much longer than this. Feels like old times."

"I've been thinking about old times. Are you sure you don't have time to crawl into bed? We could warm each other up."

"I'll be gone again as soon as I find an address."

"Gone again. Hm. You are good at that."

"Something on your mind, Becky?"

She put her chin on her right knee and looked at me for what seemed like a long time. "For the first couple of months of university, I thought you'd come to your senses and follow me."

"You mean like ... stalk you?"

"I was sure you'd show up at my door. I wrote you."

"I got the letters eventually. I'd joined up by then."

"Ironic."

"How's that?"

"That you'd join the Army but you wouldn't fight for me. I'm worth it, you know. If you'd come after me back then, things would be very different now."

"I took no for an answer. That's what I was supposed to do. We were too young — "

"I'm not saying it was all your fault."

"All my fault?"

"I just wish I'd never hooked up with Rud, is all."

"With all that's going on, to be honest, I haven't given your husband much thought."

"I'm thinking about him. He's a problem. I thought he was a problem you were going to solve for me."

I leaned against the post by the steps and looked at the sky. A clear night sky full of stars always made me feel small. Becky was making me feel smaller. "I have a radical idea for you. It's something I learned while I was away."

"Shoot."

"Here's what a lot of people don't want to hear: There isn't a solution for every problem."

"Is that the new Army motto? I don't think it will catch on. It's too defeatist."

"The Army motto is, 'This we'll defend.'"

"I thought it was 'Army of One' or 'Be All You Can Be.'"

"Those are the old slogans. The newest one is 'Army Strong.'"

"What's the difference between a motto and a slogan?"

"Sincerity. Slogans are the advertising that pulls you in. A motto? Those are the words we live and die and suffer by."

She looked up sharply and fixed me with her gaze in a way that reminded me of predatory birds. "Do you think less of me because I'm breaking my vows with my husband, Easy? If that's the case, you were there, too! I don't recall any objections — "

"No. I do not think less of you. Anybody should be able to pull out of a bad deal. Marrying Rud was a bad deal."

"The trouble comes in getting out clean with enough money so I don't have to live like an animal," she said.

"Any money left from your inheritance?"

"That's all spent. I've got no student loans because of the money they left me but that just gets me up to zero."

As someone who was living below zero, I had to search my heart for a moment to find sympathy for her financial situation.

"You know the funny thing? If my parents hadn't been killed by a drunk driver, Mom and Dad would probably take me in and lend me some money. From what I remember of them, any help I'd get would come with an extra heavy helping of 'I told you so.' I couldn't take their money. I couldn't pay the interest on it. Every conversation would be about how I fucked up. I'd rather be poor. Mom and Dad would probably take Rud's side, anyway."

"He hit you, Becky. That should be the end of it right there."

"It's not as easy as you say it is. God, I need a cigarette — "

"You gotta tear off the band-aid, Becky. Just get out and figure out the rest later."

"When everything's said and done, it's easier said than done."

I'd never experienced her country club life so Becky assumed I didn't know what I was missing. Every poor person knows what they're missing. We've got TVs. We've been to the movies. This is America. Money is the currency but envy is the engine of the whole economy.

"You're used to bouncing around," she continued. "I'm not a college student anymore. I shouldn't have to get a futon and sleep on the floor.

My ramen noodle days are behind me. People say it's freeing to have less stuff and comforts. That's not true. Besides, with a dead body in our living room, we're going to end up putting our lawyer's kids through Harvard. You can bet those vultures will take a serious bite out of Rud's money long before we get around to divorce proceedings."

"Don't blame me for the dead body in the living room, Becky. Excuse me for breathing but it was him or me."

"That's not what I meant."

"Then I don't know what you want from me."

"I want lots of things."

"I think you found the root of your problem. Don't feel bad. You're not alone."

"I wanted you to kill Rud and erase him from my life so he'd never hurt me again."

"An inheritance is cheaper than a divorce, huh?"

"I thought you were the guy who was going to save me. Can you help me or not?"

I didn't bother concealing the contempt in my tone. "Kind of busy trying to save my dad right now."

She stood. "I want more than things, Easy."

"What else?"

"To be held. To be told everything's going to be okay."

"I don't know if that's true. I'm not in the habit of lying."

"And here I thought guys like you were all about taking the next hill. I didn't think you'd settle for less. Not every problem has a solution, my ass."

"That isn't something I learned from serving. I learned it in San Diego. I did my rehab with guys who'd had their arms and legs and faces and balls blown off. You want a divorce? There is an easy solution. You just don't want to pay any price. Divorce Rud and take the hit. You want company? I'm here for you. You want a killer? I think I need a better reason to murder somebody than whether you have a slightly less fun lifestyle."

She pouted. She was sexy when she pouted. She knew it. "I didn't come here to fight. I came by for company. Where've you been all night?"

"Trying to find Dad."

"Paul told me."

"Oh?"

"He says you should be getting something for him. He says to remind you he's what's keeping you out of jail and that he's got your Ernie Sr. for even more leverage."

"Carstairs told you about Dad? I was trying to keep you out of this. What's he doing telling you?"

"He didn't tell me much but he made it clear he needs whatever you're supposed to get. 'No fooling around' were his exact words. He said you'd be okay and your dad would be okay as long as you do as you're told."

"He must be coming unglued and in a panic if he's trying to use you to put more pressure on me. What did you say to him?" I asked.

"That you're not always so good at doing what you're told but you'd do anything for your dad."

"Did Carstairs lean on you hard?"

She let out a low chuckle. "I've lived with an abusive husband. You don't think I can handle a few veiled threats? I'm not as soft as I look, just curvy."

"Did Carstairs say anything about Detective Buck?"

"According to Paul, Buck is off chasing down Micah Burmenthol's known associates. Apparently, Micah was known to police in New Jersey. That phrase 'known to police' has always struck me as coded language. All that means is 'troublemaker.'"

"He has a record? Do you know what his rap sheet says?"

"Paul didn't tell me anything more about the victim than that."

"Victim? Burmanthol would have killed me if I'd let him."

"Sorry. Paul's words. And I'm sorry for what I said. I do appreciate that you went there to talk to Rud. I'm sorry it worked out the way it did."

"The way it worked out? You mean the part where I'm still on the sunny side of dirt?" I yanked open the front door and stalked through the house to my father's desk. Becky and Sophie followed me in and watched me rifle through the drawers. Rollie Gallagher was a subcontractor for Dad. It didn't take long to find a file with tax forms with his name and address on them.

Sophie padded to a corner to curl up and sleep. Becky touched my shoulder gently. "Easy? Don't be mad at me, please. Sometimes it seems like everybody's mad at me and I can't take much more of that. Just so you understand, that's why I want the money. Life with money? It's not about being able to buy things. It's how people look at you, how they treat you. With money, you get respect — "

"No matter how you earned it? I know. You want a smoother ride with greased wheels. Like everybody — "

She kissed me hard on the lips. When she broke away, she stayed close and I could smell her shampoo, a scent of roses. "I wouldn't like it if you stayed mad at me, Easy."

"I'm angry now but I doubt I'll be able to stay that way. Not with you. We've got too much history."

She pushed me into the chair by the desk, leaned down and kissed me again. She brushed my lips with hers, going slow. Passion has a way of getting bigger before it eases off. She straddled my lap, kissing me deeper and grinding against me.

She suddenly pulled back. "Promise me you'll be careful. When the deputy talked to me about you, I got a scared feeling. Whatever you're doing for him that's keeping you out of jail is dangerous. Paul Carstairs is a very dangerous man. That damn badge gives him all the power."

"I know."

"So stay with me awhile." She began unbuttoning her blouse.

I stayed her hands. "Time's a factor. I have the information I came for. I've got to get on the road and find Sleepy Rollie Gallagher."

"Please?"

I shook my head, not without regret.

She slid to her knees. She did so not to beg me to stay and not to pray. Becky smiled coquettishly as she unbuckled my belt. "Maybe not every problem can be solved," she conceded. "Let me solve one problem for you."

Becky was persuasive. I stayed a little longer before heading to Ecorse to find Rollie Gallagher and an eighteen-wheeler full of explosives.

42

Rollie Gallagher lived an hour away in a double-wide trailer on the far side of Ecorse. I was relieved to find Dad's Kenworth parked behind the house. The truck had a fresh coat of red paint and looked better than I remembered. The blare of a television emanated from inside the trailer. I knocked but probably wasn't heard over the noise from the TV. I rapped harder on the door and the television's volume was turned down a bit. Then I heard the distinctive sound of the rack of a pump shotgun.

I stepped to the side of the door and called out. "Rollie? It's Ernest Jack's son, Easy! We need to talk!"

"Easy Jack? Jeez, I thought you got blown up over there. Didn't an IED get you?"

"I got blown up a little. It didn't take all the way."

"What do you want?"

"To talk."

"Go ahead."

"You want me to yell through the door?" He didn't answer so I added, "Dad's in trouble."

After a long pause, I heard heavy footsteps and the turn of the lock. Rollie Gallagher wore a stained gray t-shirt and dirty jorts. He peered at me for a moment. The man's eyelids rode low and he moved slowly. He looked like a tortoise who'd suffered a stroke.

"Show me your eyes," he said.

I slid my shades down my nose an inch and winced in pain at relentless daylight.

"Yeah, you gotta be Easy, I guess. I heard about you. Where is Ernie Sr. keeping himself?"

"I don't know. That's why I'm here."

He nodded. "I see." He turned and walked away. He left the door open.

I took that as my invitation to enter his home. His living room was spare. A dilapidated recliner sat pointed at a huge TV tuned to Fox News. The television was obviously a fresh purchase. A broken cardboard box for the sixty-five inch OLED screen sat behind the chair. His old TV had been much smaller. I noticed it unplugged and banished to a far corner by the entrance to the kitchen.

Beside his recliner a little bar fridge hummed loudly, competing with the sound from the television. The screen showed six panelists arguing about politics. It wasn't immediately clear what the topic was because two guys were trying to shout over each other while three women watched silently and waited patiently. The moderator failed to moderate.

Rollie rocked slightly in the recliner with a pump shotgun across his lap. He asked if I wanted a beer. "I got Moosehead."

The room had the sickly sweet smell of stale beer. I declined his offer. "When did you get back from Denver?"

"Never went. I just got back from a trip to Atlantic City, though. Only been back a day and here you are, pounding on my door."

"Dad told me you had a load of air conditioners bound for Denver."

He shook his head.

"When's the last time you saw him?"

Rollie took a swig from his beer can and his high forehead wrinkled. I took that to mean he was thinking hard. "Don't remember what day of the week but it was shortly after he got back from his last run to Canada. I imagine you're thinkin' of the day he told me to take a load of bombs away and get rid of them somehow. You were in the military. Do you know bombs?"

"A bit, yeah."

"Interesting what you Jacks get yourselves into. Make me wonder if you aren't kinda cursed. Do you believe in curses?"

I ignored the question but the answer was yes. "Dad wanted you to get rid of them? Why?"

"Your father is not a well man, Easy. I think when a fella gets toward the end of his days, he starts thinking about what he's leaving behind. He didn't think the people who wanted the bombs should have them. Since he's sick, I think he started thinking maybe he could afford to relax about his bills and do the right thing instead of the things that pay."

"Dad got religion?"

"When you got nothing else left, you get religion."

"What did you do with the cases?"

"None of your business anymore, is it?"

I put some bass and steel in my voice. "Where are the bombs, Rollie?"

He sighed. "The last time I spoke with Ernie, he didn't care what I did with them as long as the load didn't go to the people who'd placed the order. Bad customer service if you ask me."

"Are the devices still in the truck?"

Rollie searched the seat cushion under his butt, found the remote and muted the television. "Son, you really don't know what's going on, do you? Ernie got jammed up with some bad people."

"Deputy Carstairs, for one, yeah."

"I've never met him but according to your dad, that cop is a leech. Ernie also told me he left some money for you. Didn't you get it? You're supposed to be far and away by now. The people he got mixed up with, there's no comin' back from that."

"Maybe there is. I'm not ready to give up so easily, even if Dad is."

Rollie's face softened. He wasn't much older than me but he talked as if he was a wise old wizard. "You sound really young, Easy.

What you don't understand is, it's already over. Done deal. History. Casper. Ashes. Take the Barracuda and go for a ride. Don't come back."

"It's more complicated than that. I can't walk away clean. Carstairs is leaning on me to deliver that load."

"That fuckin' guy. Ernie said he wouldn't mind him so much if he didn't demand such a heavy cut. He's worse than the IRS."

"Do you know the deputy?"

Rollie shook his big head. "Ernie knows him. Your dad took care of the people end of the business. I just drive."

"So? Are the explosives in the truck or not?"

"Don't you worry about that. Just go for a drive and don't look back. That's what Ernie wanted and it's my advice. Honor thy father and thy mother, the Good Book says. Take a fuckin' hint, whistlehead! Go live and survive."

"That cop is the only thing keeping me out of jail right now."

"Got your nuts in a vise, huh? I sympathize. Been in that same vise all my life." He knocked back his beer, gulping and swallowing. He almost finished the can but had to stop to gasp and catch his breath.

I got the idea he was getting his courage from that can. He gave me what I took as a guilty look.

"Easy, when your dad left that shipment with me, my original intention was to dump the whole load into the bottom of a quarry somewhere. If it didn't go boom after I tossed it off a cliff, I figured I could take shots at the boxes with a deer rifle until it all went up in a fireball. That would make a good YouTube video. Then I found another buyer for the stuff. I don't work for Ernie anymore. Rollie's gotta think about what's good for Rollie now. Nobody else is lookin' out for me."

"Who is the new buyer?"

He shrugged. "It's an acquaintance of a friend of a friend sort of situation. They're not paying as much as Ernie's connection, but it's a fire sale. Everything must go. That stuff's too hot for me to handle. I don't want that load parked in my backyard."

"So the explosives are still in the truck."

"That don't matter. I already got a down payment. Bought me this sweet TV from BestBuy on the way back. Nice, huh?"

"Who'd you sell it to, Rollie?"

"In honor of my long association and friendship with your dad, I did not sell it to Carstairs' people if that's what you're so worried about. This is a totally separate deal. I figured I'd honored Ernie's wishes."

"What do you think your new buyer is going to do with it?"

"Not my problem, not my business or yours. You sell a customer a coffeemaker, you don't follow them home to ask if he's sticking the machine up his ass for giggles, jollies and caffeine enemas."

"Dad wouldn't have gone for your new deal, either."

"I'm just looking out for number one, Easy. I gotta make some real cash. I hate to say it but it seems you didn't get the memo. One way or another, your dad's dead already. I'm out of business with him. He said I could have Sophie's title slip and sell her, but how long is the money going to last from that old truck? I'm drowning here. You gotta understand, I'm just trying to get by. I got no rich uncle comin' to save me. All I got is that new TV and a fridge full of beer."

He sounded enough like Joshua that I felt like I was in a replay of the previous night. The difference was I liked Joshua.

"Just so you know, this isn't personal," Rollie added.

I liked Sleepy Rollie Gallagher even less when he raised the 12 gauge and pointed it at my chest. He had me cold.

"You got fifteen seconds to get off my property! Then I blast you into next Tuesday afternoon."

Time to retreat and regroup. I turned and strode for the front door. My left knee didn't like my sudden burst of speed and change of direction but I ignored the pain and kept going.

He didn't give me fifteen seconds. Rollie shot me in the back as I got to the bottom of his front steps. I fell to the ground in agony and tried to clutch at my left shoulder blade, sure it was bloody and broken. The pain was excruciating.

Rollie walked up to me and pointed his shotgun at my face, "Stings, don't it?"

"You're a mean bastard, Rollie."

"Don't be a baby about it. It was just a beanbag round."

"You're still a mean bastard."

"When I was a kid stealing apples from an old man's orchard, he got me with rock salt. I'd rather be hit by a beanbag than rock salt. Rock salt hurts worse. Probably. Never actually tried shooting myself with a beanbag but I'm guessing so."

I eyed the muzzle of the 12 gauge. At close range and pointed at my head, even a beanbag round would kill me.

"Rollie says roll over."

I obeyed. He took my pistol from my waistband. He picked up my sunglasses from the grass and put them on.

"Get up," he said. "I tried to warn you away. Some people are like moths. You tell 'em not to fly into the fire and what do they do?"

I struggled to my feet and, using the barrel as a prod, Rollie pushed me toward the eighteen-wheeler.

"Climb in the back if you're not too much of a gimp. If you can't manage that, we'll end it right here. I'll have to bury you in the woods out back with my dead dogs."

I got into the back of the Kenworth and Rollie climbed in after me. In the dim light inside the truck's box, I saw a pile of furniture blankets, a few lengths of rope and many cases of explosives. The cases looked identical to the one I found in the barn's bunker. Rollie shoved me to the floor and grabbed a length of rope from the rack. He tied my hands behind my back and then tied my ankles together.

"What's your plan, Rollie?"

"Don't know yet. I'm not big on plans. You say you know bombs. Maybe the people I've sold the bombs to could use you. They could take you off my hands. I got a bad back. I'd rather not be digging graves at midnight and hauling your carcass through the woods."

"You're a real human being, Rollie."

"I've worked for your dad long enough, helping him out. I don't think I owe him nothing more. I already threw the truck into my deal. Remember how hard I tried to be nice."

"I will remember."

He laughed and added, "I know! I am a mean bastard. But I'm the mean bastard with the gun." He was still giggling to himself as he climbed down out of the box, closed the doors and left me in darkness. He smacked the truck's body a couple of times and yelled, "If you gotta pee, hold your water. The guy is supposed to be along soon."

43

I don't know how long I sat in the dark. I fumbled with my bonds for quite some time before I got free. That didn't do me any good but it was slightly more comfortable. My back ached where the beanbag hit but pain radiated out from the site of impact on my shoulder blade. It was as if I had suddenly grown more nerves to communicate pain.

I blinked at the afternoon light as the doors to the truck's box creaked wide. Rollie stood with the 12 gauge over one shoulder. Beside him was a whip-thin guy dressed in motorcycle leathers. He was an old forty or a young fifty-five and wore his hair in a thick mullet.

"Huh," Rollie said. "He weaseled out of the ropes."

Mullet's face split into a wide smile. "You don't watch a lot of BDSM porn, do you, Sleepy? You tie a guy up right, you gotta be a cowboy or a gay cowboy who knows the ropes. A bondage guy would know how to tie somebody up right. Mostly, ropes don't work, anyway. Zip ties are better. Go with handcuffs for best success."

Rollie looked from Mullet to me and back, opened his mouth to speak and then decided against it.

Mullet looked me up and down. He'd spent so much time in the sun and wind that when he smiled, his face crinkled into horizontal slashes and lines. "Sleepy Rollie says you know the ropes when it comes to explosive devices. He also says you got cop trouble."

I gave him a quick sum-up. "A dirty cop will kill my dad and frame me for murder if I don't deliver these explosives to him." I skipped over the detail about killing a guy in self-defense. Matters were complicated enough without long explanations.

"Interesting," Mullet said.

"Is it? Feels like a horror show to me."

"Who's the cop?"

"Deputy Paul Carstairs up in Oakland County."

"And he's got your dad?"

Rollie sighed impatiently and pointed the shotgun at me again. "Can you take the whistlehead off my hands or not?"

Mullet seemed to consider this before slowly and gently placing one index finger on the barrel of the 12 gauge and guiding the muzzle off to one side. "Haste makes waste, Sleepy. What's a cop want the explosives for, Mr. Jack?"

"I have no idea but I can tell you that a billionaire wants them so — "

"Bullshit!" Rollie scoffed. He pointed his weapon at me again.

"Slow down, fat boy," Mullet said. "I like a good tale. Tell me more, Mr. Jack."

It was my turn to look him up and down and I took my time, trying to slow the play and give myself time to think. Everything about Mullet told me he was a tough guy who'd been through something bad, maybe war or prison time. If I appealed to his pride and to logic, I might talk my way out of this jam. The other jams would have to wait.

"Whatever you've got planned for this load," I said, "it can't be as profitable as selling the stuff to a billionaire, right?"

"Now I'm more interested. Go on."

"You're not somebody's dad trying to buy illegal fireworks out of the back of a truck," I said. "If you've got enough mojo, maybe you won't be pushed around by a shit-kicking cop from the boonies.

Whatever you planned for these explosives, you can buy it or buy bigger and better with whatever a billionaire can pay."

Mullet turned to Rollie. "Do you believe his story, Sleepy?"

Rollie shrugged. "Carstairs has taken a slice out of every deal Ernie Jack ever made. It's the secret economy, man. Cops know and the banks are in on it but that's not the question. The question is, who's takin' care of Rollie? I asked for twelve grand for the load and another twelve for the truck — "

"That's all?" I asked in disbelief.

"Shut up," Rollie said. "I'm talking to my customer."

Mullet waved his big hands, motioning for Rollie to slow his roll. Then he turned back to me. "Can you drive this truck, Mr. Jack?"

"Learned from my dad when I was fourteen, sure."

He bobbed his head. "Sleepy, give the man his sunglasses back. I'll hold on to his piece for him. You got something we can use as a ramp? I'll need to get my bike into the back of ... what'd you call her?"

"Sophie," Rollie said.

"Named after my dead mother," I added.

"Right. Sophie. Nice or a little creepy. Can't decide."

"What about my money?" Rollie demanded.

The man in leather spoke in the patient tone of a schoolteacher speaking to a dim child. "You got your deposit to go get the stuff. You'll get the rest when delivery is complete. Things change. Adapt. This man says he's plugged into billionaire money. The second rule of business is to spend other people's money, not your own. I like the idea of spending billionaire money on this load. You'll get a better deal if you can sit tight a little longer. That makes sense, doesn't it?"

Rollie took a moment to work this through. Then he said, "What about cash on the barrelhead and a bird in the hand — "

"A bird in the hand will shit in your hand." He gave Rollie a hard look and didn't seem to worry about the shotgun. "Did your friend tell you who I'm repping? It's not just me standing here, Sleepy. Do you doubt me?"

Rollie's chin trembled. "N-nah, I-I don't doubt you, sir."

"Damn straight. You know why? Because the first rule of business is a deal's a deal, at least until a better one comes along." He gave a reptilian smile. "I'm solid. You solid, Sleepy?"

"Solid, sure."

"S'alright, then. Patience and promiscuity are the two most underrated virtues. I don't have 'em myself but I do appreciate those virtues in other people."

"What did you plan to do with this stuff?" I asked.

"That's another story for another day," he said. "You're looking a little rough, champ. Are you up to bringing me in on your deal with this billionaire? Because you better be."

"A drowning man will grasp at anything, even the tip of a sword," I said.

Mullet gave a slow nod. "And a hungry man is an angry man. For today, I think we can do business. I'm hungry, Mr. Jack, and I'm interested in making money. I'm always on the lookout for a bigger fish and a better deal. Mind, if you cross me, you should know I am entirely prepared to fuck you up beyond all recognition. I help me first, understand? If that ends up helping you, well, that's just fine. I'm telling you this up front so we recognize each other's vibe and harmonize. People are music and business is jazz and I will tolerate no syncopated rhythms. Are you feelin' the beat I'm sendin'?"

"Uh, you kind of lost me on that last part but I get the gist. Shall we seal it with a kiss, hold hands, braid each other's hair and sing kumbaya?"

He laughed as he took off his gloves and offered his bare hand. L-O-V-E was tattooed across the knuckles of his right hand. I expected H-A-T-E on his other hand. Instead, his tatted knuckles read W-H-A-T with a big question mark on the back of his left. We shook.

"People call me Easy."

"Nobody calls me," he said. "I text. However, since I'm your new best friend and we are embarking on a mutually beneficial enterprise, you can call me Coop."

44

I drove the Kenworth back toward Lake Orion as Coop lounged in the passenger seat. He ignored the road and watched me. "How do you know Sleepy Rollie?"

"I don't. My dad hired him to drive because he couldn't anymore. Health problems."

"What kind of health problems?"

"I don't really know the details. Nothing good."

"Shitty deal, isn't it? My dad didn't know he was sick until he was dead."

I watched the road and tried not to think about becoming an orphan. If Dad's captors were worried that he'd croak on them, he must be in worse shape than I'd guessed. I wondered what and how much they'd done to him before backing off and getting him to call me in.

"So this cop who has you jammed up, he gonna frame you for that murder in Lake Orion?"

"You know about that?"

"Big news in these parts. Not hard to connect the dots. I excelled at those connecting the dots puzzles in elementary school. You know the ones? Connect the dots, make a shitty picture? Not much of a puzzle, really. More of a way to teach little kids to count while drawing a straight line. We set the bar pretty low, don't we?"

"The guy who died, that wasn't my fault. All that matters to the deputy is that this deal goes through and he gets his cut."

"A cut for him, a cut for me, a cut for Rollie. Jeez, Easy! Sounds like you're dyin' of death by a thousand cuts. You're bleedin' cash, ole son."

"I just want my dad back."

"You guys must be close."

"Not really. That has nothing to do with it."

"Interesting. What does it have to do with, Easy?"

"I owe him. I hate owing him, but I do."

"That's a tad refreshing. You know what that fat boy Rollie wants?"

"Cold beer, a big TV and porn in HD?"

Coop chuckled. "He wants what everybody wants. He only thinks he wants to sit and watch TV with unlimited pizza on speed dial. He's another tragic victim of the American dream, man. It was supposed to work out for everybody but it hardly ever does. When he was a kid, betcha he thought he was going to grow up to be Tom Cruise."

"But only Tom Cruise can Tom Cruise. It's in the Constitution somewhere."

"Exactly!" Coop crowed. "The lie that any kid can grow up to be anything is a uniquely American mind virus. It would be mean but everybody's infected. We got a whole country measuring their tiny lives against a handful of weird outliers in Hollywood and New York. When guys like Rollie don't get all the money, adoration, washboard abs and hot wives of the rich and famous, they finally understand the horror in the mirror. What people think they want and what they get, two different things, galaxies apart."

"What do you want, Coop?"

"Oh, I'm no exception. I see the game but I'm not outside of it. All anybody really wants is to escape. They want to get beyond criticism, out of their nine-to-five ... or out of their two or three lowly fucking jobs. They want to feel safe. Ha! We're walkin' the high wire without a net from the day we're born."

"The trap. That's what Dad calls it. Says we're all in it."

"Smart man, your dad."

"But still in the trap."

"No shame there. It's got everybody." For the first time, Coop looked out the window at the humble homes we passed. "What do you suppose these people do out here? What's a fun Saturday night out in the sticks?"

"I've lived out in the country. Bean suppers at the fire hall and barbecues at the Lions Club are big events."

"No wonder the whole country's fat," Coop said sourly.

"I don't know. Most people seem pretty happy."

Coop spun his head around and stared at me in a way that reminded me of Becky when she was mad. "That true, champ? You wouldn't shit a shitter, would you?"

I shrugged. "Nobody knows the inside of anybody's else's head."

"That much is true."

"They seem satisfied, anyway."

"You mean they settled."

"I don't know if they'd see it like that. We had neighbors down the road who invited us for dinner once. You know what the big occasion was?"

"Tell me."

"Dude bought a brand new John Deere ride-on mower. Aside from the day he got married and the births of his three kids, that might have been the proudest day of his life. He kept telling us it was all paid for."

Coop smiled but there was no energy in it. "Unlike the wife and kids."

"I think he watched his front lawn with binoculars," I said. "Couldn't wait for one blade of grass to grow faster than the rest so he could jump on and go round and round again. He called it pride of ownership. I wonder if he was OCD."

Coop threw his head back and laughed. I could see all the fillings in the top row of his teeth. "Well, ain't this ride elucidatin'? I learned the secret to happiness: Have small dreams!"

I smiled along with him. Then I stood on the brakes hard as I swerved to the left, nearly jackknifing the rig. Coop's right temple smacked into his window. Before we screeched to a stop, I veered right. He leaned my way just enough so I could grab his mullet and slam his face into the dash.

Stunned, he reached for the pistol he'd taken from me. I used it to bash him across the face a couple of times and popped the passenger side door open. When he hit the ground at the side of the road, his right arm was bent up behind his back. Broken. As he sat up his was a rictus grin of pain. The arm hung loosely in its socket.

I leaned out and pointed the pistol at his head. "I want you to know this is nothing personal."

"Don't shoot — "

"Your arm's broken," I said. "I'm not going to shoot you. The part that isn't personal is I'm going to have to take your bike. I'm on a deadline to save my dad. I can't stop to unload. Sorry."

He looked up at me with new eyes. "You aren't going to shoot?"

"You're unarmed. No pun intended. If you want, I guess I could shoot you in the knee if you start making a fuss."

Coop tried getting up but sat back down quickly when the pain hit. He cradled his limp right arm with his left. "Dislocated again," he said. "I guess, the shape I'm in, I'm not up to gettin' too randy and handsy."

"Don't come after me, Coop. Don't send anybody after me, either. I'm wrapping up the deal quick so by the time you get that arm in a sling, the whole thing will be Donesville."

Blood dripped down his gaunt face. Coop appeared demonic. "You are nowhere near Donesville, my friend. You're in Fucksville."

I shrugged. "Lived there all my life."

"I will come after you. You know that, right?"

"It won't matter. The deputy will have me in jail by then, I'm sure. I don't need to add another murder to the charges against me. Murder is something you should mean to do."

"Heh. Just so you know, I can get to you in jail, too, Easy."

"Then I guess I'll have to set that bridge on fire when I come to it. Don't be a spoilsport, Coop. You said yourself this is a game. Don't be a shit stain about losing."

Coop winced as he wiped the blood from his eyes. "I guess that's why they call it the dashboard. It's where you dash your face. You know, Easy, you're goin' about this all wrong. I could help you — "

"I'm in the trap. I've only got one way to go about this. In the meantime, no hard feelings."

He looked down at his arm and then back up at me. "No hard feelings?"

"I'm not getting buried in a shallow grave behind Rollie's place. He was going to bury me with his dead dogs. Thanks for that."

"You are a strange cat, Easy," he said.

"I'm aware, but I told you, I hate owing anybody. I consider us even. I hope you can see it my way."

"I do not. I have people to answer to — "

"And I've gotta go get my dad. A car will be along soon. You look pretty shady so tell them you went over the handles of your bike. Or enjoy the hike. The next town isn't that far. You'll be okay."

I slammed the door and drove north. When I glanced in the side mirror, Coop was up and walking along the side of the road, coming after me.

"Get thee behind me, Devil," I said, "and get in line."

I didn't get far at all.

45

I called Paul Carstairs. "Deputy? I've got what you want."

"Where are you?"

"On the road with a truckload of explosives and, technically, a stolen motorcycle."

"Technically?"

"Long story. The short story is I had to fight for your shipment. Dad better be okay."

"Start heading toward Waterford."

"Where will we do the exchange?"

"Close to Oxford County Regional Airport. I'll make a call and — "

"Your plan is to try to take cases of explosives through an airport?"

"I said, 'close to,' not the actual airport. Details aren't your problem. Eyes on your own paper and mind your business."

"You want me to play fetch, you better play fair. If Dad isn't at the drop, I'll blow up the whole load and you'll be shit out of luck. I'll call you back when I'm close."

It felt good to hang up on him. It didn't feel good for long. I heard the siren and then caught the flashing lights in my side mirror. I tucked the gun in the back of my pants and pulled over. I knew who it was before he got out of his cruiser. Deputy Paul Carstairs had followed me. He was smiling as he climbed out. Becky's warning came back to me. That damn badge gives him all the power. He pulled his pistol from his holster as he walked toward the cab and pointed it at me.

"I don't like being threatened, Easy. You talking about blowing up the load makes me nervous."

I popped the passenger side door open and climbed out of the cab before Carstairs could shoot me through the driver's side door. My knee ached as I hit the ground but I bolted for cover in the woods. Almost tumbling down the embankment into the ditch, I rolled and popped up. The spirit of self-preservation ignited my muscle memory. Despite my injuries, I bore down and ran through the pain. I threw my left hip forward with each stride to make up for my bum knee. It didn't give me the velocity I once had but it got me to cover.

In Basic, my instructors were fond of repeating old saws like, "How you train, so shall you fight," and "Sweat in training so you don't bleed in combat."

After training to exhaustion and gaining more experience, slogans melted away to become empty cliches. IEDs don't care how many sit-ups you can do.

I was almost to the tree line when I heard the report of Carstairs' first shot. The rounds went through branches nearby. Unless he was very fortunate, I was out of range. Pistols are best close up. If he'd brought his rifle, he would have had me. If he dared to abandon his prize, he could have chased me down.

A few steps into the woods, I dove and slid behind a birch tree. I was still wincing at the pain between my shoulder blades where Rollie shot me with the beanbag round. I made a mental note that if I survived this ordeal, somehow I would find a way to "settle Rollie's hash," as my father would say. Carstairs stood by the Kenworth's grill scanning the woods. The engine was still rumbling.

Now that I had another few seconds to think about it, I should have backed Sophie right over his damn car. Good ideas are often late for the train of thought.

By the swivel of his neck and how he bounced on his feet, he clearly did not know what to do. Carstairs could have called for backup or requested a K9 unit to track me through the woods. However, if his fellow cops weren't in on the deal, they would want to search the truck. Mazie Lane told me I was up to my neck in shit but Carstairs would find himself in hot water. Even if he tried to play it off as a routine traffic stop, the cases of explosives would end up in an evidence locker.

Breathing hard, I lay down on a bed of moss behind a tree and pulled out the pistol. Hunkering down, I waited for the deputy to follow me. I had a good position. When he stepped inside the tree line, I could empty the pistol into him.

Unfortunately, Deputy Carstairs wasn't foolish enough to follow me into the woods. "Easy!" he called. He waited for my reply. I kept silent, not wishing to give away my position.

"Easy! You're not making this easy! If you don't come out right now, I can't vouch for your father's safety!"

Now that he had the shipment, all bets were off. How had he found me? My best guess was he'd thought to put a tracker on the truck. It would be easy to do. I'd done it to him. I had not looked for any such device when I left Rollie's place. I was just glad to get out of there. But if he had used a tracker, why didn't he use it before now?

Another voice came to me. A man with a deep voice was cursing. I recognized that voice. I got to my feet and slipped to my left. When I got to the edge of the woods, I saw a face I'd only seen once before and in the moonlight. The man who'd shot Dad's dogs sat in the passenger side of the cruiser.

"I told you to let him be, you dumb fuck!"

Carstairs disappeared behind the truck and reappeared behind the patrol car. He was rightfully worried I might start shooting from the woods. If I opened up with my pistol, he could duck behind the engine block. At this range, trying to kill him was likely a waste of my ammunition.

"I had to know who the guy with the broken arm was, didn't I? How does he figure into this?"

"Why don't you ask him?"

"Easy for you to say, Eugene! I'm out front on this deal. You're the behind-the-scenes guy."

The dog killer's name was Eugene? I'd been bested by a guy named Eugene?

"I'm an operative," Eugene replied stiffly.

"Can you drive that rig, Operative?" Carstairs asked without humor.

Eugene shrugged. "Man, if I weren't doing this, I'd be driving an Uber but all I got is a rusty old Mazda. I don't drive stick."

"Shit," Carstairs said. He pulled his phone from his belt.

"Who are you calling? Triple-A?"

"We're on a tight schedule," the deputy whined. "The lady's plane will be landing soon. We've got to get this stuff out of here and away from us. I'll stay here and guard the truck. You go back and get Ernie Sr.'s hired man. What was his name again?"

"Rollie Gallagher."

"Right. We'll get him to drive the truck. You'll ride with him and I'll follow in the cruiser."

"And what about Ernest Jr.?"

The deputy scanned the woods again, searching. "Well, shit, you got a gun and I got a shotgun in the rack. Between the two of us, I'm sure we can solve that problem."

They planned to kill me but I wasn't the immediate problem. Along came Coop.

46

Coop had a hitch in his step and his right arm hung limp as he walked along the road's shoulder.

Carstairs stood in the road by the back fender of his cruiser. "Hey!"

Coop gave him a big smile that turned his face into sunburnt creases. "Did you get him?"

"Him who?"

Coop didn't slow his stride. "Who him? Him, driver! Him stole my bike! Bike in truck! Him, Easy Jack! Me, Tarzan. You speak ape?"

"This truck is abandoned," Carstairs said flatly. "There's nothing in the back, Tarzan."

Coop looked around, his eyebrows meeting in the middle. "That was suspiciously quick. He just threw me out of that truck a few hundred yards back. You must be Deputy Carstairs."

The biker wasn't an ordinary biker. As he got close, he pulled a chain out of his shirt. At the end of the chain hung a badge. It was the gold badge of an FBI agent. Coop then dropped to one knee and pulled a pistol from the small of his back with his good arm. "Federal agent! Drop that weapon!"

Taken by surprise, the deputy slowly bent from the waist. He placed his pistol on the asphalt and stood upright. The cop raised his hands slowly.

"I've been hearing things about you, Deputy. Not good things."

"That so? How about you identify yourself before we get too chatty?"

"Cooper, short for FBI agent Andrew Cooper. I was working deep undercover when I stumbled across a kidnap case. This morning I thought I'd be arresting an idiot named Rollie Gallagher. You're a bigger idiot, deputy."

"Did Easy Jack call you?"

"Hell, no! Rollie tried to sell explosives. I heard about it."

"How'd that occur, exactly?"

"Like it always happens. Rollie talked to a cousin who talked to a buddy who'd been to prison. That guy asked one of my CIs for a connection to a buyer interested in explosives."

Agent Cooper stood and kept his gun aimed at Carstairs as he stepped closer. "I usually pose as a hitman to weed out husbands and wives looking to get rid of their spouses. Crazy how things fall apart, isn't it, Deputy? We talk about investigating and deducing and that CSI shit all day but it's always the little things that trip up entrepreneurs like you. It's all about word of mouth."

"I have no idea what you're talking about," Carstairs replied. "I stopped this truck because the driver was all over the road."

"Not buying it. Easy comes off earnest. Where's his father?"

Carstairs shrugged. "I think we should pull my lawyer in on this conversation. His name is Rudyard Bench. I'd like to call him now."

"Sure, but one more question before we put you in your own handcuffs. What's the plan? If you're working with a terrorist organization, you're going to find yourself in a black site answering uncomfortable questions from interrogators who don't share my gentle nature. Trust me, you really don't want to deal with the domestic terrorism task force."

"This is ridiculous." The deputy reached for the phone on his belt again. As Cooper ordered him to keep his hands up, Eugene popped the door to the cruiser open and threw himself on the ground, raising his pistol as his belly hit the ground.

I ran forward but I was too far away to stop what happened next. If Agent Cooper had been left-handed, he might have got Eugene with his first shot. He didn't get a chance to fire a second round. Three of the operative's rounds caught the FBI agent in the chest. He dropped his weapon and slid to the ground. I fired on Eugene.

The dog killer had graduated to become a cop killer. He rolled on his side and turned his attention to me, returning fire. Bullets whined past my left ear.

I pointed and fired as quickly as I could until my revolver clicked empty. Though my target presented a low profile, one of my rounds caught him in the belly. Eugene cried out and dropped his pistol. His yellow shirt blossomed red as blood pumped through the fabric and onto the road. He gawped at me. I could see the whites all around his eyes. Perhaps he didn't really see me. He could have been looking through me into the next world. Maybe all he saw was the pain.

Carstairs scooped up his weapon as I retreated toward the safety of the woods. I was out of ammunition, anyway. I was one step from the tree line when I tripped. I didn't fall to the ground but I twisted my knee just enough to make me gasp and curse the pain.

Satisfied I was in full retreat, Carstairs ran to Cooper's still body. Though the FBI agent was probably dead, the cop popped a fresh mag into his 9mm and shot him in the head. Then he shoved the toe of his boot under the body and rolled the dead man down the embankment into the ditch.

Poor Agent Cooper. He discovered the key to happiness a little too late.

"Paul!" Eugene gasped. "I need help!"

Amped up, the deputy strode over to assess his ally's injuries. I could hear him clearly from the trees. "Thanks for shooting that guy, Eugene."

"Get me to a hospital!"

Even from where I stood, I could hear the dog killer's breaths.

They were short, quick and shallow. It was the sound of a man whose allotted number of inspirations in this world were running out.

"Gut shots are the most painful, Eugene," Carstairs replied coldly. With a casual gesture of his weapon, the deputy shot the man in the head. "Headshots are the most bloody."

He kicked Eugene's limp body down the embankment as well. The two bodies were no more than twelve feet apart.

I limped north along the edge of the forest. I hoped to find a vehicle. I couldn't risk hitchhiking. Once I got to a phone, I planned to call the FBI office in Detroit. With one of their agents dead, maybe I had enough information and leverage that they'd be looking at Carstairs hard instead of looking at me. It might have worked out but the deputy could run. He got ahead of me.

Appearing from behind a large oak, Carstairs pointed his weapon at the center of my chest. "Hi, Easy."

"Hello, Deputy Carstairs. Is this goodbye?"

"You shot Eugene," he said.

"He was in the middle of murdering Agent Cooper and then he tried to kill me."

"You got a knack for killing people in self-defense, don't you, Easy?" Carstairs grinned. He'd won and he knew it.

"Your buddy Eugene killed our dogs. Shooting him has gotta be legal, right?"

"Always the smartass." He gave a long wistful sigh. "I should shoot you dead right now — "

"But you need me to drive the truck, right? It's not that lonely a highway. People will slow down and gawk. Maybe some Good Samaritan will stop to see if you're okay — "

"Yeah, we gotta get going. If you give me a hard time, I'll shoot you in the good leg."

"I guess I have no other plans for the rest of the day."

47

Carstairs slapped handcuffs on me and shoved me into the back of his cruiser. It didn't take long for him to find a small road that wandered off into the woods. He parked the patrol car on the little rat road and we walked back through the woods toward the Kenworth.

As I limped along, I asked, "How's my dad?"

"Pretty sick."

"He wasn't that bad when I saw him last. Did you mess him up more?"

"Messing him up wasn't my department. That was Mr. Ramone's job. Your dad says you don't know what's wrong with him."

"He told me he doesn't know, either."

"I don't get you. You go away for years and then you come back determined to get in my way."

"I kept in touch on the phone once in a while."

The deputy seemed to contemplate this a moment and then dropped the words on me slowly. "Ernie knows what's wrong. It's non-Hodgkin lymphoma. You've been fighting hard to save a dead man. How's that feel?"

"Confusing. He told me he didn't know. I guess it's his pride. He never wanted to show weakness. Or maybe he thought if he said it out loud, it would be real."

My mother died on a hot August afternoon. That June, Dad came up with an idea to save her. Mom was dubious but he claimed his strategy was based more in science than superstition. "Talk in an Irish accent from now on," he urged her. "It's killing you, Sophie. Be a different person and maybe the demon will figure out it's in the wrong body."

Mom told him to leave her alone so she could have her fourth nap of the day.

"C'mon," he cajoled. "Try it for thirty days and we'll see if the tumor gets smaller. Do it for me, please. I need you. Do it for me and I'll bring you a hot fudge sundae from Dairy Queen."

Mom clearly thought Dad had lost his mind but she bargained. "I won't do it for anything less than a Peanut Buster Parfait."

"And your life."

"If you say so, Ernest."

She tried her best for sixteen days. We all spoke in Irish accents to encourage her and confuse the disease. She gave up because pretending tired her too much.

Dad was bitterly disappointed. Down in the kitchen, I consoled him in hushed tones. "It wouldn't have worked, anyway. She wasn't fooling anyone. Her Irish accent is terrible, offensive to leprechauns everywhere."

Tears leaked from his eyes as he laughed long and hard. "It really is, isn't it? Terrible!"

No matter. Her cancer was sure it had the right address. The tumors did not retreat. The disease burned through her like a wildfire in the end. Still, for those precious sixteen days that June, we laughed often, happier than we'd ever been since the day of her diagnosis.

My parents weren't alone in their superstitions, of course. Lots of people don't want to say the word cancer. They say, "C-word," instead.

And no wonder. How had Coop put it? *We're all born walking a high wire without a net.*

"Ernie's a grifter and a smuggler," Carstairs said. "You think he's worth all the fight you've put up? I doubt that FBI agent would think so."

"That's on you," I said.

"Then why are you sweating so much?" Carstairs asked.

"It's the pain."

"Sweating from pain? Didn't know that was a thing."

"It is. There are all kinds of pain, Deputy. It can be sharp or ache and burn but it can also be crushing, bright or exquisite."

"Exquisite?"

"Rollie shot me in the back with a beanbag round. That was exquisite and bright pain at first. Now it's a throbbing ache that travels up and down my spine."

"Uh-huh. And what does that guy know about our transaction?"

"Nothing."

"Your dad does his suffering in silence. I like that about Ernie."

When we got to the truck, I looked around. No one had stopped. With the bodies in the ditch and out of sight from the road, the crime scene looked unremarkable. How long it would take someone to notice Agent Cooper wasn't reporting in? The bloody scene that had transpired here might go unknown for a very long time.

The deputy handcuffed my left hand to the steering wheel and for the second time that day I pulled Sophie onto the road and headed north with a passenger holding a gun.

"You want to know why your dad didn't tell you about the lymphoma thing? He watched all his money drain away trying to save your mother or at least make her final years comfortable. When his time came, he planned to take that old Barracuda for a long drive, pick a pretty spot with a nice view and shoot himself. I imagine that's basically what a lot of people did in the Old West. Got a bad toothache out on the frontier? Shoot yourself. Got cancer? Shoot yourself. Got syphilis? Get shot by your angry wife."

Carstairs laughed at his own joke. I kept my eyes on the road. With my wrist handcuffed to the wheel, the trick I'd used to get Coop out of the cab wouldn't work twice. I'd been damned lucky the first time.

"I got a dad I don't talk to much," the deputy volunteered. "He keeps me up to speed on who's doing well in Delaware. That's what he always says. 'Doing well.' That's code for, they got more money than you. I tell him I'm a cop. I don't necessarily do very well but I do good."

"Debatable," I said.

"Those awkward phone calls aren't going to be a problem after today. I don't think I'll bother giving my dad another call again for the rest of my life. When I get mine from Mazie Lane, I'll do better than anybody I went to school with. Better than most anybody. Maybe I'll give my dear old dad one last call from an island in the Caribbean. Just to let him know, you know?"

"That you're dirty?"

"That I'll never have to worry. When I get old, I can hire a staff of cute Filipino nurses to take care of me. You know that good feeling you have when you've got a full tank of gas? Life will be like that, but multiply it by about six million. Six million dollars. I'm going to be the Six Million Dollar Man. That used to be big money back in the day. Now it's a few decent homes. Still big money to me, though."

It would have been a massive amount of money to me, too. I understood the gravitational pull of wealth. A pile of cash is a comforting thing. At least, I imagined it would be.

48

My father had a good memory for numbers and could do math. I guess that's why I had once assumed he was a good businessman. I was wrong. He'd taken on a lot of risk at the border but had not driven a hard bargain. I had to wonder, if they'd paid Dad more, would he still have had a crisis of conscience? Heroes in comic books don't get paid. If Carstairs hadn't demanded an enormous cut and the criminals had paid Dad his worth, maybe I wouldn't be in this jam at all. Dad might have gone along with it, gotten paid and we'd both be home right now with a pen full of live German shepherds. Dad was no saint. All things considered, maybe he wasn't enough of a sinner.

"I'm going to love living on a tropical island," Carstairs told me. "Pick just about any tropical island that doesn't have too many tourists or an extradition treaty. I'm going to drink margaritas for breakfast. I'll walk along the beach each night, sugar sand between my toes. No more of this running around and scrounging bullshit."

"You're just bragging now," I said.

"That was the point, yeah. Try to keep up, Easy."

"And you thought I was a smartass."

"You're a dumbass, actually. You brought in the FBI."

"Rollie stumbled into that."

"That's what the agent said. Didn't know whether to believe him. What was wrong with his arm?"

"I broke it."

"That probably didn't help his aim much. Thanks."

"You are a greasy shit, Deputy Carstairs. Do you need to plug our destination into your GPS or should I just follow the smell of dirty money?"

"No such thing as dirty money, Easy. There is only money. Our destination is not on GPS. That's how rich Mazie Lane is." Acidic resentment crept into his tone as he added, "The best payout of my life and it's couch change to her. In case nobody's ever told you, life is not fair."

"I've been to war and worked with refugees," I replied. "You're a white guy who wears a badge and a gun. You might be the biggest whiner I ever met."

"I don't like you and I've got two guns on me."

"I haven't forgotten."

Carstairs gave me directions. I drove the prize to a private airfield. The fence was topped with razor wire and there was no signage to suggest what the facility was, only signs that read: Private, No Trespassing. As we pulled up to the main gate, I heard a low buzz and the barrier slid aside for us.

"We're expected," Carstairs said. "She doesn't enjoy waiting."

"A couple of bodies in a ditch aren't a good excuse for tardiness?"

Carstairs said nothing.

The airfield wasn't much: a runway, a fueling station, a couple of steel hangars and a windsock. The control tower was an office building that had a second floor with a view.

The billionaire mastermind behind this mysterious project had come to supervise the transfer of the smuggled explosives personally. My father was nowhere in sight. There would be no exchange of the hostage for the goods. Dad had crossed them by not supplying the explosives. Arms deals are no place for a gentleman's agreement.

I wasn't going to get my dad back by asking nicely. If I got the chance to turn this mess around, I promised myself to be just as brutal as my enemies. Desert sand wasn't blowing in my eyes in Michigan and I wasn't in uniform anymore. Still, this was war. Like Coop, it seemed I'd learned my lesson too late.

On the day I left Lake Orion to serve, I felt like the road was wide and the future was filled with possibilities. The day I got out of boot camp and the day I graduated from Ranger training stood out in my mind as particularly happy days. Looking back now, that fact made me a little sad. I had been mistaken. Those were not happy days. What I'd felt was the relief. I'd gone through an ordeal and arrived on the far side of it. My sunny days were something like happiness but they were really about escape. Coop was right. We all want to escape.

By the end of this trip, I fully expected Deputy Carstairs would shoot me. He did not hesitate to kill an FBI agent or his co-conspirator. Ian Fleming said, "You only live twice: Once when you are born and once when you look death in the face." Staring death in the face now, I considered what I would miss out on. I liked the smell of fallen leaves each autumn. I would not crunch curled leaves under my feet this fall. I loved to play with dogs and train them. I think that was the only job I really enjoyed.

And Becky. She was the only woman I'd ever loved. As I parked the truck by the plane on the tarmac, I mourned the future with her I would not see.

49

Mazie Lane stood on the tarmac beside a private jet. She waved to us gaily with what looked like real warmth. "Mr. Carstairs! Mr. Jack! So good to see you both again! And you've brought me presents! Finally!"

As the cop removed my cuffs, the goon with the sad soul patch stared at me through the window. "Ramone! Deputy Carstairs here was just talking shit about you. You should shoot him."

The bodyguard gestured with his M1 Carbine to get me moving.

"Good talk, Ramone. I do enjoy a good heart-to-heart but you're smothering me."

Apparently, the deputy wasn't in the mood for pleasantries, either. His only question for the bodyguard was, "You got the money?"

"It's on the plane. Let's inspect the cargo first, shall we?" Lane replied breezily.

"Where's my father?"

"Safe," she said.

"I'd like to see him."

Lane smiled and walked to the back of the truck. Carstairs informed me I'd be helping to load the plane. "Open the truck."

I put my hand on the catch. "Wouldn't it be really cool if I opened this up and a dozen FBI agents poured out, oozing with guns and bullets and flash-bang grenades?"

The bodyguard's eyes widened for a second as he stepped in front of his boss. I opened the door to reveal nothing more than the cases of explosive devices and Coop's motorcycle.

I was going to tell the bodyguard that he had no sense of humor. Before I could say so, Ramone let out a low whistle. "1979 Harley Davidson Shovelhead Bobber!"

"He can talk!" I said.

"Where'd you get that beauty?" Ramone asked, genuinely curious about the machine.

"It was a bonus," I said. "It belonged to the FBI agent Deputy Carstairs killed on the way here."

The billionaire gave the deputy a hard look. "There's far too much talk about the Federal Bureau of Investigation here for my liking. What the hell is happening? Is he serious?"

"The deputy shot Eugene, too," I said. "After I shot him, but still —"

"I don't know who Eugene is," Lane said. "I don't want to know more about your troubles. Just load the goddamn plane." Still, she smiled like she'd asked for two lumps of sugar for her tea.

I counted forty-one cases. Adding the one Dad had kept back in the barn, the total was forty-two. According to the Hitchhiker's Guide to the Galaxy, forty-two is the answer to the ultimate question of life, the universe and everything. From where I stood, the shipment looked like the answer to a prayer from a domestic terrorist cell.

"Good thing we brought the Lear, Miss," Ramone told his employer. "The Piper Navajo wouldn't have been big enough."

"As always, Matias, I treasure your expertise."

Hers might have been a genuine display of affection but I wasn't sure that was possible for her. Perhaps she was a reptile in an elegant human suit. Matias Ramone didn't seem to have any doubts. He bobbed his head and said, "My pleasure, Miss."

"Where'd you get this guy?" I asked. "Are there killer robot pilot bodyguard butler schools I don't know about?"

If I hadn't been carrying an explosive at the time, I'm pretty sure Ramone would have chucked me under the chin with the stock of his M1. Instead, we finished loading the plane. I'd never been on a Learjet before. I wondered if they'd take me for a little ride before shoving me out over the ocean.

"You aren't planning to ram this into the Freedom Tower and do 9/11 Part Two, are you?"

Lane laughed as she poured herself a flute of champagne. "That is an interesting thought. There is a profit motive there but my companies are not heavily invested in nation building abroad. Hmph. Perhaps I've been thinking too small."

She laughed when she saw the expression on my face. "Don't worry, Easy. I promise I am not a suicide bomber. I have far too much to live for."

"Did you file a flight plan?" I asked Ramone. "Bet you did. There'll be radar records, right? Did you guys dump all your cell phones so you can't be tracked? Of course, with the resources of the FBI on you, we could be getting surveilled by drones and satellites right now, couldn't we? They could be ordering a drone strike right now. I know they say those aren't for targets on American soil but they would say that, wouldn't they? 'All enemies, foreign and domestic,' and all that. We won't know for sure that we're dead until we wake up in hell."

Ramone looked to Carstairs and remarked, "Does he ever shut up?"

"He barely stops to breathe," the deputy replied.

"Sorry. I get chatty when I'm nervous. Your crew killed an FBI agent. That is zombie criminal behavior. This is the kind of shit that does not die. When ordinary people get killed, maybe it fades away. Carstairs killed a federal agent named Andrew Cooper. He left his body in a ditch beside Eugene's body. That's not the kind of thing that goes away, not ever."

Lane looked to the cop. "This sounds like it's a situation that must be elevated to something to which I must be apprised. Explicate, Paul. Who is Eugene?"

"Nothing to worry about."

"My province is spreadsheets," Lane said. "I work with data. Give me data. Who is Eugene and why is he involved?"

"An operator I had to bring in," the cop replied. "He was a pro, no connection to me so you can never mind — "

"Eugene sat in the front seat of your patrol car," I interjected. "How many phone calls went back and forth between you two? Burmanthol is dead. That's another guy you knew. How long before federal agents from Detroit are looking at you?"

For the first time, the billionaire looked disconcerted. That gave me a warm feeling. Of course, my luck being what it is, the good times did not roll for long.

50

Mazie Lane looked at the deputy as if he had a target painted on his forehead. "Paul, when the senior Mr. Jack refused to cooperate, you assured me you could handle the situation quietly. You hired him and he is your responsibility. Do you remember our talk about how I wanted the task completed with a maximum of discretion and a minimum of drama? When I said I was concerned you'd turn the transporter into a brutally savaged corpse, you said you could handle this with a soft touch. Have you failed to deliver on our deal?"

Ramone raised his rifle but the deputy was quick and pulled his weapon. It would have been convenient if they'd shot each other and dropped dead simultaneously. However, I'm not that lucky and they weren't that eager to die.

"Mexican standoff," I said.

"Racist term. Call it a stalemate."

At that, I had to give him a smile. "Oh. Uh, sorry. Making progress, though. I feel like we're opening up to each other. Maybe we could go on a man's retreat and really get in touch with our feelings. I bet we have a lot in common. This relationship could end up nice. You make me some s'mores around a campfire and I'll braid your hair — "

The billionaire, the bodyguard and the dirty cop could agree on one thing. They all said, "Shut up!" at the same time.

"Killing the FBI agent was necessary to deliver the goods. Killing the other guy gave law enforcement a dead end."

The other guy. Not 'Eugene.' Just 'the other guy.' *That's cold,* I thought. No wonder Carstairs was a killer. He did not share toys or play well with others.

"Whatever they're planning," I told Carstairs, "it's a safer bet if there's no trail back to them. Don't worry about Mazie. She can afford the best lawyers. She is rich and untouchable. The worst she'll get is famous, maybe get a book deal or a guest spot on a reality TV show —"

"I told you to shut the fuck up, dog boy," Ramone said.

I didn't have any illusions I could talk my way back to a long and happy life with Becky. However, sowing dissension in the ranks before they blew my head off would provide a little satisfaction.

Since she wasn't holding a weapon, I focused my plea on Mazie Lane. "As soon as the deputy killed Eugene and Agent Cooper, all your plans came undone like a toddler's shoelaces. Every play, movie and book with titles like *The Perfect Crime* or *A Simple Plan* all end in a fuck up. There's a reason for that."

I turned to the men. "When the evidence piles up, she'll need a sacrificial goat. Mazie will pretend it was all Ramone's idea and go yachting somewhere in the Mediterranean. You guys? Oh, you guys are so going to jail! Don't worry, Deputy. For a former cop, prison will be a vacation for you. Of course, since you killed a cop, they might put you in Gen Pop. Ramone looks like a take-charge kinda guy. Maybe you could be his gang's bitch?"

"For God's sake, shut your pie hole, Easy!" Carstairs said.

It was a near thing. A few pounds of pressure on a trigger is almost nothing. They might have shot each other. Instead, Lane stepped behind me and kicked the spot behind my left knee hard. I went down. Pain exploded under my kneecap. It didn't feel so great on my right knee, either. She clubbed me across the back of the head for good measure. When I rolled over on my side, I saw that she'd been armed, after all. She just didn't wave it around until she was ready to use it. Her handgun was pointed at my face. It was an SVI Tiki-T. The base price on that model was over $4,000 for the weapon and one magazine. Leave it to a billionaire to pack one of the most expensive custom pistols on the market. When it comes to their toys, the rich spare no expense.

"Don't you see what he's doing?" Lane demanded.

The men did not lower their weapons immediately.

"If you think the murdered FBI agent will bring too much heat," Carstairs told them, "a murdered deputy from a local force wouldn't be cool, either."

"Everyone calm down," Lane said. "If you shoot Ramone, there's no one to fly the plane. My deal won't go through and you won't get paid. Do you want everything we've accomplished to come to nothing?"

I decided I had to risk speaking. "And if you shoot me, who's going to drive the truck away from where your plane landed?"

Mazie Lane looked down at me. Her mask was finally off. I saw the hatred in her eyes. This was someone who was rarely refused anything. It's dangerous to be surrounded by people telling you you're awesome all the time.

"If you behave, you get to live longer," she said. "You can go back to the scene of the crime with Paul and help him clean up his mess. There must be no trail, do you understand? None of all this blood you've spilled can get traced back to me."

Carstairs lowered his weapon and whined, "And what about my money?"

"You'll get it when I complete the deal on my end. You haven't held up your end of the arrangement very well, have you?" Her smile was back. It was as if she were a kindly elementary school teacher reprimanding a naughty boy.

Lane's gaze shifted back and forth between the deputy and me. "Do as you're told. Good things could happen," she said brightly.

That, I thought, *is certainly a lie.*

Then she surprised me. "To ensure your continued peaceful

cooperation, Paul will allow you a few minutes with your father. You will find that he's quite alive. It will be in your interest to make sure he stays that way. I hope you don't take this concession as a sign of weakness, Mr. Jack."

It wasn't a weakness. She was demonstrating her strength. She had so much bread she didn't mind dropping a few crumbs.

Ramone and Lane retreated toward the plane. As she turned her back on us I got the impression we had disappeared from her mind, erased from memory. Matias Ramone kept his M1 up and walked backward, his gaze never leaving us until they were safely on the plane.

"Another fine mess you've gotten us into," I told Carstairs.

"Get up. I'll take you to see Ernie Sr."

"That's unexpectedly cool of you."

"I got reasons. Nothing to do with you, stupid."

I smiled. "Sorry, your big payday didn't work out."

"If you don't shut up, I might have to pull your tongue out and shove it up your ass."

"That might help me get this bad taste out of my mouth."

I hated Carstairs and he hated me. Still, I have to give the guy a little credit: He had the grace to laugh.

51

Carstairs and I left the rig on the tarmac and walked back toward the airfield's little control tower as Ramone refueled the jet. This place might once have been an airfield for a courier business. Besides the few outbuildings and a couple of hangars, the only other evidence this place had once been a hub of activity was an old flat trailer. Its hitch was rusted and both its tires were flat.

As we neared the control tower I spotted Joshua Well's minivan on the far side of the building. I blurted, "Aw, shit," just as Joshua came out of the building's back door. "I warned you to stay away from all this and go get a regular job."

The young man bent his head to run a hand over his buzz cut, looking sheepish. "You know how it is, Easy: Treadmill life. Gotta get that cheddar. Told you baby needs a new pair of shoes. Not just an expression, neither. My daughter actually needs new booties. I want to buy a pair of red high heels for my girl so she can put 'em in the air, too, you feel me?"

The deputy didn't look happy with either of us. "Did you guys grow up together or something? This is not a fuckin' high school reunion, boys."

"We bonded hard over a mutual love of ska-punk bands from the nineties," I said. "The Mighty Mighty Bosstones were dope."

Joshua giggled.

Carstairs was not so easily amused. "You're just like Easy, so full of shit. He messed with your tire and trussed you up like a Christmas turkey by the side of the road in the middle of the night. If he did that to me, I'd have killed him twice by now."

Joshua looked from me to the deputy and gave a lopsided grin. "Naw, Easy didn't mean nothin' by it. You gotta de-escalate, man! Adjust your stimulus to response ratio to proper and proportionate. I played soccer. You don't get mad just 'cuz the other team scores on you. It's not personal."

"I didn't play soccer," Carstairs said. "I played football. It's war."

"I've been to war," I said. "This is not any of that. I still don't know what or even why this is."

"Jesus, one chatterbox was enough!" Carstairs said. "You two are giving me an ear beating. This is not a coffee klatch."

Joshua couldn't stop smiling. "I've always been bullied for my superior language skills — "

With no warning, Carstairs stepped forward and cuffed Joshua's left ear. Joshua didn't say anything besides, "Ow," but I could tell it hurt. "No abusing your teammate," I said. "It's bad form and bad leadership. I took a seminar."

My captor pointed his pistol at my crotch. "One more word."

My mouth dried up and I said nothing.

"Anyway," Joshua said, "I'm goin' for a smoke. You want anything? I could go on a run for groceries. Ernie wants something to read. I figured I'd pick him up a *Sports Illustrated* and a few incidentals. Toilet paper, some Advil, chips and beer. He wants some Speedway. We were talkin' beer. He told me I should try Mitten beer. It's made with peanut butter and — "

"Shut it, Joshua."

"Am I fired?"

"It's not that you're fired so much as your job is done."

"That's the problem with the freelance life. The gigs can be short, few and far between."

"Wait out here. Keep an eye on the gate."

"Nobody's coming to the gate, man. You sure you don't want me to run to the store? Won't take me long and Easy's dad looks in a bad way, all pale and shit." Joshua looked at me. "Sorry about your dad. He's kind of a grumpy guy but he's a good listener — "

"You weren't supposed to talk to him at all," Carstairs growled.

"Well, not for nothin', but it's pretty boring out here. No Wifi — "

"Just watch at the gate and keep your damn mouth shut."

"What about my fee? Daddy needs him some foldin' green. I love that long paper — "

"I didn't get paid yet. When I do, you do." Carstairs pointed his pistol at Joshua's head. "Got it?"

Joshua raised his hands. "Okay! Okay! I got it. Solid. Cool. Message received, five by five! I think I'll be gettin' my git on and mosey." Joshua retreated.

I was a little sorry to see him go. He talked too much but with him gone, that left me with three maniacs and my dad.

Holding me at gunpoint, Carstairs tossed me the handcuffs. "Put the bracelets on again."

"I don't look my best in jewelry. I'm more a petticoats kind of guy."

When he gestured with the gun, I complied. I didn't tighten the handcuffs to his satisfaction so he cranked them smaller with a ratcheting click. I winced in pain as the steel cut into my wrists. I wished I hadn't given up that handcuff key to Joshua when I left him by the side of the road.

As I glanced over my shoulder, Lane was boarding her private jet. She didn't look back. Giants don't worry when they step on little people. Her pet goon walked from the fuel tanks toward a hangar for something. Ramone kept the M1 with him but killing me and burying sins would be left to Carstairs.

I'd been so worried about the Young Rabbi throwing me in jail for killing Micah Burmanthol. That huge threat now seemed a tiny, unlikely eventuality that wouldn't touch me at all, like a sailboat disappearing over the horizon. Impending death focuses the mind on what's important. None of my dreams and wishes mattered. I'd be dead by midnight.

52

The first floor of the control tower was a bunch of abandoned offices with empty filing cabinets. Carstairs made me walk up the stairs in front of him. It was tempting to think I might suddenly throw myself backward and catch him off guard, tap dance on his head and knock him unconscious. My handcuffs were in front of me. If this were a movie, I'd somehow get hold of his pistol or choke him out with the cuffs. This was not a movie. His experience as a cop made him too careful around me.

I took the stairs slowly. My leg was bothering me and I wasn't in a hurry for this day to end. As long as they could use me, I would live. I wracked my brain for a weasel way out but nothing came. Some problems don't have solutions.

At the top of the stairs, the light brightened again and I squinted. The radio and radar room was dated and dusty. A few dead computer terminals and empty chairs were scattered about. The airfield's wind-sock hung dead. Beyond that I glimpsed the jet.

"Is anybody there? Help! Help!"

Dad! Finally!

His pleas emanated from behind a closed door. The big padlock on the door looked out of place. Abrasions along the door frame suggested the lock had been installed recently. Carstairs stalked over by the windows. The key to the lock lay on the desk. He tossed it to me. "Jack family reunion. Go for it."

"I'm here, Dad!" I popped the lock and pushed open the door. It was a small bathroom. Dad sat on the closed lid of the toilet. He looked haggard. Beneath his white beard stubble, his skin appeared bloodless.

His captors had been smart about his unlawful confinement. If you're going to kidnap somebody, it makes sense to chain one of their ankles to the pipes under the sink of a bathroom. Each trip to a toilet allows the captive another chance at escape. When the only seat in the room is a toilet, dreams of shenanigans are greatly diminished.

Dad looked shaky as he struggled to his feet. He gave me a bright smile at first. That faded when he spotted Carstairs behind me. "Oh," he said. "And here I thought you'd come to the rescue."

"Sorry."

"No, I'm sorry. I've been an unwilling business partner with that scumbag for years." He looked at the deputy. "I shoulda put you down like a rabid dog years ago."

"Love you, too, buddy!" Carstairs said.

"Sorry I got you tangled up in this mess, Junior. This isn't your war."

"It's my way. I chose this tangle, Dad."

His shoulders sank and tears welled in his eyes. "Thanks, kiddo. That helps me a little. I'm past the Sea of Glass. Maybe I'm headed for Tranquility. Just in time, huh?"

"Sea of Glass?" Carstairs looked nervous and raised his pistol. "If you assholes are talking in some kinda code — "

Dad and I shared one last laugh. It was bitter but it felt good. It wasn't an inside joke, exactly. It was a memory that bound us together. Even though Dad often didn't like me much more than I liked him, shared experience and a common enemy pull a family together. I don't know if that's love but it's something like it.

When my mother was dying, she attended several cancer survivor support group meetings. She didn't care for them much.

"Too much boo-hooin'!" she complained. "If they're not giving me something useful to do, there's not much point, is there? I think some of them keep comin' back like vultures, pickin' at the bones, enjoying the taste of sad stories too much. And how many times do I have to hear that putting kale and apple cider vinegar through a blender is going to make me live longer? Geez, fill me up with hot fudge sundaes and chocolate shakes and send me off happy tomorrow!"

However, Sophie Jack did attend one meeting in the last summer of her life that gave her something set in stone. One of the attendees, a breast cancer survivor who had beaten the odds and far outlived her doctors' dire predictions, read a little story. Mom copied it out in big block letters in pencil on a lined sheet of loose-leaf. She brought it home and posted it on the fridge door under a yellow butterfly magnet. The story was called "Master of the Seven Seas." It read:

THERE ARE seven seas we all must cross.

The first is the Sea of Struggle, to be born and raised.

Next comes the Sea of Pleasure. These are the teen years where the responsibilities are few and most worries are either illusions or far off along the journey.

Though the voyage may be stormy, the Sea of Love is long and it is the deepest of all seas. Our sails are full and the greatest adventures happen in this leg of the journey.

Love is followed by the Sea of Loss. As the sun dies, this passage is fraught with dangerous rocks that threaten to sink our ship.

Loss opens to a great sea called Suffering. It will be a journey in darkness. We may be forced to navigate by faith and by the stars. As the wind dies in our sails, we man our posts and stay on deck, watching for light, waiting for the far side of night. We will feel the wind in our hair again.

The calm Sea of Glass awaits with the dawn. Here, the sailing is so smooth, its surface is like a mirror. We can peer over the side and see our reflections in the water. As our ship slices on, our stores of fear are used up. The Sea of Glass yields a glimpse of the world as it really is.

It's a short sail to the Sea of Tranquility. Here, we leave our losses behind. Our hold is empty of regret. No more tears are needed.

When we finally run aground, we are grateful our work is done. On that far shore, we burn our ship and bask in the heat. In the ashes, we finally find what we came for: peace.

THIS STORY TOUCHED Mom in a way that lasted. The words inscribed on my mother's tombstone read: *To arrive here, I crossed all seven seas.*

When Mom posted that story on the refrigerator door, I think she did it for us, too. Her home-care nurse wanted to call an ambulance. Mom waved that away so, as the nurse fretted, my mother died in her own bed. She gasped her last with Dad by her side, holding her hand until her hand went limp. I was down in the kitchen, reading that story for the hundredth time, desperate to believe it.

The Sea of Tranquility also happens to be the name of a plain on the moon, of course. Apollo 11 landed there. Given that my father was kidnapped and I was handcuffed at gunpoint, tranquility felt as remote as the moon.

53

C arstairs tossed his police-issued handgun on the bathroom floor in front of my father. "Pick it up, Ernie."

Puzzled, Dad looked from the weapon to Carstairs and back. "You need a reason to shoot me? You want to make it look good?"

"Don't be stupid. It's not loaded and I won't make a mess in here unless I have to. Murders are best done in the woods when the victim is already standing in the grave." Carstairs laughed. "Of course, don't get any ideas. I've about had it with the Jack family. I'd love to shoot you both."

"He wants your fingerprints on his weapon," I said. "He's trying to set up a story for how an FBI agent and his buddy got killed."

"Tell you what, Ernie. Pick it up and I'll spare your son. He can go to jail for the murder at Rud's house but I won't kill him. Something is better than nothing. Your choice. Pick it up. I won't shoot you but if you don't, I'll shoot Easy right in front of you. It's going to be quite a mess in here."

Dad picked up the gun and made a show of putting his fingerprints all over it. "Good enough?"

"Fine. Now put it on the floor and Easy, you can kick it over toward me. Gently."

I did as I was told. Carstairs did not wear gloves as he picked it up and stuffed the empty gun back in his holster. It would have been suspicious if his fingerprints weren't on his own weapon. No doubt he'd concoct some story of how he pulled Dad and me over by the side of the road. He might even say Agent Cooper was riding with him in his cruiser.

Dad stared at the deputy and said, almost casually, "No matter what you do to us, you won't get away with this."

Carstairs let out a harsh laugh. "Oh, c'mon! Are you kidding me? 'You're not gonna get away with this!' Ha! Isn't that what they all say?"

Dad gave me a look. "I tried to keep you out of this. You shoulda run like I told you."

"Not in the mood for 'I told you so' right now, Dad."

"Sorry."

I think the last time Dad apologized to me was in his Paddling's days. It was soon after Mom died. He leaned on me hard to help him out of the bar and he threw up on my pants and shoes. Ernest Sr. didn't apologize often but at least he meant it. Given his condition, I was in a forgiving mood. I didn't want to argue in front of our kidnapper. It would be bad form.

"The clearance rate for murder in Michigan is about sixty-two percent," Carstairs said. "Most murders are simple and straightforward. When a wife dies, it's always the guy standing over her with a smoking gun and that's almost always her husband or boyfriend. Boom! Go to jail and do not pass go. The shit we're in is much more complicated. I'll be beside Detective Buck the whole way to make sure he sees things the way I need him to see them. Trust me, gentlemen, this is fucked up but the odds are very much in my favor."

"Getting your fingerprints is just his backup plan," I said. "He doesn't know what the hell he's doing. He's whistling past the graveyard — "

"Shut up, Easy."

"You haven't thought this through, Deputy. Go ahead, Shoot us now. That's a whole lot of digging you're going to have to do on your own. Are you in excellent shape? You'll have to move our corpses so we're nowhere near Mazie Lane's airfield. But it's just not two bodies. You've got four to get rid of. Are you really up to killing four men in one day and burying the bodies? That's a lot of dead weight — "

"I'll have help if I need it."

"Who? Joshua? You treat him like shit and you're worried because he's a motormouth. You gonna kill him, too? He's got a little baby girl at home. Me, Dad, the two bodies in the ditch, Joshua ... you really think you can deal with all that? This isn't the Middle Ages. You're already fucked. You just haven't figured it out yet. You got a head full of money. Your dreams are pushing out your brains."

"I'll improvise. It'll work out."

"Because wishing makes it so?" I ignored the gun in his hand and pressed my point. "Even if everything goes perfectly and you're standing over a mass grave tonight, what's to stop Mr. Ramone from coming back and killing you next? You heard the billionaire herself say she doesn't like loose ends. The FBI will bring heat you can't handle. Nobody can handle that much heat."

"With money, I can do anything." His tone told me I was getting through to him. He knew it was a lie even as he gave it air.

"You'll never see a dime, Carstairs," I said. "Mazie said she brought it all the way on that plane with her. It's right there but she's smart. She knows you haven't held up your end and it's all falling apart. Mazie wouldn't even walk twenty feet to get the money for you."

The deputy raised the pistol which, I noted, was the same handgun I'd used to kill the dog killer. He stood in the doorway, frozen and confused. He seemed unsure whether to kill us, contain us or run after his money before the jet took off.

"Okay, calm down," Dad said. He sat back down on the toilet lid. "Paul can't kill everyone. He doesn't even know who...heh." He broke into a low chuckle and stopped.

Carstairs' eyes narrowed. "What? What was that?"

"Nothin'." Dad stared at the floor.

Carstairs bulled into the room, spun me around and put the muzzle against my temple. "Talk fast. I'll kill him, I swear!"

"Okay! Okay! I'll tell you! The explosives came from somewhere, you idiot! I wanted some insurance and I had to tell somebody so, so I — "

"You told the supplier! You told him what?"

"Everything."

"I knew I shouldn't have told you what it was for."

Dad talked in the same gentle but firm tone he used on an anxious dog that might bite. "Paul, settle down. You told me because I wouldn't get the shipment unless I knew what it was for."

"You know what the bombs are for?" I asked.

"Sure. Paul assured me no one would get hurt. That promise sure turned to shit, huh?"

"And here we are," I said.

"I cooperated because I needed the money. Not for the debt collectors, Junior. For you. I wanted it for you, son. I wanted to have something more to leave you. I'm really sorry. After Sophie died, things fell apart and they never came back together for me. Not for laziness nor lack of trying. I'm just ... fucked."

My father's third apology to me was the most heartfelt, his admission was heartbreaking.

"Who's the supplier?" Carstairs demanded.

"A friend from way back. Bought my first Glocks from him. He goes by several names. The name he always used with me was Chiba."

Carstairs pressed the muzzle into the soft meat of my temple hard. I almost told him that's not how guns kill people. Bullets come out of the business end so pushing the weapon into my brain was inefficient. It didn't feel like it the right moment to educate him.

"I only have a number for his burner phone," Dad said. "He's a ghost, moves around a lot. Usually, to find him I have to go to a little bar in Saskatoon called the Fringe, drop my name and wait."

"But you've got a number."

"I get a new number for him every time I've dealt with him. It might not work anymore. It's his burner."

"I'll tell you what you're going to do, Ernie. You're gonna get ... what was his name?"

"Chiba."

"Get Chiba to come here."

"All the way from Saskatchewan?"

"I don't care what you have to do to get him here but you will. Tell him his product is defective. Tell him we have an even bigger order for him to fill. I don't care, but this ghost needs to get his ass here now. Mazie says no loose ends. That's a loose end with leverage."

"There's a plan," I said. "If the rich lady pays, that's another breadcrumb the deputy cleans up for her. If she doesn't pay, the deputy has another witness who doesn't know anything about him. He could use Chiba to get paid. Worst case scenario, he can be the hero who caught an international arms dealer. Maybe you shake down Chiba. Or you could even put it all on Mazie — "

He silenced me by pressing the muzzle into my head even harder. "You think fast, don't you, Easy? I haven't figured it all out yet but I know I need more options and some peace and quiet."

"Don't hurt Junior! I know the number. I'll talk to Chiba."

Carstairs pushed me away and pulled a cell phone from his pocket. "What's the number?"

Ashamed and angry, Dad gave him the digits.

The deputy entered the numbers and hit send.

The jet on the tarmac exploded.

One less billionaire lived in the United States of America.

54

We fell to the floor as the pressure wave hit the small building. The structure rocked and every pane of glass shattered. Though my ears rang and my senses were dulled, I'm pretty sure I heard my dad chuckle and say, "Whoops," just before the next explosion hit. That was the fuel pumps going up.

In a rage, Carstairs shot my father through the chest. Don't fire a weapon in a small room. It's deafening.

Pursuing my hobby of visiting celebrities' graves, I'd often looked up famous last words. Churchill said he was "bored with it all," before slipping into the coma from which he'd never awake. Bogart said something about how he should have swilled martinis instead of scotch. Accounts differed. Another source said Bogie's last words were to tell Lauren Bacall to hurry back from going for strawberry ice cream.

As last words go, my father's choice of "Whoops," wasn't all that bad, given the circumstances.

I had underestimated my father. Tricking Carstairs into detonating an explosive on the jet was pretty smooth. Dad was more sly than I'd thought. It was up to me to make the most of the chance at life he gave me.

The cop was on the floor, dazed and bleeding from his forehead. I rolled left and got to my feet as he fired again into my father's chest. It was petty and vindictive. Surely Dad was already dead.

Usually, the rule is to deal with the weapon before you deal with whoever's wielding it. That's typically true, but I was fairly incapacitated and not just because of the cuffs on my wrists.

I've heard a dozen tough guys brag about what they'd do against a man with a gun. Every single one of them was delusional. They all seemed to think the sloppy training they got out of a karate class at the Y would save them. They believed they could kick a pistol out of a strong man's hand. No. They can't. Kick the gun hand and the gunman tightens up with his finger on the trigger. I blame a thousand bullshit martial arts movies.

You don't kick a gun from a man's hand. You grapple for it. I lunged for the weapon and, rather than trying to pull it from him as he expected, I pressed on it with all my weight. With the muzzle against the deputy's chest, he couldn't fire. As he struggled to throw me off, I brought my bad knee down as hard as I could into a soft target: his throat.

I was half a second too slow. Carstairs pulled his jaw down so his lower teeth took the brunt of the blow. Pressing all my weight on the gun again, I managed to drive my knee into the base of his throat. My combat drill instructor called that little dent the sternal notch. It was enough to wrench the gun from his grasp. I was so surprised I fell back and the gun went spinning through the air, out into the control tower's radar room.

As Carstairs rolled on his side, choking and struggling to pull air into his lungs, another explosion rocked the building. I glanced around. Dad's hands were on his chest but he wasn't clutching at his wounds. His hands were loose, his eyes lifeless. He stared past me into the outer room. I took that as a strong suggestion. The building was on fire and quickly filling with smoke.

I fumbled with the little key ring on the deputy's belt and yanked it free. Several keys hung from the ring but I was only interested in one: the key to the cuffs. Carstairs was still trying to suck air as I freed myself and slapped one cuff on his right ankle. I put the other cuff on my father's dead wrist.

"Sorry, Dad," I said.

I didn't want to think of my father as forensic evidence. However, that's all he could be now. Whatever he had been was consigned to memory. There was no time to think beyond the moment. I would have to grieve later. Dad would have understood.

The fire brightened as the wind from the shattered windows fed the spreading flames. I surprised myself at how fast I could move. I didn't think about my knee or the pain in my back or much of anything, really. I scooped up the pistol as I ran for the stairs and kept going, plunging into the column of smoke rising up the stairwell like a chimney. The building would soon be fully engulfed.

Should I have tried to pull Deputy Carstairs from the inferno? In a perfect world, yes. Ours is not that world.

I emerged from the choking gray smoke, eyes stinging, my vision blurred. The jet had been shattered by the explosion. The truck had been parked by the jet. What little was left of the Kenworth lay on its side and was alight.

If I hadn't fallen to the ground coughing, the crack of gunfire to my right would have cut me down. I rolled left and returned fire in the direction of the unseen enemy before staggering behind the wheel of the abandoned trailer.

The wheel and the flat frame of the trailer didn't give me much cover. However, a run for the semi or a dash behind the burning building would have left me too vulnerable on open ground. I could reach Joshua's minivan but that was chancy, another run through another field of gunfire. Between bullets and flames, I didn't have many options.

Flat on my back, I checked the load in the pistol. I had a few rounds but that was all.

I dared to roll right just enough to peer around the flat tire, desperate to find a target. I saw an incredible sight that would haunt my dreams. Mazie Lane's bodyguard staggered through the smoke holding his M1 and dead set on killing me. He'd failed to protect his boss but a man bent on payback doesn't need a paycheck.

He would have shot me to death easily but for one detail: Matias Ramone was on fire.

55

Mazie Lane must have had depths that I did not appreciate. She inspired such loyalty in her bodyguard I wondered if they'd been more than employer and employee. He staggered through the billowing smoke, a zombie committed to vengeance.

His long black hair and his eyebrows were gone. His stupid soul patch and most of his clothes were also burnt off. Half his face was blistered red and black with burns. Though the explosion had not killed him outright, he would undoubtedly follow his employer into death soon.

Ramone must have been standing by one of the hangars when the bomb detonated. He would have been better off on the jet. They say death is never instantaneous. However, I doubted the billionaire had any time to realize she was on her way to whatever comes next when the shipment went critical.

The bodyguard trudged forward, dragging the M1 at his side. Every step must have been agonizing. I coughed on the smoke and he seemed to rise out of his shock minutely. In his ruined face, I could see the wheels spinning behind his eyes. He raised the rifle with difficulty and squeezed off another shot in my direction. The round went wide. Slowly, painfully, he brought the weapon tight to his hip to steady his aim.

I rolled back behind the trailer's wheel and listened as several shots went into the dirt around me. One round ricocheted off the trailer's frame. Then all I heard was the roar of the flames. When I dared to peek out again, Ramone had dropped the M1 Carbine into the dirt. He stood, staring into nothing as what was left of his pants burned away.

I rolled to my feet and ran at him, leading with the pistol. There was no rush. He was all out of fight.

Jet fuel fumes wafted off him. Matias Ramone was a walking corpse, too stubborn to die. Burns covered at least two-thirds of his body. Though his burning pain must have been exquisite, he said nothing. Looking into Ramone's eyes, I sensed he was only dimly aware of my presence.

"Ramone? What was all this about?"

He remained silent. I repeated the question, louder this time.

The man turned his head slightly and winced, searching for me or for an answer, I don't know. Then he sank to his knees. His burned mouth gaped and closed over and over like a fish out of water. A thin, tortured wheeze came from his tortured lungs. It sounded as if he was struggling to breathe through thick spider webs.

Ramone reached for the pistol in my hand. As he placed a burnt paw over my hand, I felt the sizzling heat of his burnt skin. His red, swollen skin threatened to crack at the effort of raising his arm. Weak and helpless, he leaned forward, guiding the muzzle to his forehead. His gaze was a silent plea.

I showed him mercy.

Matias Ramone dropped dead into the dirt at my feet.

In the distance, I heard a high voice yell something. Between the roar of the flames and my dulled hearing, I couldn't make out what was said. I spun around to see Deputy Carstairs limping heavily as he emerged from the smoke. He staggered around the corner of the building, yelling something I couldn't decipher.

It is amazing to ponder the variables that create a future. Before this airfield was owned by Mazie Lane, someone had commissioned an architect to plan the design. If the company had a larger budget, maybe they would have sprung for a more ambitious terminal. However, the airfield's tower was only a two-story building. Whoever made that decision — God knew how many years ago — had unwittingly provided an escape route for Paul Carstairs. He hadn't followed me down the stairs to safety. He'd jumped through the shattered windows.

Then I heard him. He was cursing in general and at me in particular. His voice was high, still feeling the effects of getting kneed in the sternal notch.

I wondered how he had escaped the handcuffs. I didn't have to wait for long. He held a small blade in his left hand. It was covered in blood that belonged, no doubt, to my father. Bloody handcuffs trailed behind the cop, still attached to his ankle. In his right hand, he held his service revolver. He took a shot in my direction. Apparently, he had reloaded.

I lunged toward the cover of the thickening smoke. Carstairs fired again. His shots went wild. Anger makes us stupid. It was as if he was more concerned with the quantity of rounds fired rather than quality of his aim.

I stumbled and the deputy's key ring dropped into the dirt in front of me. Nerve pain screamed up from my left knee and my right leg was slow to get me up and going. It felt like I was carrying a few hundred pounds on my shoulders. Gravity was suddenly too strong. Overwhelming exhaustion threatened to swallow me. I had succeeded in ignoring the pain to escape the fire but my reserves were almost gone. I'd only managed to struggle up into a crouch when Joshua roared up in his minivan and placed the vehicle between Carstairs and me.

Joshua looked at me for a second before jumping out of his vehicle. He scooped the key ring off the ground. "Get the fuck up!" He reached under my armpit to yank me to my feet and pushed me into his vehicle.

Another shot rang out as Joshua slammed the accelerator to the floor. Even though he was the one driving, he shouted, "Go! Go! Go!"

It might have ended there if we had tried running over Carstairs. It was just as likely he'd have shot us through the windshield. We drove toward the gate. I was surprised to find the gate was open and said so.

"Not an accident," Joshua said. "As soon as I came downstairs I rolled it back and blocked the track with a rock. That man put hands on me. He was going to kill me!"

"Still might," I said.

"Days like this almost make me want to work in a shoe store or something. Almost."

He didn't say it to be funny but I couldn't help chuckling. Joshua didn't speak again until we were on the road and far from the airfield. He kept glancing in his mirrors. "I don't think he's comin' after us."

"He's got nothing to drive. He's stuck for now."

Looking through the rear window, I could see the column of black smoke from the burning jet for a long time.

"This presents Deputy Carstairs with quite a conundrum," Joshua said. "How's he going to explain it?"

"He's a cop. He'll find a way to blame somebody else. He'll say he was kidnapped or something, probably by you and me. That's what I'd do if I were him."

"Then we're each other's alibi. We gotta get the smell of jet fuel off us. Maybe go hang out in Atlantic City and go gamble. We're lucky to be alive. You gotta capitalize on a lucky streak while it's hot."

"Joshua, if you thought Carstairs was going to kill you, why didn't you take off? You had the van. The gate was open."

"What? So he can kill me at home and maybe get my boo and baby, too? If he wanted me dead or locked up, it wouldn't take much. Hangin' out with the crazy rich and powerful is mad dangerous voodoo, Easy. People like that can indulge their whims. I've hung out with poor people engaging in various and sundry illegal activities. I feel safer with us lowlifes. Unless they're crazy, stupid or crazy stupid, a lowlife has to plan things out if he's going to take a shot at you. Guys like that deputy and his crowd, they don't know fear and never missed a meal, neither. I was thinking maybe I should shoot him and take you and your dad home."

"Dad didn't make it."

"Sorry about that, Easy."

"He blew up the plane before he left."

"That was him? Huh. Well, good for the old man! Vengeance is his!"

"Thanks for picking me up on your way, Joshua."

"No hard feelings?"

"Nope, we're good," I said.

"Cool. So what's next?"

"Next?"

"Yeah, like ... what's the big plan? I was hoping you had some ideas. I'm fresh out. Maybe I've gotta get on the road, head west and keep going until I hit salt water."

"What then?"

"Head south until I hit water again. Then maybe I should learn to swim."

My mind reeled. What would I tell the FBI and the Young Rabbi? Agent Cooper's motorcycle was in the back of the truck. They'd piece that together eventually. I'd survived the blast but, with Carstairs alive and lying, I was still in the trap.

"Well?" Joshua pressed. "Whaddaya got? I don't want to leave my little girl behind. I got aunties still livin' in the Philippines but I can't go live there."

"Why not?"

"Spiders, man! I hate spiders. You ever seen a Redback spider? Fuck, no. I'd rather swim to Antarctica."

"Gimme a minute," I said. I rubbed my sore knee and waited for the pain signals bombarding my brain to settle to a dull roar. As the pain diminished, I remembered something they told us in Group in San Diego. It was a mantra so common that somebody posted a homemade sign on the corkboard behind the coffee machine. The scrawl in Sharpie read: Lessons must be repeated until they are learned.

Since my homecoming to Lake Orion, my mistake was trying to pretend everything was normal. For me, civilian life was another war.

Becky's words came back to me, too: *Remember who you are, Easy.*

Carstairs had to get his injuries treated. He would have to try to explain why he was found by an exploded jet and three dead bodies. We had the night, at least.

"While the deputy figures out his lies, we better get busy," I said.

"Doin' what?"

"Figuring out our lies and backing them up."

"What are you thinking, Easy?" Joshua's voice shook.

"Something extreme that's crazy in Michigan but you might see it happen in a war zone. You're not going to like it, but I guess it's better than trying to live peacefully with scary spiders in the Philippines. The first thing I'm going to need is some painkillers. Then we can get to work."

Joshua nodded and went silent, finally out of words because he'd used them all. He was ready to follow me. I was ready to lead again.

In the field, my crew called me the Night Man because of my preference for the graveyard shift. Whether standing on guard or on night patrol, I felt safe peering through a Sightmark digital night vision rifle scope. Darkness is soothing. During daylight hours odds are more even.

I had a lot of chaos to put in order. I would have to go deeper. Following the nightmare through to the end is how we wake up.

56

Detective Jerry Buck dropped Carstairs off at the deputy's house in an unmarked car around eight o'clock the next morning. If the pair had spoken in the car, they didn't look friendly. Carstairs slammed his door. The Young Rabbi rolled down his window to say something. The deputy ignored him and limped up the driveway.

He didn't use crutches but his limp was so pronounced I suspected he'd rolled his ankle badly when he threw himself out of the second story window. That was likely why he hadn't run up and shot me in the head when he had the chance.

The Young Rabbi pulled out and drove away. Cops often get special treatment when it comes to giving official statements about their crimes. They aren't held on bail. Instead, meetings get set up so they can recover from the shock of whatever they've experienced. When he did start answering questions, Carstairs would have a union rep or some agent of a police association present in addition to an attorney. Another bit of luck, but not for him.

I still had the deputy's key ring, a thought that probably didn't strike the cop until he got to his front door. I had no worries about the burglar alarm this time. I had deactivated it at the touch of a button on his house keys.

The deputy circled around to the back of the house. From the window, I saw where he hid the backup key I'd failed to find. It was tucked under the barbecue's propane tank.

I pulled back from the window and crept into the living room at the front of the house. Carstairs came in through the sliding glass doors at the back. His slow, heavy footsteps told me he'd head to the bedroom soon. Maybe he was as exhausted as I was.

He stopped in the kitchen. I heard water running in the sink. He refilled his glass twice. As he walked into the living room, he was taking off his gear, leaving it behind him on the floor. Carstairs gasped when he found me sitting in his leather chair. In one gloved hand, I held one of Dad's pistols from the bunker. I trained the weapon on his midsection.

"I didn't tell them you were involved. I didn't tell them anything yet."

"What do you plan to tell them?"

"Your father's body and the truck were there so obviously I had to place him there. I told them I pulled Ernie over for speeding and Ramone took me hostage. Hit me on the head. I've got a concussion so maybe I've got some short-term memory loss."

"Amnesia? You think they'll buy that? This isn't a Spanish soap opera."

"I'm a decorated officer — "

"Spare me. What did you tell them about Agent Cooper?"

"They don't know about him yet. When they do, I'll pin that on Ramone, too. I had a lot of time to think while I got patched up. Buck's really interested in what a billionaire was doing hauling a load of explosives. I'm the victim."

"The Young Rabbi and the FBI will want to know all the logistics. Who fired when. Where were you when thus and so occurred? You think you can cover the five Ws?"

"Huh?"

"The five Ws: Who, what, where, when, why. They'll also be very interested in the how, Deputy. That's a lot of questions."

"I can sell an arms deal gone wrong. Dealing with shady people, bad things do happen."

"That is true."

"I could come out clean on the other side of this. Maybe I'll retire a hero and write a book, sell it to the movies. Maybe the estate of Mazie Lane would be interested in paying me enough to shut me up. There are still a lot of possibilities, Easy."

"And what about me?"

Carstairs gave me a reptilian grin. "I can offer you a cut of whatever I get. What if I can make that deal with the billionaire's estate, for instance — "

"Desperation makes people dumb, Deputy. That sounds like a dumb and unlikely plan. I think you could come out on the other end of this with no jail time but the rest is a fantasy. It's too complicated and you are *way* too desperate, man. If I let you live, maybe you'll be working on the dock at the back of a Costco this time next year. More likely you'd go to jail and take me with you."

"Have you forgotten the murder of Micah Burmanthol? I can offer you your freedom. I can keep you out of jail for this and for the thing that happened at the Bench house."

"Or I could take my chances that the justice system is just."

Carstairs laughed harder at that suggestion than a cop ought to. I got out of the chair and motioned him toward the bathroom off his bedroom. "I have one question," I said. "What was all this about? What were they going to do with the explosives?"

"Well, I'll tell you — "

That's when he attacked me. Or tried to, anyway. I smacked him across the face with the pistol and shoved him back. He stumbled into the bathroom door. I shoved him again. His freshly messed up ankle was worse than my bum knee so he fell. Lying on the bathroom floor, he looked around, bewildered.

Eugene the Dog Killer was draped over the toilet. Joshua and I had tried to sit him up but the corpse was not cooperative. I decided "draped" would have to be good enough. Agent Cooper lay face up in the bathtub. We'd run a chain from his ankle to the plumbing, just as Dad had been chained up.

"You can spin a story but I kinda doubt you'd fool the Young Rabbi," I said. "Buck seems pretty bright. You might be able to fool a jury. Juries are notoriously soft on cops, even when they're as bad as you. That's not what really bothers me about your plan, though."

I had already placed the gun in Eugene's hand. All I had to do was lean down and fire low, as if it was the dog killer throwing shots into the deputy's belly.

"Wait!" he pleaded."I'll tell them everything. I'll get you off on self-defense for Burmanthol. I'll confess to everything. And there's a shoebox full of money in the front hall closet. It's the deposit Mazie Lane paid me. You can take that, too."

"Doubtful."

"It's there and it's real, I swear. All you gotta do is look. I skimmed some off the top of Mazie's deal. She paid me to find a connection to a supplier. I told her the buy was much more expensive than it was. I mean, what could be the harm? She's a real estate mogul. She didn't know the going rate for a shipment of plastique! I sent Ernie off with two-thirds of the money for the buy and squirreled away the rest for a rainy day. It's raining for me but it's your lucky day, Easy."

"Funny. Micah Burmanthol offered me a chance to buy my life. That did not work out. And here we are, full circle."

"Listen, Easy, I know you're pissed but we can make a deal."

"You've convinced me. I'll take the money."

"Really?"

"But no deal." I let the first few rounds go wide by a few inches because it was fun to watch him think he was shot. Then I put two slugs in his belly.

Deputy Carstairs moaned.

"You know what really bothers me? Any guesses on why I won't take you up on your offer? No? What really bothers me is you killed my dad."

He moaned some more.

"Abdominal wounds are the worst, aren't they, Paul? Didn't you tell Eugene that? Funny. It feels like it's okay to call you Paul now."

He gasped. "See you in Hell, Easy."

"Tell them who sent you. And shut the fuck up. You're the bad guy, you don't get the last word."

He kept talking, though. He summoned enough energy that I heard him out in the living room when I picked his cell phone from the floor. He was still yelling when I retrieved the shoebox full of money from his closet. I even heard him when I was outside the house, strolling toward my ride with the shoebox under my arm.

Paul Carstairs' shouts of pain and anger were cut short when I hit send and detonated the last device. Dad was embarrassed about how little money he could will to me. I'd dug up the bomb he'd left in the bunker. That was his most valuable gift. In the end I had an outstanding amount of money, anyway.

I did what it took, Dad. I landed the fish.

The house went up in a fireball that would confound forensic analysis. I pitched the cell phone back into the fire before walking down the street. The morning sun was bright and most people were at work. I pulled on my big sunglasses and kept going.

A few faces peeked out from windows of nearby houses. No one was looking at me. They were either grabbing their phones to call the fire department or staring at the scene of destruction.

Down the street, I slid into the minivan beside Joshua. He handed Paul Carstairs' little pug over to me and the little dog licked my hand.

"Drive, but slow," I instructed.

"What did he say?"

I scratched Edmond behind the ears thoughtfully. "The deputy had a lot to say. I didn't care for it."

Joshua glanced in the rearview mirror. "I'm going to be less loquacious around you from now on."

"Do you think you'd like to adopt Edmond? He's pretty cute. Everybody loves dogs."

Joshua glanced at me. "That's it? What are you gonna do now, Easy?"

"There are some loose ends to trip over. I've got a car back in the woods I need to clean up, get some detailing done. The cops will come around eventually. They'll have lots of questions. Most of that is simple. My dad's truck was there because he smuggled explosives for them. That is the truth. We're each other's alibi. Stick to the story and we're clear, at least from what happened at the airfield. If I don't get pinched for Micah Burmanthol, maybe I'll take Dad's car for a road trip along Route 66. Dad always wanted to take the Barracuda out that way but never got around to it."

"When they see his corpse chained to a piece of pipe in a burning building — "

"Not for us to speculate about the evil deeds of bad men, Joshua. If forced to guess, I'd suspect that somebody got greedy. People betray others often, usually over money. My dad got caught up in something that went over his head. Who knows why the explosives went off? That's what they're supposed to do. Maybe somebody got careless."

Joshua nodded. "And until then, we keep our mouths shut."

"Can you do that?" I asked.

"Believe it or not? Yeah. I can't be away from my baby girl."

"There is one thing that bothers me, Joshua — "

"Only one thing?"

"Carstairs didn't tell you what the bomb plot was?"

"For real? I swear, no. I'm just a helpin' hand. Nothing's changed since you had me at your mercy. Nobody listens to Joshua and nobody tells Joshua nothin' neither. It'd be a better world if they listened to me, I tell you that. What's eating you, Easy?"

"Coupla things. Mazie Lane had no idea who Eugene was. Carstairs called him his operator, like an independent operator. They were happy to use the dead body at the Bench house as leverage but she didn't know anything about him. Micah Burmanthol was hired by Carstairs, too."

"Who cares who hired who? Criminal enterprises don't generally have an extensive Human Resources department do they?"

I shrugged. "She cared enough to micromanage this thing herself but she didn't know that? Doesn't fit. Worse ... much worse ... Deputy

Carstairs and Eugene came up on me after I left Rollie's place. How did they know to pull me over then and there?"

"Rollie must have called Carstairs."

"Doubt it. Rollie was trying to make his own deal. He accidentally found an FBI agent in a haystack of potential arms dealers. He thought he had big money coming. Besides, he was scared of Coop. It's not Rollie who narced me out to Carstairs."

The little dog in my lap curled up and fell asleep. I envied Edmond, partly because he could sleep. It had been a long time since I slept. He also didn't know he was mortal. Dogs don't worry about death. Treated right, they live until they die, happy and oblivious.

"I am feeling sad and disappointed, Joshua. Only one person knew I was headed to Rollie's place. Think how much simpler my life would have been if I were spayed."

57

Becky sat in the rocking chair on the porch when I arrived home. Sophie sat at her feet. I took a long breath before facing her. My meds were on the kitchen table. I was looking forward to a shower, a change of clothes and a couple of caps of Tylenol.

When I stepped out of the driver's side of the vehicle, the German shepherd raced toward me. For anyone else, that would have been scary. However, the dog ran in circles several times, tail wagging the whole time. Eventually, he settled down enough for me to rub behind his ears and the thick fur of his chest.

"Whose van is that?" Becky asked.

"A friend's."

"Where have you been?"

"Visiting with the friend."

"Dolores called me. The whole damn town is in an uproar. Paul Carstairs' house exploded this morning. It's still burning!"

"I talked to Dolores soon after you did," I said. "We had a long chat. She said you were pretty broken up about the fire, like crying and inconsolable."

Becky shifted back and forth on the balls of her bare feet. "Paul was in there, wasn't he?"

"Was he?" I asked.

"As soon as I heard, I knew."

We stared at each other. She looked ready to burst into tears again. The distance between us was no more than a few yards but the chasm had never been greater.

"Alright, something's on your mind. What else did that bitch tell you?"

"I thought Dolores was your bestest bestie in all of Lake Orion."

"Easy, if you've got something to say, say it."

"Dolores says I've got Rud all wrong. She says he was only an asshole to me because I'm sleeping with his wife. That's on you and me. When I think back on it, that's pretty reasonable."

"Rud hit me."

"You said that but now I'm wondering if you did that to yourself to set me up, to get me riled up and running to your rescue — "

"What? You think I'm the first abused wife in the history of the world who really ran into a door?"

"I don't know, Becky, but I have some concerns. Everybody's got scars. I knew a guy in the Army who had crosses burned into his skin, all over his torso. I have scars, too. I think maybe your scars are all on the inside. You bragged that you could lie convincingly. I should have believed you. You and Carstairs ... you were a couple, weren't you?"

"No," she said.

I didn't believe her.

"Carstairs told me he dreamed of getting away to a tropical island with a lot of money. Were you going to do that with him?"

"How could you say that?"

"When I went over to your house to talk to your husband, you were hoping I'd kill him so you could get all his money. You made it clear you needed more than a divorce settlement would get you. Given all the cash Carstairs was going to get, that was greedy, wasn't it? If the plan was for me to kill Rud, what was Micah Burmanthol doing there?"

Becky dropped the facade and dug in her purse. She pulled out a pistol. I was pretty sure it was the gun that belonged to Micah

Burmanthol, the one I'd asked her find in the yard, the one she'd claimed was not there. I was ashamed how deeply I'd fallen for her and her lies.

"Sophie! *Look*," I ordered.

The German shepherd went on alert and growled.

"Don't make me shoot the dog, Easy. He's is the last thing left that belongs to your family that your dad named Sophie. Buncha freaks."

"Dad loved Mom so much he would have called the coffeepot Sophie if it had occurred to him. He didn't care much about naming conventions and gender norms."

She laughed a little. I would miss that laugh.

"What happened to you, Becky? We used to be … well, us."

"You should know, Easy. You're the one who was always talking about feeling trapped in Lake Orion. All my life people have underestimated me. Even when I became valedictorian they were staring at my tits, as if I'm too pretty to be smart. I'm the entire fucking package but men are only interested in the fucking. Women hate me because somehow being me isn't fair to the also-rans. I am so sick of that shit. You know what's worse? I even believed them for a little while."

"It's hard to be all you can be when a whole town has made up their minds about you since you got out of diapers," I said. "I understand that part, Becky. Believe me, I do."

"You know what, Easy? I really can't remember a time when someone didn't think I owed them something. Poor pretty Becky, the orphaned princess who needs rescuing. When they think you owe them, they act like they own you."

"I know that feeling."

"I found a way out," she declared. "When Rud introduced me to his hoity-toity friends in California, I was the one who made the connection with Mazie. People like her, they're always looking for ways to have a little bit more than everything. Rud didn't see the potential there but I did. He wouldn't have the balls to do anything even if he did see it. Mazie knew important people who could make government contracts happen. She had an idea but she needed me to put the dirty details together. I was the poor little orphan girl from nowhere who knew a smuggler back in Michigan but she needed me!"

Becky was ranting. Sophie picked up her energy. The dog was getting skittish, ready to attack. Holding the German shepherd's collar, I felt him vibrating. Potential energy coiled through his muscles, about to become kinetic.

"You and your family have always had a badass reputation," Becky said. "I knew a gun smuggler from childhood. There are only six degrees of separation between any two people on Earth. I figured your dad had to be one degree away from an arms dealer. I knew how to use that."

"Use Dad, you mean."

"Your father always liked me. He could have warned you away from me but I guess he didn't want to break your little heart."

"Actually he did warn me away. Trouble is, I'm not spayed."

She laughed. "Well, that was fun, too. You were always easy, Easy."

"Was it just manipulation or was it nostalgia sex?"

"Call it a thank you for playing your part. I learned something. All you have to do to get everything you want is be a little ruthless. I don't have problems. I solve them.

I eyed the gun in her hand. "So you are ruthless now, huh? Ready to shoot me?"

Becky gave a smile I'd never seen cross her face. She looked cruel. "Ruthless. Totally without ruth."

"Why get rid of Rud?"

"I met Paul at a charity golf event. From the moment we met, I knew I had to ditch my husband. Beating him up wouldn't do the job. I got Paul to bring in Micah Burmanthol. Some master assassin he turned out to be, huh? He was pissed at you for the night he and Eugene came here to kill the dogs. He let emotion get the better of him, didn't he?"

"Was it you or Carstairs who got them to kill the dogs?"

"My idea. I figured if you thought Rud sent them, that should have been motivation enough to get you to go in there hot and heavy, guns blazing."

"I guess I was still trying to act like a civilian then. Did you give Micah a key to the back door, too?"

"He was supposed to make it look like you and Rud killed each other, open and shut. That asshole messed up big time. Money is much more important than vengeance. Now that I won't get the money, I guess I'll have to settle for vengeance."

A tear slipped down Becky's cheek as she pointed the gun. "Everything's so messed up. You and I had puppy love, no pun intended. Rud was convenient and had some money. Paul could have had a lot more money. Truth is, I really loved Paul. There's a balance to things and you've tipped the scales, Easy. I loved Paul so much that now I hate you."

Focused on the handgun pointed at his master, Sophie barked harshly. I knelt beside the dog, holding him back. "I get it. Nobody will underestimate you anymore, Becky. But what was it all for? What was the grand plan?"

"Fiber optics."

"What?"

"The Seven Mile Bridge in Florida has forty-four spans and an aqueduct. It carries all the fiber optic cables that provide telecommunications to and from the Lower Keys. Mazie had the political connections to get the contract to rebuild it."

"But to get the contract to rebuild it, Mazie had to destroy it first," I said. "That's some convoluted Lex Luthor shit, right there."

Becky's cheeks were still wet but she managed another of her scary smiles. "It would have worked. I was the one who suggested we wait for hurricane season. Blow it and blame it on climate change."

"That definitely wouldn't have worked — "

Angry, she aimed at my head carefully, closing one eye in a long deadly wink. "Sure it would. Mazie had the politicians in her pocket. Everything's fake news now. Nobody trusts the media or experts anymore. We'd blow the bridge and anything that stood in our way would be just another conspiracy theory."

"Mrs. Bench? This is not an optimal happenstance."

Becky whirled to find Joshua standing at the end of the porch by the bug zapper.

"This will not do and, just so you know, cannot stand." Joshua held his cell phone high, recording everything.

"Who the fuck are you?"

"People call me loquacious. I'm the buddy with the van and Easy's my Soldier Boy. Don't be pointing no peashooter at my Soldier Boy, Mrs. Bench."

"It's over, Becky. Let go."

"No." A defiant smile crawled across her face that reminded me of Mazie Lane when she was threatening me.

"Easy said you were smart," Joshua offered. "Pardon me for stating the obvious hangin' out there like a sweet pair of 38Ds stuffed in a 34B push-up. I mean, I do hear your pain but we all got pain. May I humbly suggest maybe you're too desperate to make sure everybody knows how smart you are? My mom teaches school. She says, 'When first we practice to deceive, we're fucked up, tangled up and failing to perceive.' I know that's not the original quote about practicing to deceive but Mom said it better."

I felt sorry for Becky then. She had escaped Lake Orion. She might have been okay if she kept going and started over completely. Instead, she came back, still trying to prove something, still trapped in the dark reflections she saw in the eyes of others.

Becky had taken a few beats to process the fact that someone else besides Sophie and I were in on the conversation. Knowing that her confessions were recorded, she made a snap decision. We saw her next move coming. Joshua and I weren't so different from the woman with the gun in her trembling hand. I would like to think it's not true but in the same position, we'd probably do the same thing. Becky swung the pistol on Joshua as he dove for cover.

I let go of Sophie's collar as I gave the command I didn't want to use. "Sweetie pie!"

The German shepherd raced up the steps and leaped at Becky's gun arm, just as I'd trained him to do. The dog broke three bones in her hand before I could stop him.

"Don't feel too bad about getting your confession recorded," I told her. "The first night the billionaire showed up, I got outflanked by a goon with a rifle in that same spot. My new best friend hiked in from the road just like Mr. Ramone did that night."

Becky barely heard me. She was crying. "Take me to a hospital!"

"You'll be okay. I have to take you to the Young Rabbi first."

"I hate you so much, Easy!"

"That's the really sad thing, Becky. I still love you a little."

Becky told me from the beginning she wasn't my girlfriend. She was my girl-*fiend*. She was right.

58

"Which brings back me to you," I said. "You've been quiet a long time. Did you think I forgot about you and our little walk in the woods? Have you enjoyed my account of all the hijinks and shenanigans? Did you think you looked thinner than the way I described you?" I shone the flashlight on Rollie's restraints. "Your wrists are pretty red. I told you not to fuss with those zip ties."

We kept moving slowly, careful not to trip amid traitorous moon shadows and tree roots.

"It's late and I can barely see where I'm going," Rollie said. "Let's go back, crack a few beers and talk about this. You don't have to do this, Easy."

He was doing that thing all victims do, using my name to try to make me think of him as a human being instead of a target.

"You know what happens when somebody disappears?" I asked him. "Pretty much nothing. It has always fascinated me that there are at least 100,000 active missing person cases in this country every year. If there's no body, there's no murder. If this were a murder case, that would be different. Murder cases can drag on for years. Leads can go cold but cops don't forget about murders."

"You're going to kill me?"

"Your grave's already dug, Rollie. Over the next hill, I think. Remember how you were going to bury me in the backyard with your dead dogs? That was cold, man."

"What do you want?"

"*Mm* ... nothing."

"Your father wouldn't want you to do this."

"Dad probably wouldn't. Mom would have understood. She killed a boy who threatened me. Did you know that?"

"I assumed it was Ernie who killed that kid on the road with the postal truck."

"Mom was quite the hard charger, even when she was sick. Maybe especially because she was sick. Having so little to lose is kind of a superpower."

Rollie stopped and knelt on the wet ground. "I am begging you, please don't kill me. There must be something — "

"Dad said the name of the guy who sold the explosives was named Chiba. Do you know that name?"

"Chiba, yes. His friends call him Sonny. He was your dad's Canadian supplier. Ernie made contact with him through some girl at the Fringe in Saskatoon, a waitress named Darla."

"And you know this how?"

"When your dad was hospitalized last year, I had to go to Saskatoon for him to pick up some automatic rifles, a few grenades and a whole lot of bump stocks."

"Darla, huh?"

"Yes, she's a little redhead. Really cute with a tiny turned up nose. Looks like one of Santa's elves except for the scorpion tattoo."

"Thank you, Rollie. I think that's all I need to know." I raised the shotgun and pulled the trigger. The beanbag round to the sternum at close range would probably stop his heart. That's why I shot him in the belly. It took him a long time to get his breath back but Rollie survived. I escorted him back to his house, cut him free of the zip ties and dumped him in his favorite chair. I even found his remote and turned on the TV for him.

Before I left, I whispered in his ear that he'd never seen me. "The local cops and the FBI will come calling. Carstairs' cruiser is still parked on a back road down the way a piece. When they come here, tell them exactly what happened except you never shot me with a beanbag. It wasn't me who drove off with Coop, either. It was my dad. He's going to have to take the responsibility but it's okay. He'd do anything to protect his son. That's how I'll always remember him and Mom."

Rollie nodded and grunted, rubbing his bruised abdomen gingerly.

"If anybody asks, you had quite a fall when you went for a walk in the woods. And Rollie? If you mess this up, we'll go for another walk. That journey will be one-way."

Rollie understood.

I slipped out to enjoy the walk back to the Barracuda in the cool crisp night air. I felt clean. It would be fall soon. I always liked Lake Orion in autumn. The sweet smell of fallen leaves is the smell of death but it's also a reminder of childhood innocence, going back to school and new beginnings. I loved crushing crunchy dead leaves under my feet.

When I got back to the Barracuda I leaned back on the hood and looked straight up at the night sky. I could almost imagine being in space, free of gravity, outside of everything familiar. A good look at the Milky Way makes everyone feel small. Starlight is weak by the time it reaches Earth. The stars that sent that white light might not even be there anymore. Every night sky is a time machine showing us what was, not necessarily what is.

If I had a time machine, I would go back to the night of that party when I barked in Victor Down's face and he fell in the pool. If I'd stayed home that night, Victor wouldn't have lost his big toe. Sophie Jack wouldn't have felt the need to run him off the road with a postal truck. I probably wouldn't have got together with Becky.

Given the vastness of the universe, sometimes it feels like nothing we do really matters. Looking around, most everybody is still in the trap. There is no order to things. Some people take that as a license to do whatever the hell they want. I figured somebody's got to impose some order on the world. The world won't do it for itself. That is the legacy I inherited.

And Paul Carstairs' money, of course. I gave some to Joshua so he could stay out of trouble a while. When the heat died down, I paid a visit to Paddling's and left Billy the wannabe actor a big tip. I gave him enough to get him started in Hollywood. He left with Amy last week to start a new life. Becky and I didn't work out but I think Billy and Amy have a chance. Everybody deserves a chance.

I said goodnight to the sky and climbed into the Barracuda. Sophie popped up in the back seat and barked once. "We gotta come up with a new name for you," I told the German shepherd. "Any suggestions?"

The dog whined, wiggling his butt, eager to go.

"No? Nothing? Really? Lot of help you are. It's okay. I forget sometimes, you're a dog and I'm pretty much talking to myself most of the time, aren't I? They say it's the PTSD. I call it thinking things through. Maybe the cure for my PTSD is a little more traumatic stress in the service of a good cause."

The dog stared at me, waiting.

"Your vocabulary is small but you do seem well-intentioned," I told him. "Never mind, doggo! We'll come up with a good name. In the meantime, how about it? You up for a road trip? Let's go north. There's an arms dealer up there. We should take a look at his stock. Then maybe we should make sure he never sells dangerous ordnance to anybody else again. What do you say?

The German shepherd's wagging tail beat against the Barracuda's back seat.

I checked my watch. Midnight is my time. I am back working the graveyard shift.

I am the Night Man.

MORE CRIME THRILLERS LIKE THIS

Books (and their authors) live and die by reviews. If you enjoyed *The Night Man*, please leave a review wherever you purchased this book. Thank you!

The next *Night Man* thriller, *In Dark Hours*, hits in fall 2020. I write in a variety of genres. If mystery and suspense and lots of gunplay are your reading pleasure, you may especially enjoy the following killer crime thrillers.

Cheers!
  RCC

P.S. Here's your universal Amazon link: author.to/RobertChazzChute

The Hit Man Series

Bigger Than Jesus (#1 in this series)

"I found myself rooting for the guy with the gun and the Armani suit." ~ Armand Rosamilia, author of *Dirty Deeds*

"Wickedly real and violently funny!" ~ Claude Bouchard, author of *The Vigilante Series*

Are you still a bad guy if you kill people who are much worse? Jesus (it's pronounced "*Hay-soose*") Diaz is the funny hit man caught in the gears of The Machine. Jesus craves what we all want: the love of a bad woman and bags of cash. The mob wants him dead. To escape New York will take wit and grit. He's got plenty of both.

Higher Than Jesus

Killing a guy on Christmas is bad luck. Jesus Diaz is hunted by the FBI and the mob. He's also failing miserably at group therapy. From the bad streets of Chicago to the White House, secrets are revealed as badasses burn. Arms deals go sideways. Vicodin brings you up. Willow, the glamazon of your dreams, goes down. The stakes crank ever higher. You wanted a life in movies? Your life is a movie but Happily Ever After could prove elusive. Strap in for a deadly new year.

Hollywood Jesus

The unluckiest assassin meets his deadliest opponent yet. Teaming up with a rising star to break up a human trafficking ring, the action gets rough. Jesus Diaz is tougher, or at least he'd like to think so. You're going to love Jesus!

The Divine Assassin's Playbook

The first three books in the *Hit Man Series* are now available in ebook and paperback. Enjoy *Bigger Than Jesus*, *Higher Than Jesus* and *Hollywood Jesus* all in one massive adventure binge.

Resurrection, A Hit Man Novel

The divine assassin is back! Jesus Diaz returns in this new killer crime thriller packed with fast action and witty dialogue. (*Psst!* You can even enjoy it as a stand alone novel.)

His first love was Lily Vasquez. Hunted by mob assassins, she is on a rampage to stop her would-be killers. When Big Denny sends Jesus after her to settle the score, all bets are off. Follow the trail of blood, mayhem and vigilante justice from England to Miami and back to New York. Strap in for a crazy ride that will keep you up all night.

~

Brooklyn in the Mean Time

"Sucks you in and refuses to let go! A true master of his craft!" ~ Alex Kimmell, author of *The Key to Everything*

Family secrets are murder. When a wayward son returns home, uncovering the past could kill his future. Dangerous men want their money back and Chazz is on the run. When he discovers a side of his father he never knew, big mistakes must be buried if Chazz is to survive. Digging up the old ugly with his brother could get Chazz killed long before a drug lord's hitman shows up to collect.

Bumbling his way through '90s New York, encounter a new kind of psychological crime novel. Funny, dark and compelling, you're in for a great read on a fast ride as soon as you begin *Brooklyn in the Mean Time*.

~

Sometime Soon, Somewhere Close

Check the locks and leave all the lights on. Get ready to devour this dark collection of crime fiction in one sitting.

Enter the mind of an experienced serial killer in Chicago. Meet a stalker in Edmonton and an aspiring murderer in Detroit. Feel the creeping dread as the truth about a missing fisherman in Nova Scotia is revealed. Will you forgive the bullied boy who finds a nasty way out of his torture?

These seven stories will give you a night to remember.

ALL BOOKS BY THIS AUTHOR

~ THE CRIME THRILLERS ~

Bigger Than Jesus

Higher Than Jesus

Hollywood Jesus

The Divine Assassin's Playbook

(The first three novels in the Hit Man Series.)

Resurrection, A Hit Man Novel

Brooklyn in the Mean Time

The Night Man

Sometime Soon, Somewhere Close,

A Collection of Dark Crimes

~ DYSTOPIAN & APOCALYPTIC FICTION ~

This Plague of Days, Season 1

This Plague of Days, Season 2

This Plague of Days, Season 3

This Plague of Days, Omnibus Edition

Amid Mortal Words

ABOUT THE AUTHOR

Robert Chazz Chute is a former crime journalist and an award-winning writer. He pens killer crime thrillers, suspense and apocalyptic science fiction. He lives in Other London.

Ex Parte Press is always on the hunt for Super Readers. To find out more about RCC's books, please visit his author site at AllThatChazz.com and subscribe to the newsletter for deals and updates.

BONUS: If you really love his books and want even more Chazz, join Fans of Robert Chazz Chute on Facebook for daily updates and chat.

facebook.com/robert.c.chute

twitter.com/RChazzChute

instagram.com/robertchazzchute

www.ingramcontent.com/pod-product-compliance
Lightning Source LLC
Chambersburg PA
CBHW020417260626
47156CB00007B/2425